The Lady Most
Willing . . .

The Lady Most Willing . . .

A Novel in Three Parts

Julia Quinn
Eloisa James
Connie Brockway

HARPER LUXE

An Imprint of HarperCollinsPublishers

HarperCollins books may be purchased for educational, business, or sales promotional use. For information, please e-mail the Special Markets Department at SPsales@harpercollins.com.

FIRST HARPERLUXE EDITION

HarperLuxe™ is a trademark of HarperCollins Publishers

Library of Congress Cataloging-in-Publication Data is available upon request.

ISBN: 978-0-06-222305-0

13 14 ID/RRD 10 9 8 7 6 5 4 3 2 1

For our husbands . . .

. . . Paul. He might not throw cabers,
but give him a pair of scissors,
and he can slice a wasp in half in mid-air.
As far as I'm concerned, that's the
modern-day equivalent of slaying dragons.

—JQ

. . . Alessandro, because we met on a blind date,
and although it didn't take place in a Scottish castle,
one might argue that our characters
find themselves in a similarly happy situation.

—EJ

. . . the good Dr. Brockway, whom I forgive
for not gaining a single pound since the day we wed.
No truer love has a woman than this.

—CB

Prologue

Some said the legendary storm of 1819 that screamed down from the north pushed madness ahead of it. Others said the only madness exhibited that night was born inside a bottle of contraband whiskey. And then there were those who claimed that magic rode vanguard to the snow, sweeping the halls of Finovair Castle and inspiring its laird to heights of greatness . . .

Or something along those lines.

All that's known for certain is that it was a chilly December day when Taran Ferguson led his clansmen to the brow of a hill from which they could see Bellemere Castle glowing like a jewel in the dark Highland night. As his men told the story later, the wind whipped Taran's tartan back from his shoulders as he forced his steed to paw the air, then brought the magnificent beast back down to earth.

Nearly disbalanced, 'tis true, but that was part of the miracle: he'd drunk a bottle of whiskey and kept his seat.

"A glorious and sacred task lays ahead of us this night," he bellowed. "Our cause is just, our purpose noble! Down yonder sits the Earl of Maycott . . . The *English* Earl of Maycott!"

This brought forth a roar from his men. And perhaps a belch or two.

"He sits amongst his gold cups and fine china," Taran continued grandiosely, "seeking to worm his way into our good graces by bidding the finest Highland families to dine and dance with him."

His clansmen glowered back at him: none of them, including Taran, had been invited. Not that they'd wanted to be. Or so they told themselves.

"No English interloper will seduce a Scottish lassie on my watch," Taran shouted. "Scotland is for the Scots!"

There was another obligatory roar of approval from his men.

"Ye ken full well that I have been sowing wild oats since my dear wife died, some twenty years ago," Taran continued. "But sadly, laddies, ye also know that none of those seeds bore fruit, for it takes a rich field indeed to nourish a seed as mighty as that of the Ferguson."

Taran had the good sense not to wait to see how this was received. "My line is threatened with extinction. Aye. Extinction! And where, I ask you, will you all be then? Where will your children be without a Ferguson laird to see to their well-being?"

"A better place than we are now," one of the men muttered, pulling his tartan closer against the screaming wind.

Taran ignored him. "Yet all is not lost! You ken I have two nephews by my younger sisters."

Unhappy mutters met this statement. One of Ferguson's sisters had married a refugee from the French Revolution, a penniless comte. The other had wed an English earl who turned out to be as disagreeable as he was English.

Taran raised his hand, quieting the grumblers. "It's the half-French one, Rocheforte, who'll inherit my castle." He paused dramatically. "Think on it, lads. If my Frenchie nephew marries a Scotswoman, his son will be one of us—a true Scotsman!!" He slashed the air with his broadsword so vehemently the momentum nearly carried him off his saddle, but at the last moment he righted himself. "Or mostly. And it's the same for my English nevvy as well."

"I'm sorry to tell you but the earl is engaged to an Englishwoman!" one of the men called out. "Me wife's cousin lives in London and wrote about it to me wife."

"Oakley was going to be wed," Taran said briskly, "but he caught his intended practicing steps with her dancing master that were never meant to see a ballroom floor." He paused dramatically. "Her *French* dancing master."

"Didn't you just say your other nephew is French?" one of his men asked, rubbing his hands on his kilt for warmth.

Taran brushed this aside. "It pains me to say it, but neither lad can be trusted to find a bride worthy of Finovair. And marry they must, or our birthright will crumble to dust."

"Half there already," someone muttered.

"It behooves us"—Taran paused, so pleased with the word he thought it bore repeating—"it *behooves* us, my fine companions, to make sure both my nevvies marry Scotswomen. Or at the very least, someone with enough blunt—"

"Get to the bloody point!" shouted someone with freezing fingers and a wife at home. "What are we doing here?"

No one could fault Taran for missing a good exit line. "What are we doing?" Taran bellowed back. "*What are we doing?*" He rose in his stirrups and, wielding the great broadsword of the Ferguson over his head, shouted,

"We're going to get us some brides!"

Chapter 1

Finovair Castle
Kilkarnity, Scotland
December 1819

"Remind me again, *why* are we here?"

Byron Wotton, Earl of Oakley, took a forti-fying gulp of his whiskey and nudged his chair closer to the fire. Castles were notoriously difficult to heat, but it was bloody *freezing* at Finovair. He knew his uncle was short on funds, but surely something could have been done about the arctic breeze that ran like a snake through the sitting room.

"I believe you left a woman at the altar," his cousin Robin said with an arched brow.

"We were a month away from the wedding," Byron shot back, perfectly aware that he had risen—or rather, descended—to Robin's bait. "As well you know."

He might have pointed out that he'd caught his fiancée in the arms of her dancing master, but really, what was the point? Robin knew the whole story already.

"As for me," Robin said, leaning forward to rub his hands together near the fire, "I'm here for the food."

Anyone else might have taken it as the dry riposte Robin had intended it to be, but Byron knew better. With nothing to his name but a defunct French title, Robert Parles (Robin to everyone but his mother), quite likely *had* come to Finovair for the food.

A rush of cold air hit Byron in the face, and he bit off a curse. "Did someone leave a window open?" he asked, scowling as he glanced around the room. The sun had gone down hours before, taking with it its pathetic delusion of warmth.

Byron stomped to his feet and crossed the room to inspect the windows. Several were cracked. He peered out, into the worsening storm. Was someone out there? No, no one would be so mad as to—

"What happened to Uncle Taran?" Byron asked suddenly.

"Hmmm?" Robin had let his head loll against the back of his chair. He did not open his eyes.

"I haven't seen him since supper. Have you?"

Robin snorted and sat up straighter. "You missed the show. After you went off to God knows where—"

"The library," Byron muttered.

"—Taran got up on the table in his kilt. And let me tell you"—Robin gave a shudder—"that is *not* a kilt one cares to peer under."

"He got up on the table?" Byron could not help but echo. It was outlandish, even for Uncle Taran.

Robin gave a one-shouldered shrug. "Some of his liegemen came to drink with him after supper, and the next thing I knew, he was on the table, thumping his chest and raving about the glories of the past, when men were men and Scottish men were thrice as manly. Then he called for his claymore and the whole lot of them disappeared."

"You didn't think to ask them where they were going?" Because that was the first thing Byron would have demanded.

Robin eyes met his with the barest hint of amusement. "No."

Byron started to comment, but he was cut off by the welcome sound of their uncle, bellowing outside the castle.

"Speak of the devil," Byron said, with some relief. Their uncle was a bosky nuisance, but neither of them wanted to find him facedown in a snowdrift.

"Best go drag him to the fire and thaw him out," Robin said, putting down his glass. "Garvie says we're in for a three-day blow."

They left the great hall and pushed open the huge front door, where they discovered a small clutch of their uncle's clansmen milling about the keep, thumping their chests and clapping one another on the back. They wore full Highland kit, kilts and fur cloaks, and the torches they carried sputtered beneath a thickening snowfall. Taran stood at their center, grinning like a madman.

"God, look at all those knees," Robin murmured.

"Whose carriage is that?" Byron asked, peering at a gleaming black vehicle drawn up just where the torchlight gave way to darkness.

Taran pushed his way through his men. "I've brought you brides!" he shouted over his shoulder to his nephews. "Come out here, lasses!" He pulled open the door of the carriage with a flourish.

A fresh, pretty face appeared for a moment, and then a slender hand grasped the inside handle. "There are no brides here," she said smartly. The door slammed shut.

Byron stared in shock. "Bloody hell!" he breathed. He looked at Robin. Even as his cousin's brows rose, a smile was growing on his handsome face. "This is not amusing, Rob. That was a *lady.*"

"Damned right that was a lady," Taran bellowed. "A spirited one, too. I got three of them with money, birth, and looks enough." He pointed a gnarled finger at Robin. "You'll pick one of these, nephew, or I'll do it myself and lock the two of you in a room until you have to get married." He glanced at Byron. "You might as well take one, too," he added magnanimously.

Byron started down the steps with a groan.

Taran gave the door a sharp tug and a dark-haired girl tumbled out. "Lads, this first lady be—" He stopped. Stared. "Catriona Burns, what in the devil are you doing here?" he demanded.

"You abducted me!" the dark-haired young lady retorted, hands on her hips.

"Well, if I did it were a mistake," Taran said. He looked over at Byron and Robin. "Don't even think about this one, lads. Nice lass, no money."

Byron heard her outraged gasp even above the sound of Robin's hopeless laughter.

"Move aside, Catriona. The rest of you lassies get out here," Taran bellowed, peering into the carriage. "My nephew needs to take a good look before he chooses one of you for his bride."

"I cannot believe that you visited an outrage of this nature on young ladies," Byron stated, shooting his uncle a murderous look. Taran was a moth-eaten bear of a man, still more brawn than beef, dark hair shot through with the same silver that colored his beard. He didn't look cracked, though he obviously was.

Byron reached the carriage just in time to offer an arm to the lady who appeared in the open door. In the light of the torches, snowflakes drifted onto hair the color of dark rubies.

"There's a good one!" Taran announced. "Fiona Chisholm. She's a bit long on the shelf, but I brought her younger sister, too, if'n you want a more tender lamb. Each of them has a tidy fortune."

"I deeply apologize for my uncle's lunacy," Byron said, bowing over Miss Chisholm's hand once she was on the ground. "You must be feeling nearly hysterical with fright."

There was laughter rather than terror in the young lady's eyes. "Having long acquaintance with the laird, I am not as frightened as I might be. You have the advantage, sir," she said, dropping a curtsy.

"Byron Wotton, Earl of Oakley."

"Lord Oakley, it is a pleasure to meet you."

"This is my younger nephew. Lives in England," Taran put in. "Robin there will be inheriting Finovair. He's the one ye're here to marry."

Robin had crossed the courtyard and now moved to stand at Byron's side. "Robert Parles, Comte de

Rocheforte," he said cheerfully. "Call me Robin. Pleased to meet you, Miss Burns, Miss Chisholm."

Byron handed Miss Chisholm to him and put his hand out to help yet another lady, this one smaller, with curling toasty brown hair, delicate features, and brilliant, deep-set brown eyes.

"Maycott's daughter," Taran said proudly. "Lady Cecily. She's the best of the bunch: worth a fortune and pretty as a penny. Though"—he lowered his voice— "she *is* English. But she's been out a fair few seasons now, too, and shouldn't be too picky at this point."

The lady's eyes grew round.

"Uncle, I implore you to shut your mouth," Byron said. "Lady Cecily, I can find no words to apologize for the terrible imposition committed against you."

Lady Cecily seemed about to reply when Robin edged Byron aside, taking her hand and bowing. "Oh, I don't think I can apologize," he said. "No one's ever kidnapped a lady on my behalf before. But then," he continued, grinning wolfishly, "no one has ever had to."

The girl's eyes widened again, and even in the fitful torchlight one could see her cheeks turn rosy. For a second, Robin froze, staring down at her. Then he abruptly looked away, releasing her hand, and stepped past her, craning his neck to peer into the carriage.

"Who else is left in there, Uncle? One of George's girls? I always fancied marrying into royalty."

"This is a serious business!" their uncle said with a scowl. "Only one left, I think. Fiona's sister."

His ancient lieutenant nodded gravely.

Byron ground his teeth. "Robin, please escort Miss Burns, Miss Chisholm, and Lady Cecily into the castle. It's freezing, and they aren't wearing cloaks."

"Didn't have time for that," Taran said cheerfully. "I snatched them straight out of the ballroom. Marilla Chisholm, there's no hiding in that carriage," he bellowed.

The last young lady appeared, pausing dramatically at the top of the carriage's steps. She was very young, very blond, and very beautiful, and she swayed gently. "What is happening?" she cried, her voice wavering. "Oh, what is to become of us?"

"You are perfectly safe, Miss Marilla." Byron held out a hand to support her as she stepped down. "I am Lord Oakley. I offer our deepest apologies, and my assurance as a gentleman that you will be speedily returned to your family."

"No, she won't," Taran said. "Snow's already closed the pass. Should be two to three days before anyone makes it through." He pushed the carriage door shut. "Let's get inside. It's as cold as a witch's teat out here, and we're done."

The carriage door slammed open again and an exquisite Hoby boot landed decisively on the ground. A deep, irritated voice said, "Not quite!"

Byron's jaw dropped.

Robin turned around. "Holy hell, Uncle, you've kidnapped the Duke of Bretton!"

Chapter 2

Catriona Burns was a practical girl. One had to be, living as she did in the Highlands of Scotland. When it was December the seventeenth, and the sun rose for barely six hours per day, and the temperature hovered somewhere between freezing and dead, one had to be prepared for anything.

But not *this*.

It was two in the miserable morning, she'd lost feeling in at least eight of her toes, and she was standing outside in three inches of snow. With an earl. And a French comte. And a *duke*. Who'd been kidnapped.

"Taran Ferguson, you insufferable miscreant," she practically yelled. "What do you think you are *doing*?"

"Aye, well, y'see . . ." He scratched his head, glanced at the carriage as if it might offer advice, and then shrugged.

"You're drunk," she accused.

His mouth twisted so far to the right it seemed to turn his head. "Just a wee bit."

"You kidnapped the Duke of Bretton!"

"Well now, that was a mistake . . ." He frowned, turning to his loyal retainers. "How *did* we end up with him?"

"Indeed," bit off the duke. Normally speaking, Catriona would not have found him terribly fearsome. He was a rather good-looking fellow, with thick, dark hair, and deep-set eyes, but there was nothing wild or untamed about him.

That said, when the Duke of Bretton speared Taran Ferguson with a furious stare, even Catriona took a step back.

"What were you doing in the carriage?" Taran demanded.

"It was *my carriage!*" roared the duke.

There was a moment of silence—well, except for the French comte, who wouldn't stop laughing—and then Taran finally said, "Oh."

"Who," the duke demanded, "are you?"

"Taran Ferguson. I do apologize for the error." He motioned toward Lady Cecily, then waved his hand past both Chisholm sisters. "We only meant to snatch the women."

Marilla Chisholm let out a delicate cry of distress, leading Catriona to let out an indelicate grunt of annoyance. She'd known Marilla for every one of her twenty-one years, and there was no way she was the least bit distressed. She'd been trapped in a carriage with a duke, only to be deposited at the feet of two other titled gentlemen.

Please. This was Marilla's wildest dream come true, and then inflicted upon the rest of them. Catriona looked over at Marilla's older sister, Fiona, but whatever she was thinking, it was well hidden behind her spectacles.

"Bret," said one of the men—the stiff and serious one who had already apologized six times.

The duke's head snapped around, and Catriona saw his eyes widen. "Oakley?" he asked, sounding well and truly shocked.

Lord Oakley jerked his head toward Taran and said, "He's our uncle."

"*Our?*" the duke echoed.

Lord Rocheforte—or was it Mr. Rocheforte? Catriona didn't know, he was *French*, for heaven's sake, for all that he sounded British. Whoever he was, he clearly saw no gravity in the situation, for he just grinned and held up his hand. "Hallo, Bret," he said in a jolly voice.

"Good God," the duke swore. "You too?"

Catriona looked back and forth between the trio of men. They had that air about them—five hundred years of breeding and a membership to White's. One didn't have to venture far beyond the Highlands of Scotland to know that once one reached a certain social level, everyone knew everyone. These three had probably shared a room at Eton.

"Didn't realize you were in Scotland," Mr. Lord Rocheforte said to the duke.

The duke cursed under his breath, following that up with: "Forgot the two of you were related."

"It still quite frequently comes as a shock to me, too," Lord Oakley said in a dry voice. Then he cleared his throat and added, "I must apologize on behalf of my uncle." He jerked his head furiously toward Taran. "Apparently, he—"

"I can speak for myself," Taran cut in.

"No," Lord Oakley said, "you cannot."

"Don't you speak to me like that, boy!"

Oakley turned to Taran with a fury that even outstripped the duke's. "Your judgment—"

"He was asleep in the carriage," Catriona blurted out, jumping into the fray. The men went silent for long enough to stare at her, so she quickly added, "When you and your men threw us inside. His Grace was already there, asleep."

"Did he wake up?" Mr. Lord Rocheforte murmured.

Catriona blinked, not sure if she was meant to actually answer. But she had a feeling that if she did not maintain control of the conversation, the other three men would come to blows, so she said, "Not right away."

"It was right easy," Taran boasted. "We just went in, snatched them, and left. No one even put up a fuss."

Lord Oakley let out a long, agonized breath. "How is that possible? Surely your parents . . ."

Fiona Chisholm cleared her throat. "I think the guests thought it was all part of the entertainment."

Rocheforte started laughing again.

"How can you find this funny?" Lord Oakley demanded.

"How can you not?" Rocheforte sputtered.

"I feel faint," Marilla twittered.

"You do not," Catriona snapped. Because really, the whole thing was bad enough without Marilla's nonsense.

Marilla gasped in outrage, and Catriona had no doubt that she would have hissed something monstrously insulting if they had not an audience of unmarried gentlemen.

"Might we go inside?" the Duke of Bretton asked, each syllable icy sharp.

"Of course," Lord Oakley replied quickly. "Come in, everyone. We will get this sorted out and have everyone *back on their way home*"—he glared at his uncle at that—"posthaste."

"We can't go home," Catriona said.

"What do you mean?"

"The roads are impassable."

Lord Oakley stared at her.

"It's a miracle we even made it here," she told him. "We certainly cannot return tonight. There is no moon, and"—she looked up at the sky—"it's going to snow again."

"How do you know?" Lord Oakley asked, with perhaps more than a touch of desperation.

She tried not to stare at him as if he were an idiot, she really did, but his white-blond hair was practically glowing in the moonlight, and with his mouth still open in horror, he looked like a traumatized owl. "I have lived here my entire life," she finally said. "I know when it's going to snow."

His reply was something that should never be uttered in front of a gently born female, but given the circumstances, Catriona opted to take no offense.

"Let's get inside," he muttered, and after a moment of confusion, they all piled into the castle.

Catriona had been to Finovair Castle, of course; Taran Ferguson and his crumbling abode was the Burnses' third-closest neighbor. But she'd never been so late at night, after most of the fires had been allowed to die down. It was so cold the air had teeth, and none of the young ladies was wearing a coat or pelisse. Catriona's gown had been sensibly tailored with long sleeves, as had Fiona's, but Lady Cecily's powder blue confection had little cap sleeves, and Marilla's practically bared her shoulders.

"There's a fire in the drawing room," Lord Oakley said, hurrying everyone along. It was difficult to believe that he was related to Taran; they looked nothing alike, and as they passed the candlelit sconces, Catriona could see that Lord Oakley's features were uncommonly stern and severe.

As opposed to Mr. Lord Rocheforte, who had one of those faces that looked as if it didn't know how *not* to smile. He was chuckling as they made their way through the cavernous great hall, although Catriona did hear him say to the duke, "Oh, come now, Bret, surely you see the humor in this."

Catriona pricked up her ears, but she didn't hear "Bret's" response. She didn't dare steal a glance at the duke, not when they were all in such close proximity. There was something about him that made her feel uneasy, and it wasn't just the fact that he was certainly the highest-ranking individual to whom she had ever been introduced.

Except she *hadn't* been introduced to him. She'd only watched him from across the Maycott ballroom, as had the rest of the local peons. The Earl of Maycott was one of the richest men in England, and heaven only knew why he had wanted his own Scottish castle, but want it he had, badly enough to spend a fortune restoring Bellemere to a level of magnificence that Catriona was fairly certain it had never enjoyed, even when it was in its supposed glory.

Once the work was completed, the Maycotts had decided to hold a ball, inviting a few of their London friends but, for the most part, the local gentry. Only so that their first annual Icicle Ball would be a crush.

Or at least that was what the local gossips said. And while Catriona knew better than to believe everything she heard, she *always* listened.

The Chisholm daughters had been brought to meet the duke, of course. They were heiresses, quite possibly the only heiresses this corner of Scotland had ever seen, and they'd each had a season in London. But not Catriona. Her father was a local squire, and her mother was the daughter of a local squire, and as Catriona fully expected one day to marry a local squire, she didn't see much sense in begging an introduction to the visiting aristocracy.

Until.

Catriona still wasn't sure how she had come to be snatched up along with Lady Cecily and the Chisholm daughters, but she'd been the first to be tossed into the carriage. She'd landed squarely atop the duke, who responded first with a snore, and then with a frisky hand to her bottom.

Then he'd called her Delilah and started nuzzling her neck!

She'd jumped away before she could dwell upon the fact that it all felt rather nice, and then the duke had fallen back asleep.

Someone, Catriona had decided acerbically, had got into the Maycotts' good brandy.

Catriona had only a minute alone with the sleeping duke before the other three ladies were tossed into the carriage, and then he *had* woken up. She shuddered to think how much brandy he'd have had to drink to sleep through *that*. Marilla was shrieking, Lady Cecily was banging on the ceiling with her fist, and Fiona was yelling at Marilla, trying to get her to shut up.

Sisters the Chisholm girls might be, but there had never been any love lost there.

The duke had tried to get everyone to be quiet, but even he wasn't able to break through the din until he bellowed, "Silence!"

It was at that moment that Catriona realized that the other ladies had not yet noticed he was in the carriage. Lady Cecily's jaw dropped so fast Catriona was surprised it stayed hinged. And Marilla—good Lord, but Catriona had never liked Marilla—she had been immediately tossed onto his lap by a nonexistent bump in the road.

He had not, Catriona had noticed with some satisfaction, responded by squeezing *her* bottom.

She wasn't certain how long they'd been trapped in the swiftly moving carriage. Ninety minutes at least, perhaps two hours. Long enough for the duke to announce that no one was to utter a sound until they arrived at their godforsaken destination. Then he went back to sleep.

Or if not sleep, then a crackingly good imitation of it. Even Marilla had not dared to disturb him.

But whatever good sense Marilla possessed had fled when she'd stepped out of the carriage, because now she was chattering to the duke like an outraged magpie, clutching his arm—his arm!—as she went on about "shocking" this and "insupportable" that.

The duke gave a little tug, but Marilla had no intention of releasing her prey, and he gave up. Catriona could only think that he'd decided the heat of her hand was worth the annoyance.

Catriona couldn't fault him for that. *She'd* have cuddled up to Marilla just then if it meant raising her temperature a few degrees. The only people who didn't seem to be shivering madly were Taran's two nephews, who, it had to be said, were almost as pleasing to the eye as the duke, and not the sort of men one would think would need to have women snatched from a party.

Then again, Taran Ferguson was as eccentric as the summer day was long. And the last time she'd seen him he'd been going on about the fate of Finovair after he was dead and in the ground, so she supposed she shouldn't be too surprised that he'd go to such lengths to secure brides for his nephews.

Lord Oakley led the entire crowd into a small sitting room off the great hall. It was shabby but clean, just like most of Finovair, and most importantly, there was a fire in the grate. Everyone rushed forward, desperate to warm his limbs.

"We'll need blankets," Oakley directed.

"Got some in that trunk," Taran replied, jerking his head toward an ancient chest near the wall. His nephews went to retrieve them, and soon they were passing the blankets along like a chain until everyone had one draped across his shoulders. The wool was rough and scratchy, and Catriona wouldn't have been surprised if a flotilla of moths had come spewing forth, but she didn't care. She would have donned a hair shirt for warmth at that point.

"Once again," Lord Oakley said to the ladies, "I must apologize on behalf of my uncle. I can't even begin to imagine what he might have been thinking—"

"You *know* what I was thinking," Taran cut in. "Robin's dragging his feet, pussyfooting around—"

"*Uncle*," Oakley said warningly.

"As no one is going anywhere tonight," Mr. Rocheforte said, "we might as well get some sleep."

"Oh, but we must all be introduced," Marilla said grandly.

"Of course," Taran said, with great enthusiasm. "Where are my manners?"

"There are so many possible replies I can hardly bring myself to choose," the duke said.

"I am, as you all know, the laird of Finovair," Taran announced. "And these are my two nephews, Oakley and Rocheforte, but I call them Byron and Robin."

"Byron?" Fiona Chisholm murmured.

Lord Oakley glared at her.

"You seem to be the Duke of Bretton," Taran continued, "although I don't know why you're here."

"It was my carriage," Bretton growled.

Taran looked back at his men, one of whom was still toting his claymore. "That's what I don't understand. Didn't we *bring* a carriage of our own?"

"Uncle," Rocheforte reminded him, "the introductions?"

"Right. Maycott's probably busted it up for kindling by now, anyway." Taran let out a sorrowful sigh. "Speaking of Maycott, though, this one is his daughter Cecilia."

"Cecily," Lady Cecily corrected. It was the first word she had spoken since their arrival.

Taran blinked in surprise. "Really?"

"Really," Lady Cecily confirmed, one of her brows lifting in a delicately wry arch.

"Hmmph. So sorry about that. It's a lovely name."

"Thank you," she replied, with a gracious tilt of her head. She was remarkably pretty, Catriona thought, although not in a flashy, intimidating way like Marilla, whose blond curls and sparkling blue eyes were the stuff of legend.

"These two are the Chisholm sisters," Taran continued, motioning to Fiona and Marilla. "Fiona's the elder and Marilla's the younger. They're good Scottish ladies, but they have been down to London. Got a little polish, I hear. And that's about it."

Catriona cleared her throat.

"Oh, right!" Taran exclaimed. "So sorry. This one is Catriona Burns. We took her by mistake."

"Ye said the one in the blue dress," one of Taran's men protested. Catriona had met him before. She was fairly certain his name was Hamish.

Taran jabbed a finger toward Lady Cecily. "That one's wearing a blue dress."

Hamish shrugged and jerked his head toward Catriona. "So is Miss Burns. And they have the same coloring."

It was true. Brown hair, dark eyes. But while Lady Cecily was delicate, and moved with an ethereal grace, Catriona was . . . Well, she didn't know what she was. But she wasn't delicate. And she probably wasn't graceful, either. She generally tried not to dance for long enough to know for sure.

Taran looked back and forth between the two brunettes for a comically long few seconds. "Right, well, the problem is," he finally said to Catriona, "I wasn't expecting you. I don't have a room ready."

"You will give her my room," the duke commanded.

"I don't have a room for you, either," Taran said.

Lord Oakley groaned.

"It's very kind of you to have rooms prepared," Marilla said prettily.

Catriona could only gape. Taran Ferguson had kidnapped her and she was *thanking* him?

"I'm not really sure where to put you," Taran said slowly. He looked over at the sofa, frowning thoughtfully.

That was *it.* "Taran Ferguson," Catriona fumed. "I am not going to sleep on the sitting room sofa!"

He scratched his head. "Well, now, it'd be a sight more comfortable than the floor."

"And I am not going to sleep on the floor!"

The duke stepped forward, his eyes deadly. "Mr. Ferguson, I suggest you find a chamber for the lady."

"I don't really—"

"Or you will answer to me."

Silence fell. Catriona looked over at the duke, stunned that he would come so fiercely to her defense.

"Miss Burns may share a room with me," Lady Cecily said. Catriona shot her a look of gratitude.

"Can't do," Taran said. "There's only the one small bed."

"Put the sisters together," the duke suggested imperiously.

"Already have," Taran replied. "You'll be sharing a bed, lassies," he said to the Chisholm sisters, "but it's comfortable enough. Never had any royal visits here, so no need to get any of our extra bedrooms fancied up."

"We have two very nice guest rooms at our home," Marilla said. "We once hosted the Earl of Mayne."

"In 1726," Fiona muttered.

"Well, it's still the Mayne room," Marilla said with a sniff, "and if any of you came to visit, that is where we would put you. Well, except maybe you," she said, blinking in Catriona's direction.

"Marilla!" Fiona gasped.

"She lives just five miles away," Marilla protested. "She would hardly need a guest room."

"One apparently never knows when one might need an extra guest room," the duke said dryly.

"So true," Marilla said. "So very, very true." She looked over at him with that annoyingly catlike tilt of her head and batted her eyelashes. "Are you always so very, very wise?"

Bretton, apparently at the end of his rope, just looked at her and said baldly, "Yes."

Catriona choked on laughter, then feigned a few coughs when the duke turned to her with an arched brow. Oh dear heavens, was he serious? She'd thought he was merely trying to shake off Marilla.

"Well," Taran declared, filling the awkward silence, "we'll find something for everyone. In the meantime, let's get the rest of you settled. Where is Mrs. McVittie? Oh, there you are!"

His housekeeper nodded from the doorway.

He flicked a hand toward every female besides Catriona. "See these three up to their rooms. And, ah, Robin and Byron, why don't you go as well. Just to make sure everything is as it should be."

Lord Oakley shook his head. "As it should be," he repeated in disbelief.

"Give Lady Cecilia the blue room, or at least the one that used to be blue, and Miss— Well, actually, it really doesn't matter. Give them whichever room they want." Taran turned back to Catriona and the duke, who were still standing by the fire. "I'll see what I can find for the two of you."

"Bretton can have my room," Lord Oakley said, standing in the doorway as everyone else filed out.

"No, really," the duke responded, his voice a mocking monotone, "I couldn't possibly inconvenience you."

Lord Oakley rolled his eyes and exited into the great hall.

It was only then that Catriona realized she had been left quite alone with the Duke of Bretton.

Chapter 3

John Shevington had been the Duke of Bretton since the age of forty-three days, and as such, he had been inflicted with a legion of tutors, each of whom had been given the task of making certain that the young duke would be able to handle any situation in which an aristocratic young man might reasonably expect to find himself.

Reasonably.

Astonishingly, his tutors had not considered the possibility that he might find himself accidentally kidnapped by a stark raving lunatic, trapped in a carriage (his own carriage, mind you) for two hours with four unmarried ladies, one of whom had groped him three times before he used a bump in the road as an excuse to toss her across the carriage. And if that hadn't been enough, he'd been deposited into a barely heated castle guarded by a roving pack of ancient retainers hobbling along with weapons attached to their kilts.

Dear Lord, he *fervently* didn't want a stiff wind to lift any of those kilts.

Bret glanced over at the young lady who'd been left in the sitting room with him, the one old Ferguson claimed had been snatched by accident. Miss Burns, he thought her name was. She seemed to know Taran Ferguson better than any of the other erstwhile captives, so he asked her, "Do you think our host will find rooms for us?"

She huddled closer to the fire. "I can almost guarantee he's already forgotten he's meant to be looking."

"You seem to be well acquainted with our host, Miss . . . It was Miss Burns, wasn't it?"

"Everyone knows Taran," she said, then seemed to remember herself and added, "Your Grace."

He nodded. She seemed a sensible young lady, thankfully not given to hysterics. Although it had to be said, he'd come close to cheering her on when she'd given old Ferguson a tongue-lashing. Hell, he'd been hoping she'd wallop the old codger.

Miss Burns returned his gesture with a smile and nod of her own, then turned back to the fire. They'd both been standing in front of it for several minutes, but if her fingers were anything like his, they still felt frozen from the inside out.

If he'd had a coat he would have given it to her. But his coat was back at Bellemere, along with the rest of his things. He'd meant to stay for only two days; it was a convenient place to stop and rest his horses on the way back to Castle Bretton from the Charters shooting party in Ross-shire. In retrospect, he should have just remained with his friends for the holiday; only a fool took to the roads in Scotland at this time of year.

But he'd always had a sentimental streak when it came to Castle Bretton at Christmastime. He might make his home in London for much of the year, but he couldn't imagine being anywhere else when the Yule log was lit and Mrs. Plitherton's famous Christmas pudding was brought to the table. He had almost no family with whom to celebrate—just his mother and whichever of her maiden sisters chose to join them. But the lack of Shevingtons had made the holiday a jollier, less formal affair, with songs and dancing, and the whole of the household—from the butler down to the scullery maids—joining in on the fun.

Now it seemed his tradition would be broken by Taran Ferguson, the improbable uncle of both Oakley and Rocheforte.

Oakley and Rocheforte. He'd nearly fallen over when he saw them. He'd known Oakley since . . . well, since he'd punched him in the eye their first week at Eton and gotten a bloody lip in return. But it had all been good since then.

As for Rocheforte, Bret didn't know him well, but he'd always seemed an amiable, devil-may-care sort of fellow.

Bret glanced out the window, not that he could see anything. "When you said it was going to snow tonight," he said to Miss Burns, "had you any thoughts as to the amount? Or duration?"

She turned to him with frank dark eyes. "Are you asking me when we might be able to leave?"

He liked a woman who got to the point. "Precisely that."

She grimaced. "It may well be three days, Your Grace. Or more."

"Good Lord," he heard himself say.

"My thoughts exactly."

He cleared his throat. "Has Mr. Ferguson ever done . . . *this* before?"

Her lips pressed together with what he thought might be amusement. "Do you mean kidnap a duke?"

"Kidnap anyone," he clarified.

"Not to my knowledge, but he did run bare-arsed through the village last May Day."

Bret blinked. Had she just used the word "arse"? He tried to recall the last time he'd heard a gentlewoman do so. He was fairly certain the answer was never. Then, as he watched the firelight flickering across her skin, he decided he didn't care.

Miss Burns wasn't beautiful, not in the way Lady Cecily was, with her rosebud mouth and heart-shaped face. But she had something. Her eyes, he decided. Dark as night, and blazingly direct. You couldn't see what she was thinking, not with eyes so dark.

But you could *feel* it.

"Your Grace?" she murmured, and he realized he'd been staring.

"I'm sorry," he said automatically. "You were saying?"

Her brows rose a fraction of an inch. "Do you mean," she asked with careful disbelief, "for me to continue the story about Taran Ferguson going bare-arsed through the village?"

"Precisely," he clipped, since if he spoke in any other tone of voice, he might have to admit to himself that he was blushing.

Which he was quite certain he did not do.

She paused. "Well," she said, clearing her throat, "there was a wager."

This he found interesting. "Do many Scottish wagers involve racing about unattired?"

"Not at all, Your Grace." And then, just when he thought he might have offended her, the corners of her lips made the slightest indentation of a smile, and she added, "The air is far too chilly for that."

He smothered a laugh.

"I believe the wager had something to do with making the vicar's wife faint. There was no requirement for nudity." Her eyes gave a slight heavenward tilt of exasperation. "That was Taran's invention entirely."

"Did he win?"

"Of course not," Miss Burns scoffed. "It would take more than his scrawny backside to make a Scotswoman faint."

"Scrawny, eh?" Bret murmured. "Then you looked?"

"I could scarcely *not*. He ran down the lane whooping like a banshee."

For a moment he stared. She looked so lovely standing there by the fire, her thick hair just starting to come loose from its pins. Everything about her looked prim and proper and perfectly appropriate.

Except her expression. She'd rolled her eyes, and scrunched her nose, and he thought she might have just snorted at him.

Snorted. He tried to remember the last time he'd heard a gentlewoman do *that* in his presence. Probably the last time one had said "arse."

And then the laugh that had been fizzing within him finally broke free. It started small, with just a silent shake, and then before he knew it, he was roaring, bent over from the strength of it, rolling and rumbling in his belly, coming out in great, big, beary guffaws.

He tried to remember the last time he'd laughed like this.

Wiping the tears from his eyes, he looked over at Miss Burns, who, while not doubled over, was laughing right along with him. She was clearly trying to maintain some dignity, keeping her lips pressed together, but her shoulders were shaking, and finally, she sagged against the wall and gasped for breath.

"Oh my," she said, waving a hand in front of her face for no apparent reason. "Oh my." She looked at him, her eyes meeting his with a direct gaze that he suspected was as much a part of her as her arms and legs. "I don't even know what we're laughing about," she said with a helpless smile.

"Nor I," he admitted.

The laughter fell softly away.

"We must be hungry," she said quietly.

"Or cold."

"Insensible," she whispered.

He stepped toward her. He couldn't not. "Completely."

And then he kissed her. Right there in front of the fire in Taran Ferguson's sitting room, he did the one thing he shouldn't do.

He kissed her.

When the duke stepped away, Catriona felt cold. Colder than when she'd been in the carriage. Colder than when she'd been standing in the snow. Even with the fire burning brightly at her back, she was cold.

This wasn't the cold of temperature. It was the cold of loss.

His lips had been on hers. His arms had been around her. And then they weren't.

It was as simple as that.

She looked up at him. His eyes—good heavens, they were blue. How had she not noticed it? They were like a loch in summer, except a loch didn't have little flecks of midnight, and it couldn't stare straight into her soul.

"I should apologize," he murmured, staring at her with something approaching wonder.

"But you won't?"

He shook his head. "It would be a lie."

"And you never lie." It wasn't a question. She knew it was true.

"Not about something like this."

She felt her tongue dart out to moisten her lips. "Have you done this before?"

A small smile played across his features. "Kissed a woman?"

"Kissed a stranger."

He paused, but for only a moment. "No."

She shouldn't ask, she knew she shouldn't. But she did, anyway. "Why not?"

His head tilted to the side, just an inch or so, and he was peering at her face with the most remarkable expression. He was studying her, Catriona realized. No, he was *memorizing* her.

Then his smile turned sheepish, and she *knew*. She simply knew that his was not a face that often turned sheepish. He was as befuddled by the moment as she was.

It was amazing how much better that made her feel.

"I don't believe I've ever met a stranger I wanted to kiss," he murmured.

"Nor have I," she said quietly.

He moved his head slightly, acknowledging her comment and waiting. Waiting for . . .

"Until now," she whispered. Because it wouldn't be fair not to say it.

His hand touched her cheek, and then he was kissing her again, and for the first time in her life, Catriona considered believing in magic and fairies and all those other fey creatures. Because surely there could be no other explanation. Something was raging within her body, rushing through her veins, and she just wanted . . .

Him.

She wanted him in every possible way.

Dear God above.

With a gasp she broke away, stumbling back, away from the fire and away from the duke.

She would have stumbled away from herself if she could have figured out how to do it.

"Well," she said, brushing at her skirts as if everything were normal, and she hadn't just thrown herself at a man who probably took tea with the king. "Well," she said again.

"Well," he repeated.

She looked up sharply. Was he mocking her?

But his eyes were warm. No, they were hot. And they made her feel things in parts of her she was quite sure she wasn't supposed to know about until she was in her marriage bed. "Stop that," she said.

"Stop what?"

"Looking at me. Like . . . like . . ."

He smiled slowly. "Like I like you?"

"No!"

"Like I think you kiss very well?"

"Oh God," she moaned, covering her face with her hands. It was not her habit to blaspheme, but then it was not her habit to kiss a duke, and it was definitely not her habit to be thrown into a carriage and transported ten snowy miles across impassable roads.

"I promise you," she said, her face still in her hands, "I don't usually do this."

"This I know," he said.

She looked up.

He smiled again, that lazy, boyish tilt of his lips that flipped her insides upside down. "The madness of the moment. Of the entire evening. Surely we can all be forgiven uncharacteristic behavior. But I must say . . ."

His words trailed off, and Catriona found herself holding her breath.

"I'm honored that your moment of uncharacteristic madness was with me."

She backed up a step. Not because she feared him but because she feared herself. "I'm a respectable lady."

"I know."

She swallowed nervously. "I would appreciate it if you didn't . . . ehrm . . ." She couldn't finish the statement. He would know what she meant.

The duke turned to face the fire, holding his hands out toward the warmth. It was as clear a signal as any that they would put their momentary insanity behind them. "I am just as susceptible to the strangeness of the situation," he remarked. "I don't usually do this sort of thing, either."

Delilah.

Catriona fairly jumped. Back in the carriage, when he'd been intoxicated . . . He'd called her Delilah.

He obviously did this sort of thing with *her.*

"Where's Taran?" she practically groaned.

"Didn't you say he likely forgot about us?"

She sighed.

"Oakley won't," the duke said.

She turned and blinked. "I beg your pardon."

"Lord Oakley. He won't forget to find us rooms. I've known him for years. The only thing that is making this bearable is that he must be dying inside over all this."

"You don't like him?"

"On the contrary. I've long considered him a friend. It's why I enjoy his misery so much."

Men were very strange, Catriona decided.

"He's quite proper," the duke explained.

"And you're not?" She bit her lip. She should not have asked that.

The duke did not turn, but she saw a faint smile play across his mouth. "I'm not as proper as he is," he said. Then he glanced her way. "Apparently."

Catriona blushed. To the tips of her toes, she blushed.

The duke shrugged and turned back to the fire. "Trust me when I tell you that nothing could give him greater agony than to be party to something like this. I'm sure he'd much rather be the aggrieved than the perpetrator."

"But he's not—"

"Oh, he'll still feel like he is. Ferguson is his uncle."

"I suppose." She was quiet for a moment, then asked, "What about the other one?"

"Rocheforte, you mean?" he asked, after the tiniest pause.

She nodded. "Yes, although . . . Is he Mr. Rocheforte or Lord Rocheforte? I feel quite awkward not knowing what to call him. I've never met a French comte before."

The duke gave a little shrug. "Mr. Rocheforte, I believe. It would depend upon the recent Royal Charter."

Catriona had no idea what he was talking about.

"He won't mind whatever you call him," the duke continued. "He takes nothing seriously. He never has."

Catriona was silent for a moment. "An odd set of cousins," she finally said.

"Yes, they are." Then he turned to her abruptly and commanded, "Tell me about the rest of them."

For a moment she just stared in surprise. His tone had been so imperious. But she did not take offense. It was likely a more usual tone of voice than the one he had been using. He was a duke, after all.

"We're to be stuck together for several days," he said. "I should know who everyone is."

"Oh. Well . . ." She cleared her throat. "There is Lady Cecily, of course. But her father is the Earl of Maycott. Since you were at Bellemere, you must know her already."

"A bit," he said offhandedly.

"Well, that's more than I know of her. Her family has been renovating Bellemere for nearly two years. It seems a folly to me, but . . ." She shrugged.

"You're quite practical, aren't you?"

"May I take it as a compliment?"

"Of course," he murmured.

She smiled to herself. "I don't think the Maycotts plan to be in residence for more than two weeks per year. It seems an inordinate amount of money to spend on a house one rarely uses."

"It's lovely, though."

"Well, yes. And I cannot complain. The village has not been prosperous since—" She stopped herself. Better not introduce politics with an Englishman. Especially one who likely owned half of England. "The

Earl of Maycott has provided many jobs for the villagers, and for that I am grateful."

"And the others?" he asked.

"The Chisholm sisters," Catriona said. Dear heavens, how to explain *them*? "They are half sisters, actually, and . . . not terribly fond of each other. I don't really know Fiona that well—it's Marilla who is my same age." She pressed her lips together, trying to adhere to the whole if-you-don't-have-anything-nice-to-say doctrine. "They've both been down to London, of course," she finally said.

"Have you?" the duke asked.

"Been to London?" she asked with surprise. "Of course not. But I had a season in Edinburgh. Well, not really a season, but several families do gather for a few weeks."

"I like Edinburgh," he said agreeably.

"I do, too."

And just like that she realized that she no longer felt on edge with him. She did not know how it was possible, that she could kiss a man until she barely remembered how to speak, and then just a few minutes later could feel utterly normal.

But she did.

And of course that was when Lord Oakley returned, scowling mightily. "My apologies," he said the moment he entered the room. "Miss Burns, we've found a room for you. I'm sorry to say it's not elegant, but it is clean."

"Thank you," she said.

"You can have my room, Bret," Lord Oakley said.

"And where will you sleep?"

Lord Oakley waved off the question. "Robin will be down in a moment. He'll show you the way." He turned back to Catriona. "May I show you to your chamber, Miss Burns? I apologize for the lack of a chaperone, but there isn't a female available who might take my place. And I assure you, your virtue is safe with me."

Catriona glanced over at the duke. She trusted him, she realized, although she could not have articulated why. He gave a little nod, so she said, "That will not be a problem, Lord Oakley. Your escort is the least improper event of the evening, I'm sure."

Lord Oakley gave a tired smile. "This way, if you please."

She took his arm and headed out of the sitting room. After a few twists and turns, she realized she'd be sleeping in the servants' quarters. But after all that had happened, she decided that as long as she had a blanket, she didn't care.

Chapter 4

The following morning

Catriona had always been an early riser and was well used to breaking her fast with only herself for company, but when she walked into the dining room, the Duke of Bretton was already seated at the table, slathering butter on a piece of toast.

"Good morning, Miss Burns," he said, coming instantly to his feet.

Catriona dipped into a brief curtsy, bowing her head less out of respect than the desire to hide the faint blush that had stolen across her cheeks.

She'd kissed him the night before. She'd kissed a duke. Good heavens, her first kiss and she had to start with a *duke*?

"Are you enjoying your breakfast?" she asked, turning to the well-laid sideboard. Whatever Taran Ferguson's faults, he'd provided an excellent morning meal. There were two kinds of meat, eggs prepared three ways, salted herring, and toast and scones. And, of course, homemade butter and jam.

"In all honesty," the duke said, "I can't remember the last time I enjoyed a breakfast more."

"Mrs. McVittie is the best housekeeper in the district," Catriona confirmed, loading her plate with food. "I don't know why she stays at Finovair. Everyone is always trying to steal her away."

"I recommend the scones," Bretton said.

Catriona nodded as she took a seat across from him. "I always recommend Mrs. McVittie's scones."

"I wonder why we can't get them right in England?" he mused.

"I shall not answer that," Catriona said pertly, "for fear of insulting an entire country."

He chuckled at that, as she'd hoped he would. She needed to keep this conversation light, her observations wry. If she could manage that, she could forget that less than twelve hours earlier, his lips had been on hers. Or at the very least, make *him* forget it.

It was going to be a very long few days if he thought she was pining after him. Good heavens, if he so much

as thought she might be trying to trap him into marriage, he'd run screaming for the trees.

A distinctly non-noble Scotswoman and an English
duke. It was ludicrous.

"You'll have to pour your own tea," the duke said
with a nod toward the pot. "One of Ferguson's . . .
Well, I don't know what you'd call him, certainly not a
footman . . ."

"Men," Catriona said.

The duke looked up at her, clearly startled.

"One of his men," she said quickly. "That's what he
calls them. I don't think there's a one below the age of
sixty, but they are fiercely loyal."

"Indeed," Bretton said in a very dry tone.

"Loyal enough to steal women from a ballroom,"
Catriona said for him, for surely that was what he had
meant.

Bretton looked to his left and then his right, presumably to make sure none of Taran's men were in earshot.
"Whatever he wishes to call the gentleman who was
here earlier, I would not trust his grizzled hands to aim
the tea into the cup."

"I see," Catriona murmured, and she reached out to
pour for herself.

"It is probably no longer hot," the duke said.

"I shall endure."

He smiled faintly into his own teacup.

"Would you like some more?" Catriona asked. At his nod, she refilled his cup with the lukewarm tea, then set about spreading jam on her scone.

"Did you sleep well?" he asked.

"No," she answered, "but I did not expect to." She would not complain about having been put in a maid's room. In truth, she'd been grateful just to get a bed; she'd been half expecting Taran to try to stick her out in the stables. Still, the tiny garret room had lacked a fireplace, and although Lord Oakley had handed her three blankets, they were all quite thin.

At least with Mrs. McVittie as the housekeeper, Catriona could be assured that the mattress was aired out and clean. Bedbugs truly would have been the final insult.

"And you, Your Grace? Did you sleep well?" she asked politely. He'd been given Lord Oakley's room, which had to have been more comfortable than hers. Certainly not up to ducal standards, but still, presumably the best that Finovair had to offer.

"I'm afraid not, but as you said, I shall endure." The duke cut off a piece of bacon, ate it, and then asked, "Is it always this cold?"

"In December?" Her lips parted with surprise . . . and perhaps a bit of disappointment. Surely he had not just asked her such a stupid question. And here she'd been thinking she rather liked the highborn Englishman. "Er, yes."

He did not so much roll his eyes as flick them upward in impatience. "No, I meant *here*. At Finovair. I was shivering all night."

"Didn't you have a fire in your room?"

"Yes, but I fear it was a mirage. And it was dead by morning."

Catriona gave him a sympathetic nod. "My father says it's why Scots marry young."

At this, the duke paused. "I beg your pardon?"

"For warmth," she clarified. "It's tremendously difficult to heat these old castles. I usually sleep with my dog."

Bretton nearly spit out his tea.

"Laugh all you want," Catriona said with an arch little smile, "but Limmerick weighs seven stone. He's like a giant furry hot water bottle that never goes cold."

"Limmerick?"

She turned back to her food. "My grandfather was Irish."

"Since I can only assume Ferguson did not loose the dogs on you," Bretton said dryly, "were you warm enough last night?"

"Not really." She shrugged, resigned to her fate. "I'm in a maid's room. No fireplace, I'm afraid. And, as you surmised, no dog."

His expression turned ominous. "You were put in the servants' hall?"

"'Hall' might be a bit of a stretch," Catriona demurred.

"Bloody . . . sorry," the duke apologized, but not before Catriona heard the beginnings of "hell." "I will speak to Oakley immediately," he said. "I will not have you insulted by—"

"It's hardly an insult," she interrupted. "No more so, at least, than being informed I was kidnapped by accident." She set down her toast and regarded him with an arched brow. "If I must go through the bother of being kidnapped, I should have liked it to have been deliberate."

The duke stared at her for a moment, then smiled, almost reluctantly. "I commend you on maintaining your good humor."

"There is nothing else to do," she said with a shrug. "We are stuck here for the foreseeable future. It behooves no one to flounce about in hysterics."

He nodded approvingly, then said, "Still, the arrangement is unacceptable. I told Oakley you could have my room."

"Not to put too fine a point on it," Catriona said, trying not to be delighted at his ire on her behalf, "but your room is his room, and the last thing he will wish to do is offend the dignity of a duke."

"I have been kidnapped by a caber-wielding relic," Bretton muttered. "My dignity has already suffered a mortal blow."

Catriona tried not to laugh; she really did.

"Oh, go ahead," he told her.

She brought her serviette to her lips, smothered her giggle, then adopted a most serious expression before saying, "It was a claymore, Your Grace, not a caber."

"There's a difference?"

"If Hamish had been wielding a caber, you'd hardly be talking about it over breakfast."

He stared at her blankly.

"It's a log, Your Grace. A *log*. And it's not really used for fighting. We just like to toss them about. Well, the men do."

A good long moment passed before Bretton said, "You Scots have very strange games."

Her brows rose daringly, then she turned back to her tea.

"What does that mean?" he demanded.

"I'm sure I have no idea what you are talking about."

"That *look*," he accused.

"Look?" she echoed.

His eyes narrowed. "You don't think I can toss a caber."

"Well, I know *I* can't toss a caber."

"You're a *woman*," he sputtered.

"Yes," she said.

"I can toss a bloody caber."

She arched a brow. "The question would really be, how far?"

He must have realized he'd begun to resemble a strutting peacock, because he had the grace to look a little bit sheepish. And then he completely surprised her by saying, "A few inches, at the very least."

Catriona held her supercilious expression for precisely two seconds before she lost control entirely and burst out laughing. "Oh my," she gasped, wiping her eyes. "Oh my."

Which was precisely the moment Marilla chose to enter the dining room. Marilla, who Catriona was certain rarely rose before noon. Clearly, someone had tipped her off that the duke was an early riser.

"You're very jolly, Catriona," Marilla said. Although from Marilla's lips, it sounded more like an accusation.

Catriona opened her mouth to reply, but anything that might have resembled an intelligent comment died upon her lips. For Marilla had abandoned her thoroughly impractical evening dress in favor of a heavy brocade gown dating from sometime in the prior century.

Not that *that* would have given Catriona pause. She was all for making do, and if Taran's wardrobes contained nothing but leftovers from Georgian times, then so be it. But Marilla had chosen a dress of the deepest, darkest, most sensual red, with a tightly corseted waist and a square-cut neckline that dipped far lower than it ought.

"Isn't it lovely?" Marilla said, smoothing her hand along the skirt. "There was an entire trunk full of gowns in the attic. One of Taran's men brought it down."

Catriona just stared, speechless. As for the duke, he couldn't seem to take his eyes off Marilla's breasts, which trembled like barely set custard with every movement. Catriona would have been irritated, except that she couldn't take her eyes off them, either. They had been pushed up so high the tops had gone completely flat. She could have balanced a dinner plate on them without losing a crumb.

"Marilla," Catriona suggested, "perhaps you should . . . er . . ."

"I couldn't possibly wear the same gown two days in a row," Marilla remarked.

Catriona, clad in the same green velvet she'd been wearing the night before, decided to refrain from comment.

"It's a bit like a masquerade," Marilla said with a jaunty little flick of her wrist.

Catriona and the duke gasped in unison, as Marilla very nearly tumbled free. But Marilla must not have noticed, because she kept jaunting about, chattering on about her room, her sister, her dress . . . and with every movement, Catriona flinched, terrified that Marilla's breasts were going to burst forth and pummel them all.

"Miss Marilla," the duke said, finally rising to his feet. He cleared his throat. Twice. "I hope you're hungry. Mr. Ferguson's housekeeper has outdone herself."

"Oh, I rarely eat more than a square of toast in the morning," Marilla replied. She looked down at the feast before her, then added, "With jam, of course."

"You might wish to make an exception for this morning," Catriona said as the duke sat back down. "You will need your strength. His Grace has expressed an interest in caber tossing."

"Caber tossing?" Marilla echoed. "How very, very noble you are to take an interest in our Scottish customs, Your Grace."

Catriona wasn't sure how this made him noble, much less very, very noble, but she decided to let that point pass in favor of: "I think it will be great fun. As long as the duke is here in Scotland, he may as well learn some of our traditions."

"It will be cold," Marilla pointed out.

Marilla was right, of course. It would be viciously cold, and were Catriona arguing the point with anyone else, she would have abandoned the suggestion in favor of a hot toddy by the fire. But Marilla had always been a thorn in her side, and more to the point, she kept *jiggling* herself at the duke.

"It will be invigorating," Catriona said. Then added, "Of course we will have to cover up."

"I think it's a grand idea," the duke said.

"You do?" Catriona asked.

"You do?" Marilla echoed, followed by: "Of course you do. You have such a very fine sense of sportsmanship, Your Grace."

"Very, very fine," Catriona muttered.

"Although we might want to wait until the snow lets up," he said.

Marilla placed a fluttery hand on her heart. "Is it still snowing, then?"

Catriona motioned to the window. "The window is right in front of you."

Marilla ignored her. "Oh, what will become of us?"

"I recommend bacon," Catriona said flatly. "Surely we will need reserves to keep ourselves going for the duration."

The duke made a choking sort of sound.

"Well," Marilla said, "perhaps just a piece."

Or three, apparently.

Marilla came over to the table with her toast, jam, and bacon and sat at the duke's right, her chair somehow sliding to within inches of his. She smiled prettily at him as her breasts very nearly poked into his arm.

Catriona could only stare in wonderment. Surely those old-fashioned corsets could not have been comfortable. Marilla's chest preceded the rest of her by at least six inches.

"Did you sleep well?" the duke asked, valiantly trying to keep his eyes aloft.

"Oh heavens, no," Marilla replied, laying a hand on his arm. "I was frightfully cold."

"Perhaps Mr. Ferguson might lend you a dog," he murmured.

Marilla blinked her pretty blue eyes.

Catriona, on the other hand, choked on her tea.

"And my bed was frightfully stiff and hard," Marilla continued, sighing tremulously. She turned to the duke with melting eyes. "What about yours?"

"My . . . er . . . *what?*"

"Your bed, Your Grace," Marilla murmured. "Was it stiff and hard?"

Catriona thought Bretton might expire on the spot. And what was that . . . a blush? He was blushing! He was!

"But the pillows were nice," Marilla continued. "I do love a soft pillow, don't you?"

The duke's eyes immediately fell to Marilla's soft pillows. Catriona couldn't fault him for that; so did hers. It was rather like Taran's scrawny arse when he'd run through the village trying to shock the vicar's wife. It was impossible not to look.

"Ehrm . . . I . . . ehrm . . ." The duke picked up his teacup and drained the dregs.

"How long do you think it will be before someone saves us?" Marilla said in a breathy voice.

"We are hardly in danger, Miss Marilla," Bretton replied.

"Still." She sighed dramatically. "Ripped from our homes."

"From Lady Cecily's home," Catriona corrected, still focusing on her food. She couldn't look up. She really couldn't. The way Marilla was shaking about, she was terrified by what she might see.

"Still," Marilla said, with a touch less sweetness and light than the "still" she'd directed at the duke.

"Whatever shall we do to occupy ourselves?" she continued.

"I believe Miss Burns suggested tossing a caber," Bretton remarked.

Marilla blinked. "Oh, but you cannot be serious."

Catriona looked up just in time to see him give a falsely modest shrug. "I don't see why I couldn't give it a try," he murmured. "Besides, did you not just praise my fine sense of sportsmanship?"

"But Your Grace," Marilla said. "Have you ever seen a caber?"

"Miss Burns tells me it's a log."

"Yes, but it's— Oh!"

"Oh my heavens, I'm so sorry," Catriona said. "I have no idea how my jam flew off my spoon like that."

Marilla's eyes narrowed to slits, but she said nothing as she picked up her serviette and wiped the red blob off her chest before it slid into the deep, dark crevasse between her breasts.

If the duke thought that a caber was a simple little log, Catriona wasn't going to let Marilla tell him otherwise.

"Oh dear me," Marilla said, leaning toward the duke. "I can't reach the butter."

Bretton dutifully reached out for the butter, which was to his right, and Catriona watched with amazement as Marilla scooted even closer to him while he wasn't looking at her. When he turned around, she was just a few inches away, batting her lashes like butterfly wings.

If Catriona hadn't disliked Marilla for so many years, she would have been impressed. Really, one had to give the girl credit for persistence.

The duke shot Catriona a look that said clearly, *Save me*, and she was trying to figure out precisely how she might accomplish this when they all heard the sound of approaching footsteps. Lord Oakley arrived on the scene, and Bretton shot to his feet to greet his friend.

"Oakley!" he said, with enough enthusiasm that Lord Oakley's expression took on a vague tinge of alarm.

"Bret," Lord Oakley said slowly, glancing about the room as if waiting for someone to jump out and yell, "Surprise!"

"Join us," the duke ordered. "Now."

"Good morning, Lord Oakley," Marilla said.

Oakley glanced down at her and flinched.

"You remember Miss Marilla," Bretton said.

"Oh, don't be silly," Marilla said with a laugh that set her all a-quivering. "How could he possibly forget any of us?"

Lord Oakley made haste to the sideboard, piling his plate with food.

"Miss Burns and I were just finishing," Bretton said quickly.

Catriona felt her lips part, and she almost said, *We were?* But the duke shot her a look of such desperation, all she could do was nod and grunt, "Mmm-hmm," over the giant forkful of eggs she'd just thrust into her mouth.

"You may keep Miss Marilla company," the duke said to Lord Oakley.

Catriona shoveled two more bites of food into her mouth, watching Marilla as she eyed Lord Oakley assessingly.

The poor man was an earl, Catriona thought with a twinge of guilt. Marilla was going to be on to him like . . .

Well, like she'd been on to the duke.

Still, Catriona couldn't be expected to save everyone from Marilla, and the duke had asked first . . .

Silently, but still. She'd got his meaning.

"Miss Burns?" the duke said, holding out his arm impatiently.

She nodded and held up a hand in a just-one-moment gesture as she gulped down the rest of her tea.

"We're going for a walk," the duke said to Lord Oakley.

"That sounds lovely," Marilla said.

"Oh, but you must finish your breakfast," Catriona said quickly. "And keep Lord Oakley company."

"I would love that above all things," Marilla said. She turned to Lord Oakley, who had taken a seat next to her, and smiled seductively at him over her bosom.

Catriona thought she might have heard Lord Oakley gulp. But she couldn't be sure. The duke had already taken her arm and was hauling her toward the door.

Chapter 5

Bret did not let go of Miss Burns's arm until they had put three full rooms between them and Marilla Chisholm. Only then did he turn to her and say, "Thank you." And then, because once was not even remotely enough: "*Thank you.*"

"You're quite welcome," she said, looking down at something in her hand.

"You brought a scone?" he asked.

She shrugged. "I was still hungry."

His fault. But surely she'd forgive him.

She glanced toward the door through which they'd just come. "I think I may have left a trail of crumbs."

"My deepest apologies," Bret said, "but I—"

"There is no need to apologize," Miss Burns said, "as long as you don't mind if I finish eating while we're standing here."

"Please."

She took a dainty little bite, then said, "I thought Marilla was going to attack you."

"Is she always so . . ."

"Forward?"

A kinder version of the word he might have used. "Yes," he said.

"No," Miss Burns admitted. "But you're a duke." She looked up from her food, her eyes large and filled with the same amusement that played across her lips. "Sorry."

"That I'm a duke?"

"It can't be a good thing at times like this."

He opened his mouth to say . . .

What?

His mouth hung open. What had he meant to say?

"Your Grace?" She looked at him curiously.

"You're right," he said. Because as lovely as it was to be a duke, and it *was*—really, what sort of idiot complained about money, power, and prestige?—it still had to be said, with Marilla Chisholm on the prowl, life as a stablehand was looking rather tempting.

"I'm sure most of the time it's delightful," she said, licking strawberry jam from her fingers. "Being a duke, I mean."

He stared, unable to take his eyes from her mouth, from her lips, pink and full. And her tongue, darting out to capture every last bit of sticky-sweet jam.

Her tongue. Why was he staring at her tongue?

"You needn't worry about me," she said.

He blinked his way up from her mouth back to her eyes. "I beg your pardon?"

"Dangling after you," she explained, sounding somewhat relieved to get it out in the open. "And I think you're safe from Fiona as well."

"Fiona?"

"The elder Miss Chisholm. She's as unlike Marilla as, well, as I am, I suppose. She has no intention to marry."

Bret regarded Miss Burns curiously. "Does that mean that you don't, either?"

"Oh no, I do. But I don't intend to marry *you*."

"Of course not," he said stiffly, because a man did have his pride. His first marriage rejection, and he had not even proposed.

Her eyes met his, and for the briefest moment, her gaze was devoid of levity. "It would be very foolish of me to even consider it," she said quietly.

There didn't seem to be an appropriate response. To agree would be a grave insult, and yet of course she was correct. He knew his position; he had a duty to marry well. The dukedom was thriving, but it had always been wealthier in land than in funds. The Duchesses of Bretton always entered the family with a dowry. It would be highly impractical otherwise.

He hadn't given marriage much thought, really, except to think—*not yet.* He needed someone well-born, who came with money, but whoever she turned out to be, he didn't need her right away.

And yet, if he *were* to choose a duchess . . .

He looked at Miss Burns, peering into her bottomless brown eyes before his gaze dropped to the corner of her lips, where a tiny spot of strawberry jam lay temptingly pink and sweet.

"You're not going to marry me," he murmured.

"Well, no." She sounded confused.

"So what you're saying," he said with soft calculation, "is that, for my own safety, I ought to remain in your company for the duration of our incarceration."

"No!" she exclaimed, clearly horrified by his leap of logic. "That's not what I meant at all."

"But it makes sense," he pressed. "Surely you can see the wisdom of it."

"Not for me!" When he did not answer quickly enough, she planted her hands on her hips. "I have a reputation to consider, even if you do not."

"True, but we need not steal away from the rest, as delightful as that sounds."

She blushed. He quite liked that she blushed.

"All I really need," he continued, "is for you to act as a deterrent."

"A deterrent?" she choked out.

"A human shield, if you will."

"*What?*"

"I cannot be left alone with that woman," he said, and he felt no remorse at the low desperation in his voice. "Please, if you have any care for your fellow man."

Her lips clamped together in a suspicious line. "I'm not certain what *I* get out of the equation."

"You mean besides the joy of my delightful company?"

"Yes," she said, with an impressive lack of inflection, "besides that."

He chuckled. "I shall be honest . . . I don't know. The joy of thwarting Miss Marilla?"

Her head tilted thoughtfully to the side. "That would be a joy," she conceded.

He waited for a few more seconds, then said simply, "Please."

Her lips parted, but whatever word she'd had resting on her tongue remained there for an endless frozen moment. "All right," she finally agreed. "But if there is a hint—even a whisper—of anything improper . . ."

"You can be assured there will not."

"You can't kiss me again," she said in a low voice.

Normally, he would have pointed out that she had been doing her fair share of the kissing, but he was far too desperate for her agreement to argue. "I will do my best," he said.

Her eyes narrowed.

"It is all I can promise," he said quite truthfully.

"Very well," she said. "What shall we do?"

"Do?"

"Or hadn't you thought that far ahead?"

"Apparently not," he said, flashing her what he hoped was a winning grin.

"We can't just stand here all day in the old buttery."

For the first time, Bret paused to take a look about. They were in a pass-through room, with one door that opened to the great hall, and another that was presently shut but probably led to the kitchens. There were a couple of tables, but other than that, the small chamber was mostly empty, save for a few ancient barrels in the corner. "Is that where we are?" he remarked.

She gave him a look of mild disdain. "You do know what a buttery is, don't you?"

"Of course I do. I *live* in a castle."

"An English castle," she said with a sniff.

"It's a *castle*," he ground out. Not as ancient as Finovair, of course, but the Brettons predated the Tudors by at least two hundred years.

"You do know that we don't make butter in a buttery?" Miss Burns said.

"We don't make anything in the buttery," he shot back. And then, when her face still did not release its expression of skepticism, he said, "The buttery was where one got a beer. From wooden butts." He raised a brow. "Satisfied?"

"This was hardly a test."

"Wasn't it, though?" he countered. But he felt a smile approaching. It was a little frightening how much he was enjoying himself.

"We Scots are proud of our history," she admitted.

He gazed longingly at the dried-up old barrel. "I could use a beer right now."

"Beer? A duke?"

"Bait to which I shall not rise," he said archly.

She smiled at that.

"I suppose you'll say it's too early for spirits of any kind," he grumbled.

"Not this morning I won't," she said with feeling.

He regarded her with curiosity. And admiration.

"Well, let's see," she said, ticking off her fingers. "I was kidnapped . . ."

"So was I," he pointed out.

". . . thrown into a carriage . . ."

"You have me there," he acknowledged.

". . . groped . . ."

"By whom?" he demanded.

"You," she said, seemingly without ire, "but don't worry, I got away very quickly."

"Now see here," Bret sputtered. He had never claimed to understand the female mind, but he did understand the female body, and there was no way she hadn't enjoyed the previous night's kiss every bit as much as he did. "When I kissed you . . ."

"I'm not talking about the kiss," she said.

He stared at her, flummoxed.

She cleared her throat. "It was when . . . ah . . . Never mind."

"Oh no, you don't," he warned. "You cannot introduce such a topic and then not follow through."

"In the carriage," she mumbled. And then: "Why *were* you in the carriage?"

"It was my carriage," he reminded her.

"Yes, but the rest of us were in the ballroom."

He shrugged. "I was tired." It was true. And bored, too, although he would not tell her that. The Maycotts' Icicle Ball had been pleasant enough, but he'd really wanted to be home.

"I suppose it was late—" Miss Burns started to say.

"Don't change the subject," he cut in.

She didn't even try to look innocent.

"The groping," he reminded her.

Her cheeks went every bit as pink as they should. "You were asleep," she mumbled.

He had groped her while he was *asleep*? "I'm sure you must be mistaken."

That got her goat. "You called me Delilah," she ground out.

"Oh." He had a sinking suspicion that his cheeks were also going every bit as pink as they should. Which was to say, quite a lot.

"Who's Delilah?" she asked.

"No one whom you would ever have cause to meet."

"Who's Delilah?"

This could not end well. "Surely this is not an appropriate—"

"*Who's Delilah?*"

He paused, taking a good look at her face. Miss Burns was lovely with her color high and eyes flashing. His eyes dropped to her lips, and there it was again, that amazing, overwhelming desire to kiss her. It wasn't an urge so much as a *need*. He could stop himself if he had to, but oh, what a sad and colorless place the world would be if he did.

"What are you looking at?" she asked suspiciously.

"Are you jealous?" he asked with a slow smile.

"Of course not. We just got through—"

"You're jealous," he declared.

"I said I'm not— What are you doing?"

"Kicking the door shut," he said, just as he did so. It was a small room, and only three steps were required to bring him back to her side. "About that kiss," he said, pulling her into his arms.

Her lips parted, just in time for his to brush gently against them.

"I said I would do my best," he murmured.

"Your best not to kiss me," she reminded him, her voice trembling softly into a whisper.

He nibbled at her lower lip, then gently explored the corner of her mouth. "My best, apparently, has nothing to do with *not* kissing you."

She made some sort of inarticulate sound. But it wasn't a no. It definitely wasn't a no.

Bret deepened the kiss, nearly shuddering with desire when he felt her body relax against his. He didn't know what it was about this woman, what mystery she possessed that made him want to possess *her*. But he did. He wanted her with an intensity that should have terrified him. He'd never dallied with gently bred women, and he wasn't angling for a bride. Catriona Burns was all wrong for him, in almost every possible way.

Almost.

Because the thing was, when she was in his arms . . .
No, even when she was merely in the room with him . . .

He was happy.

Not content, not pleased. Happy. Joyful.

Good God, he sounded like a hymn.

But that was what it felt like, as if a chorus of angels were singing through him, infusing him with such pleasure that he could not contain it. It spilled out through his smile, through his kiss and his hands, and he had to share it with her. He had to make her feel it, too.

"Please tell me you're enjoying this," he begged.

"I shouldn't," she said raggedly.

"But you do."

"I do," she admitted, moaning as his hands cupped her bottom.

"You don't lie," he said, hearing his smile in his words.

"Not about this."

"Catriona," he murmured, then drew back a few inches. "Do people call you Cat?"

"Never."

He gazed down at her for a moment, his first inclination to declare that *he* would call her that. He wanted something special for her, something all his own. But it didn't fit, he realized. She would never be Cat. Her eyes were too round, too open and honest. There was nothing slinky about her, nothing cunning or calculated.

Which wasn't to say she wasn't enormously clever.

And witty.

And sensible.

"Who is Delilah?" she whispered. *While she was kissing him.*

And stubborn, apparently.

He pulled back, just far enough to settle his nose against hers. "She was my mistress," he said, unable to be anything but honest with her.

"Was?"

If his life had been written by Shakespeare, he might have said that Delilah had entered the past tense of his story when he first laid eyes on Catriona. That he had been so squarely struck by Cupid's arrow that all other women were made insubstantial and colorless.

But the truth was, Bret had broken it off with "Delicious Delilah" some weeks earlier. It was exhausting keeping company with London's most renowned opera singer. Forget her temperament, which was full of drama, both on and off the stage. It was the other *men* who were driving him to the edge. He couldn't get a quiet drink at White's without a pack of young bucks edging over to his table with winks and leers and drunken elbows jabbing in his shoulder.

Even at the Icicle Ball he'd been accosted by a pack of young men dying to talk to him about the legendary lady. To say nothing of the rude and raunchy gestures, as if the young dandies could approximate Delilah's curves by cupping their hands in front of them.

If it was going to be that much *work* to be with a woman, she ought to be someone whose company he could not live without.

He drew back another inch, and then another, regarding Miss Burns—*Catriona*—with something approaching wonder. "Was," he affirmed softly. "I do not have a mistress right now. I could not, I think . . ."

Now that I've met you.

But he didn't say it. How could he say it? It couldn't possibly be true. A man didn't fall in love, or like, or anything more than lust in so short a time. It did not happen. And it certainly did not happen to him.

"I think you have bewitched me," he whispered, because surely that had to be it. It did not matter that he did not believe in fairies or witches or magic of any sort.

He bent down to kiss her again, surrendering himself to the enchantment, but the moment his lips touched hers, they heard a commotion in the great hall, followed by a terrible sound.

Taran Ferguson, bellowing Catriona's name.

Chapter 6

Catriona supposed she should be thankful. Kissing the duke again was the last thing she should be doing, and it was difficult to imagine anything that might more quickly extinguish her desire than the possibility of Taran Ferguson barging in on them.

"I might have to kill him," the duke muttered, pulling reluctantly away.

"Catriona Burns!" Taran bellowed.

"I've got to go see what he wants," she said, trying to smooth her skirts. Did she look rumpled? She *felt* rumpled.

Bretton stepped away with a nod toward the door, but before she could head out into the great hall, Taran burst into the buttery, his eyes narrowing when they settled on its occupants.

"Catriona Burns," he accused. "What the devil are you doing here?"

"You kidnapped me," she reminded him.

"Not on purpose!"

Normally, she would have blistered him with a scathing retort, but it was difficult to maintain the moral high ground when Taran had just caught her alone with the Duke of Bretton.

"Ye're under my roof, lassie," Taran said sternly, "which means ye're under my protection."

"He did not just say that," the duke remarked, to no one in particular.

"Oh no, you don't," Catriona said furiously, jabbing her finger into Taran's shoulder. "I wouldn't be in this situation if it weren't for you. You don't get to claim dominion—"

"I'll not return you to your father as damaged goods," Taran cut in.

"I *know* you did not just say *that*," the duke said in a terrifyingly quiet voice. "Because if you did, I might have to kill you."

"Eh," Taran grunted, "you were already planning on that." He waved an impatiently dismissive hand at the duke and turned back to Catriona. "You cannot be left alone with him."

"You left me alone with him last night," Catriona reminded him.

Taran looked at her blankly.

"When you were supposedly trying to find us rooms," she added.

Taran cleared his throat. "Ach, well. You can't be alone with him anymore. I have known your father for thirty years. I'll not dishonor him by leaving you alone in the bloody buttery with the Duke of Breedon."

"Bretton," came the duke's clipped voice.

"He knows your name," Catriona said to the duke, although she did not take her eyes off Taran. "He's just being contrary."

"I don't care what his name is—"

"You should," Bretton murmured. "You really should."

"—he's not spending another moment alone with you," Taran finished. His large hand made a circle around Catriona's wrist. "Come along."

"Let go of me, Taran," Catriona retorted, trying to shake him off. Good heavens, if her life grew any more farcical she'd have to take to the stage.

"I suggest you release Miss Burns," Bretton said, and although his voice was light and conversational, there was no mistaking the edge of steel beneath his words.

Taran stared at him with a shocked expression before making a great show of letting go of her wrist.

"You know, Taran," Catriona said, shaking out her hand, "while I appreciate your concern for my good name, has it even once occurred to you that the other ladies deserve the same consideration?"

"It's different," Taran grunted.

Whatever patience she'd had with the man snapped entirely. "*How?*"

Taran jerked his head at the duke, who was still regarding him icily. "He's not going to marry you."

"I realize that," Catriona shot back, "but your nephew is hardly going to marry all three of the other young ladies."

"I have two nephews," Taran muttered.

"*Taran,*" Catriona ground out.

But Taran Ferguson had never been one for logic or consistency. He crossed his beefy arms, jutted out his chin, and stared down at her like a hawk.

An infantile hawk.

"Fine," Catriona said with a sigh. "I'll come with you, there's no need to be so dramatic."

"No!" the duke said suddenly.

Catriona turned. So did Taran.

The duke pointed his index finger at her. "You promised."

Taran's head whipped back and forth between the two of them. "What is he talking about?"

Marilla.

"I have to go with him," Catriona said, tipping her head toward Taran. She had told Bretton that she could not spend the day alone with him. Finovair might be remote, and the circumstances of their gathering might be unusual (to say the least), but the rules of propriety could not be abandoned completely. When all was said and done, the Duke of Bretton was not going to marry Miss Catriona Burns of Kilkarnity. And Marilla Chisholm would still be the biggest gossip north of Dunbar.

Catriona might be headstrong, but she was no rebel, and she did not think she could face a life as a social pariah. More to the point, she did not think her parents could face it.

She would not shame them that way. She could not.

With a weary sigh, she looked at the duke, willing herself not to drown in his blue eyes, and said, "Taran is right."

Taran uncrossed his arms and let out a sound that would have put a crow to shame.

"Much as it pains me to admit it," Catriona ground out.

"Then I'm coming with you," the duke said.

Catriona tried to ignore the warm bubble of pleasure his words brought forth. She liked the Duke of Bretton.

It didn't matter if he sought her company as protection from Marilla. Because somewhere, deep down where she was afraid to acknowledge it, she knew that Marilla wasn't the only reason he was insisting upon remaining by her side.

He liked her, too.

And even though nothing could ever come of it, Catriona decided that for once she was going to be utterly impractical and seize the day. Well, perhaps not *utterly.* She had, after all, just agreed with Taran that she should not remain alone in Bretton's company. But if she was going to be stuck here at Finovair for heaven only knew how long, then by God she was going to enjoy herself.

"Taran," she said, turning back to the older man with a devilish smile, "do you have a caber?"

"I'm cold," Marilla whined.

"Stuff it," Catriona said, without sparing her a glance. The men—Bretton, Oakley, and Rocheforte—were gathered around Taran, who was clearly relishing his role as man-in-charge. Catriona couldn't hear what he was saying, but he was waving his arms with great vigor.

"Oh, look," Marilla said, with a decided lack of interest. "Here comes my sister."

Catriona pulled her attention away from the men to see Fiona Chisholm dashing across the snow-covered lawn, hugging an ancient cloak around her. Catriona could see that she, too, had chosen to wear the same long-sleeved gown she'd had on the night before.

"Have they started yet?" Fiona asked breathlessly.

"I thought you were planning on remaining in your room all day," Marilla said in a sulky voice.

"I was, but then Mrs. McVittie told me that they were bringing out a caber." Fiona's eyes danced merrily behind her spectacles. "There is no way I would miss this."

"Taran won't let us get too close," Marilla complained. "He said the caber field is no place for the sexes to mingle."

"When did he become such a stickler for propriety?" Fiona asked.

"You'd be surprised," Catriona muttered.

The three ladies stood in silence for a few moments, instinctively huddling together for warmth as they watched the men from afar. Catriona still couldn't believe they were going to try to toss a caber, although truth be told, it hadn't required much prodding on her part. The men had been almost absurdly eager to show off their prowess; truly, the only difficulty had lay in obtaining a caber. And even that hadn't been that difficult. Taran's men were presently hauling it up from the west field.

Taran said something that made the men laugh, and then Rocheforte grinned and raised his arms as if to make his muscles bulge. Catriona felt herself grinning along with him. She'd had no cause to speak with him this day, but he certainly did seem an easygoing sort.

"Do you know where Lady Cecily is?" Fiona asked.

"No, I haven't seen her at all," Catriona replied. "Of course I've been stuck with Taran since breakfast."

"Except when you ran off with the duke," Marilla said in a waspish voice.

Fiona turned to Catriona with unconcealed interest.

"I didn't run off with the duke," Catriona retorted. "We merely finished breakfast at the same time."

"And left me alone," Marilla sniffed.

"With the Earl of Oakley!"

"You had breakfast with Lord Oakley?" Fiona asked her sister.

"I *was* having breakfast with the Duke of Bretton until Catriona ran off with him," Marilla said.

Catriona let out an exasperated sigh. There had never been any point in arguing with Marilla. Instead, she turned to Fiona and asked, "What have you been doing all day?"

"Altering dresses," Fiona told her. "That's probably what's caught up Lady Cecily, too. Did no one tell you about the trunks that were brought down from the attic?"

"Not until I saw Marilla at breakfast," Catriona told her. "My room is in an entirely different part of the castle."

"The servants' wing," Marilla murmured, not taking her eyes off the men. Lord Oakley was laughing at something that his cousin had said. He looked quite different when he smiled. Much more pleasing to the eye, Catriona decided.

Although still nothing compared to the duke.

Fiona gave her sister an annoyed glance before turning back to Catriona. "If you're comfortable in the dress you came with, you're not missing out. Most of the gowns in Taran's attic were for ladies of more ample endowment than we possess."

Marilla shot her a supercilious look.

"Well, than some of us possess," Fiona corrected. "You really should have let me take your gown out a bit, Marilla."

Marilla ignored her. Fiona shrugged and turned back to Catriona. "Do you think they know what a caber is?" she asked, the corners of her lips tilting into a tiny smile.

"His Grace is aware that it is a log," Catriona replied, biting back a smile of her own. "Of what length or girth he imagines it, I do not know."

"The other two are part Scottish," Fiona mused. "They must be, if they are related to Taran."

"I've never seen them here before."

"Nor I." There was a beat of silence, then Fiona murmured, "It's possible . . ."

". . . that they have absolutely no idea what they're getting into?" Catriona finished for her.

Fiona grinned in response.

"Well, I think you're very unwise to have suggested this," Marilla announced. "When they see the caber and realize they can't lift it, they are going to feel like fools. And men do *not* like being made fun of."

"That presupposes that none of them are in possession of a sense of humor," Catriona responded. She looked over at the men again. Or rather, *still.* She hadn't taken her eyes off them even once. The duke appeared to be having a grand time, laughing heartily at something Mr. Rocheforte had said.

Then he turned, and their eyes met.

And he smiled. Grinned, really.

Catriona's heart stopped. She felt it, thumping loud, then skipping three beats.

"Did you see that?" Marilla said excitedly. "His Grace just smiled at me."

"I thought he was looking at Catriona," Fiona said.

"Don't be silly."

"Bait to which I shall not rise," Catriona murmured.

"What did you say?" Marilla demanded.

Catriona didn't bother to answer.

"Oh, look," Fiona said. "Here come the men with the caber. I daresay the snow is making it easier to transport."

Catriona craned her neck to watch as four of Taran's men brought the caber into view. It was an enormous thing, at least fifteen feet long. They'd looped chains around the enormous log, pulling it along like a sleigh.

"Time to prove your manhood, boys!" Taran announced, loudly enough for the women to hear. His arm swept through the air in a majestic arc. "The ancient, ceremonial caber."

It was gloriously massive. At least sixteen stone and thick as a man's leg.

Catriona felt her lips pressing together, hard, just to keep from laughing. She couldn't see the expressions on Lord Oakley's or Mr. Rocheforte's faces, but the Duke of Bretton's mouth had come positively unhinged.

"Respect the caber!" Taran yelled. "Ye're going first, Duke!"

Bretton stared at it.

"Now remember," Taran said loudly, "it doesn't matter how far you throw it, it's all about landing it on its end."

"You're joking," the duke said.

"It'll balance," Taran assured him, "if you do it right."

Catriona tried not to giggle.

"Excuse me," the duke said.

"Pfft. Brrrght." All sorts of ungraceful noises were spit forth from Catriona's mouth until she finally just gave up and laughed.

"Uh-oh," Fiona said, but Catriona was laughing too hard to have any idea what she was talking about.

"Catriona," Fiona said in a warning voice.

"Oh! Oh!" Catriona yelped, gasping for breath.

"I told you so," Marilla crowed.

Catriona wiped her eyes and looked up just in time to see the duke barreling toward her. "Your Grace," she chirped, the squeaky noise just about all she could manage.

He pointed a finger at her. "You said it was a log."

"It *is* a log," she said, not that her words were remotely intelligible through her giggles.

"It's a bloody maypole!"

"Oh, I think it's bigger than a maypole."

His lips clamped together in a straight line, but he couldn't fool her. The Duke of Bretton, it seemed, was in possession of an excellent sense of humor. In three seconds, he'd be laughing just as hard as she was.

"Still think you can toss it?" Catriona said daringly.

He stepped forward. To the rest of the observers, he must have looked furious, but she could see the mirth dancing in his eyes. "Not . . . even . . . an . . . inch."

And then she lost herself entirely. She laughed so hard she doubled over, so hard she feared she might faint from lack of breath. "Your face! Your face!" she gasped. "You should have seen your face!"

"Catriona!" Marilla exclaimed, horrified. And it was true, Catriona supposed. One wasn't supposed to talk to a duke in such a way.

But his face! His face! It had been priceless.

She laughed even harder, grabbing on to Fiona for support. The other men had ambled over, grinning at her uncontrollable mirth, and out of the corner of her eye, Catriona saw that Lady Cecily had joined the party, too. The poor girl was clad in some sort of antique mourning gown, the heavy black bombazine dragging through the snow.

"Miss Burns needs air," the duke announced, and before anyone could offer an opinion, he scooped her up in his arms and said, "I'm taking her inside."

And just like that, all the chill left the air. Catriona allowed herself the indulgence of resting her cheek against Bretton's chest, and as she lay there, listening to the steady beat of his heart, she could not help but think that this was where she was meant to be.

But then, of course, Lord Oakley had to spoil the whole thing. "You're taking her inside so that she might get air?"

"Shut up," the duke said.

Catriona had a feeling she might be falling in love.

"Wait!" Taran yelled, tramping over through the snow. "She needs a chaperone!"

"I'll go," Fiona offered.

Taran blinked in surprise. "You will?"

"I'm cold," Fiona said with a deceptively placid smile. "And I still have sewing to complete before supper."

"Do you think you might help me?" Lady Cecily asked, fidgeting beneath her cloak. "Nothing they brought down fits, and I am a terrible hand with a needle."

"Of course," Fiona said. "Why don't you come with me? We'll take tea in my room and see to the gowns."

"You're supposed to be chaperoning Miss Burns," Taran reminded her.

"Oh, but Catriona will take tea with us as well," Fiona said. She looked over at Catriona. "If that is amenable."

"I would be delighted," Catriona said, although not, perhaps, as delighted as this very moment, wrapped as she was in Bretton's arms.

"Marilla, you must stay and watch the caber tossing," Fiona instructed. Marilla looked about to argue, but then Fiona added, "The gentlemen must have an audience."

Marilla must have decided that one earl plus one French comte equaled something more than a duke, because her expression quicksilvered into one of utter enchantment. "I cannot imagine a more pleasing activity." She placed a delicate hand on Lord Oakley's muscular arm. "It is all so very, very exciting."

"Very," Catriona thought she heard Lady Cecily say under her breath.

"Back to the caber, then!" Taran hollered. "The old laird and his nephews," he chortled, elbowing Mr. Rocheforte in the ribs. "The way it should be, vying to impress the fairest maiden in the county."

Mr. Rocheforte smiled, but it was a queasy thing, quite unlike his normal expression.

"That's the one I wanted for you in the first place," Taran said in a loud whisper. "Prettiest girl in town. She's got some money. *And* she's Scottish."

Mr. Rocheforte said something Catriona could not hear, and then Taran's bushy brows came together as he grumbled, "It was a whisper! Nobody heard me."

And then, before anyone could contradict, Taran pumped a fist in the air and once again yelled, "To the caber!"

"To the house," Fiona Chisholm said in urgent response, and she hurried off, Lady Cecily right at her heels.

As for the duke, his pace back to Finovair was much more measured. Catriona, snug and warm in his arms, could find no reason to complain.

Chapter 7

B y the time Bret reached the drawing room, Miss
Chisholm and Lady Cecily were nowhere to be
found. "Your friends seem to have deserted us," he said
to Catriona as he set her down upon an ancient chaise
longue.

"Perhaps we were meant to follow them to Fiona's
room?"

"Oh, but I could not venture into a lady's chamber,"
Bret said, placing one hand over his heart for emphasis.

Catriona gave a look that was dubious in the extreme.

"And at any rate," he added, "I don't know where
her room is."

Catriona cocked her head, then said, "Do you know,
neither do I."

He grinned at that. "We seem to be stuck here, then."

"On our own," she said, a small smile touching her lips.

"You're not concerned for your reputation?"

She tilted her head toward the door. "The door is open."

"Pity, that," Bret murmured. He perched on the table directly across from her, testing it first before settling his entire weight; like everything in Finovair, it was chipped and rickety.

"Your Grace!"

"I think you should call me by my given name, don't you?"

"Absolutely not," she said firmly. "And at any rate, I don't know what it is."

"John," he said, and he tried to remember the last time anyone had called him such. His mother did, but only occasionally. His friends all called him Bret. He thought of himself as Bret. But as he looked at Catriona Burns, who had already shifted herself to a sitting position on the chaise, he wondered what it would be like to have someone in his life who would call him John.

"I heard Lord Oakley call you Bret," Catriona said.

"Many people do," he said with a small shrug. He looked down, finding it suddenly awkward to meet her gaze. The conversation had made him wistful, almost self-conscious—a sensation to which he had never been accustomed.

But this feeling that seemed to wash over him whenever he was with Catriona—it was growing, changing. He'd thought it lust, then desire, and then something that was far, far sweeter. But now, swirling amid all this was an unfamiliar longing. For her, certainly for her, but also for something else. For a feeling, for an existence.

For someone to know him, completely.

And the strangest part was, he wasn't scared.

"I couldn't possibly call you Bret in front of the others," Catriona said, pulling his attention back to her face.

"No," he agreed softly. It would be improper in the extreme, not that anything in the past day had been proper, normal, or customary.

"And I should not call you Bret when we are alone," she added, but there was the tiniest question in her voice.

He brought her hand to his lips. "I would not want that."

Her eyes widened with surprise, and—dare he hope it?—disappointment. "You wouldn't?"

"John," he said, with quiet determination. "You must call me John."

"But nobody else does," she whispered.

He gazed at her over her hand, thinking he could stare at her forever. "I know," he said, and at that moment something within him shifted. He knew—and by all that was holy, he hoped she knew, too—that their lives would never be the same.

Catriona stopped at her small garret before making her way to Fiona's bedchamber for tea. She needed a moment. She needed a thousand moments.

She needed to breathe.

She needed to think.

She needed to find a way to face her friends and speak like a normal human being.

Because she did not feel like a normal human being, and she very much feared that Fiona and Lady Cecily would take one look at her and know that she'd been kissing the Duke of Bretton in the sitting room with the door open, and before he'd finally pulled away, his hands had been on her skin, and she'd liked it.

Good God above, she'd liked it.

If he hadn't stopped, she didn't know if she could have done so. But he had lifted his lips from hers, cradled her face in his hands, and looked into her eyes with such tenderness. And then he'd whispered, "Say my name."

"John." She'd barely been able to make a sound, but he was staring at her lips; surely he'd seen his name upon them.

He'd taken her hand, helped her to her feet, and said something about her joining the other ladies before they became concerned. Then he bowed and headed to the nearest exit.

"You're going outside?" she asked. "It's freezing out there."

"I know," he replied, his voice a little strange. He bowed, then said, "Until supper."

And so Catriona made her own way through Finovair's twisty halls, gathering her thoughts, tidying her appearance in her room, and then finally locating Fiona's sparse bedchamber.

Tea had already arrived, and Fiona and Lady Cecily were deep in conversation. Fiona was expertly pulling a seam out of an ancient blue gown. Lady Cecily was sucking on her finger.

"I've stabbed myself," Cecily said.

Fiona shook her head. "I told you to let me do it."

"I know," Cecily replied. "I just didn't want to feel so useless."

"I should think," Catriona opined as she took a seat next to Fiona on the bed, "that given all we've been through, we're entitled to feel anything we please."

The two ladies turned to her with identical expressions. Expressions which, Catriona was alarmed to realize, she did not know how to interpret. Finally, after she could no longer stand it, she turned to Fiona (since she could hardly be so rude to an earl's daughter she'd met only the day before) and said, "What?"

"You've fallen in love with the Duke of Bretton," Fiona said.

"Oh, don't be ridiculous," Catriona tried to scoff. But her voice did not come out as briskly as she would have liked.

Fiona stared at her from behind her vexing little spectacles, lifting her auburn brows as if to say—

Well, Catriona didn't know what she might be saying, or rather, implying, since it wasn't as if Fiona could speak with her eyebrows. Still and all, Catriona knew she had to nip this in the bud, so she said, very firmly, "You can't fall in love with someone on so short an acquaintance." It was what she believed. It was what she'd always believed.

"Actually," Lady Cecily said softly, "I think you can."

That got the other ladies' attention, so much so that Lady Cecily blushed and explained, "My parents have a love match. It has made me a romantic, I suppose."

There was a moment of silence, and then Catriona, grateful for a change of subject, voiced the obvious question. "What do you suppose they are all thinking?"

"Our parents?" Fiona asked.

Catriona nodded.

"They'll be angry, of course," Fiona said slowly, "but once they realize it's only Taran who has taken us, they won't worry for our lives. Or our virtue," she added, almost as an afterthought.

"They won't?" Lady Cecily asked.

"No," Catriona agreed. "Taran may leave our reputations in tatters, but we will be returned every bit as alive and virginal as when we were taken."

And then, with an aching gasp, she realized what she'd said. But if Fiona took offense, she did not show it. In fact, Fiona's voice was completely unaffected as she explained, "It is well known that while Taran's sense of honor is unique, it does exist. He would never allow us to be harmed in any way."

Catriona wanted to say that she had never believed the gossip about Fiona, but she could hardly bring up the subject in front of Lady Cecily. Now she felt a little knot of shame in the pit of her stomach. Why hadn't she gone out of her way to offer Fiona her support? It was true that their paths hadn't often crossed; Catriona had always been much more likely to come across Marilla at local gatherings.

"I'm afraid I won't be able to have a dress altered for you before supper this evening," Fiona said to Lady Cecily, expertly steering the conversation back to mundane waters. She frowned down at the ice blue brocade in her hands. "I promised Marilla I'd finish this one first. Then I'll do yours."

"Surely Marilla can wait," Catriona said. "Didn't you already see to that red dress she was wearing today?"

Fiona snorted. "If I had seen to that red dress, you can be sure I'd have yanked the bodice up a few inches."

"But what about you?" Lady Cecily asked. "I insist that you see to your own gown before mine."

"Nonsense," Fiona replied. "I can—"

"I will not take no for an answer," Lady Cecily said forcefully, "and even if you alter a frock for me, I won't wear it until yours is done."

Fiona looked up at her and blinked behind her spectacles. "That is very generous of you," she finally said.

Lady Cecily shrugged, as if walking around in ill-fitting gowns was nothing to the daughter of an earl. "There is nothing to be gained by complaining about our situation," she said.

"Try telling that to my sister," Fiona muttered.

Catriona and Lady Cecily looked at her with identical expressions of sympathy.

Fiona just rolled her eyes and went back to her sewing. A few moments later, Lady Cecily turned to Catriona and asked, "Have Mr. Ferguson's nephews visited Finovair before?"

Catriona shook her head. "First of all, no one calls him Mr. Ferguson. It's always Taran. I don't know why; it's not as if we're so shockingly familiar with anyone else. And secondly, I'm not sure." She glanced over at Fiona. "We were talking about that earlier. Certainly, I've never met them."

"Nor I," Fiona agreed.

"Do you know them?" Catriona asked Cecily. "I would think you would have been much more likely to cross their paths in London."

"I know of them, of course," Lady Cecily said, "and I've been introduced to Lord Oakley. But not the Comte de Rocheforte."

"Why not?" Fiona asked.

Lady Cecily appeared to hesitate, and a faint blush stole across her cheeks. "I suppose our paths did not cross."

That was a clanker if ever Catriona had heard one. But she certainly wasn't going to say anything about it.

Fiona, however, must not have shared her reticence, because she murmured, "He strikes me as a bit of a rake."

"Yes," Lady Cecily admitted. "I imagine that's why our paths did not cross."

"It seems to me that he ought *not* to be a rake," Catriona said.

Lady Cecily turned to face her with wide, interested eyes. "What do you mean?"

"Just that his is such a ready smile. I haven't shared more than two words with him, but he strikes me as being altogether too *nice* to be a rake."

"He is very handsome, of course," Fiona observed.

"Well, *perhaps*," Catriona murmured.

Fiona grinned. "You're just saying that because you have fallen in love with the duke."

"I haven't!" Catriona insisted.

Fiona replied with an arch look, then said, "You may thank me later for securing you time alone in the drawing room."

Lady Cecily pressed her lips together—presumably so as not to laugh—then said, "I *have* been introduced to the Duke of Bretton."

"Really?" Fiona asked with great interest, saving Catriona the trouble of pretending that she wasn't dying for more information.

"Oh yes. Not that I would pretend any great friendship, but our fathers were at Cambridge together. The duke generally pencils his name on my dance card whenever our paths cross at a ball."

Catriona wondered what it would be like to dance in John's arms, to feel his hand pressing gently at the small of her back. He would hold her close, maybe even a little too close for propriety, and she would feel the heat of him rippling through the air until it landed on her like a kiss.

She felt herself growing warm, which was ludicrous. It was the dead of winter, barely a week before Christmas, and she was trapped in Taran Ferguson's underheated, crumbledown castle. She should be freezing. But apparently, the mere thought of the Duke of Bretton sent her into an overheated tizzy.

"Would you like some tea?" Fiona asked.

"*Yes!*" Catriona responded, with perhaps more eagerness than the question called for.

"It only just arrived before you got here," Fiona told her, "but it wasn't hot even then."

"It's quite all right," Catriona said quickly, thinking she could almost do with an iced lemonade right now, she felt so flushed. She set to work preparing her cup, moving slowly and methodically, needing the time to compose herself.

"Do either of you know what our plans for supper are?" Lady Cecily asked.

"Mrs. McVittie's already laid the table," Catriona said. She'd seen it after she'd left the duke—*John*, she reminded herself—in the sitting room. She'd been discombobulated, but not so much that she hadn't stopped to inspect the seating arrangements. Taran had been at the head, with Marilla on his right, followed by Mr. Rocheforte, Fiona, the duke, Lady Cecily, Lord Oakley, Catriona, and then back to Taran.

Catriona had switched with Lady Cecily, certain no one (except possibly Taran) would be the wiser.

"Please tell me I'm not seated next to Taran," Fiona said.

"Marilla has that honor," Catriona replied. She gave a sympathetic look to Lady Cecily (but not so sympathetic that she regretted having switched their spots). "And you, I'm afraid."

"That's all right, I suppose." Lady Cecily took a sip of her tea. "Did you by any chance see who was on my other side?"

"I think it was Lord Oakley, but I'm not entirely positive," Catriona fibbed. There was no need for anyone to know she'd memorized the seating arrangements.

"Oh." Lady Cecily brought her cup to her lips again. "How perfectly pleasant."

The conversation stalled at that, and then, after Fiona had put her attention back to her needlework, Lady Cecily blurted, "Are either of you chilled? I'm chilled."

"The tea isn't very hot," Catriona said, since the sudden statement seemed to call for some sort of reply.

"And the fire's gone quite low," Lady Cecily added. "Perhaps I should find someone to tend to it."

"Well, I can do that," Catriona said, coming to her feet. It didn't matter how gently bred a woman was. In the Highlands, everyone needed to know how to tend a fire.

"But I think I need a blanket," Lady Cecily said. "This . . . I mean, it's not even really a shawl . . ." She fussed with the piece of fabric draped over her shoulders and made for the door. "Perhaps if I lie down."

"That was very odd," Fiona said, once Lady Cecily had hurried out the door.

Not so odd, Catriona thought fifteen minutes later. It just so happened she had to walk through the dining room to get back to her own bedchamber. When she inspected the place settings, she saw that someone had been busy with the name cards. Lady Cecily and Marilla had exchanged positions.

Catriona shrugged. As long as she remained next to the duke, she didn't care where anyone else was sitting.

Chapter 8

Later in the evening

By the time Bret came down for supper, he was a changed man.

For one thing, he was talking to himself, something he was not accustomed to doing.

"I have a plan," he said under his breath as he headed down the stairs. "A plan. I am a man with a plan." He paused, letting his eyebrows rise at the sound of that. A man with a plan. Ridiculous.

And yet rather catchy.

Which might have explained why he was humming. He never hummed. Or did he? Honestly, he couldn't recall. If he did hum, no one had ever mentioned it.

Catriona would notice if he hummed. She would even say something. And she would have plenty of opportunity to do so, because he was going to marry her.

All he needed was a quiet moment away from the motley crew of guests to propose. He didn't have a proper ring, but he did have the House of Bretton signet ring. It had been placed on his thumb as soon as the digit was large enough so it wouldn't fall off. The ring had moved from finger to finger as he grew, finally settling on his pinkie. It had been in his family for generations, the gold forged during the time of the Plantagenets, the sapphire in the middle scavenged from some Roman ruin. A face had been etched in the gem, an ancient goddess that some Bretton of old had probably rechristened the Virgin Mary.

It meant the world to him. It was the symbol of his family, his past, his heritage. And he wanted to place it on Catriona's finger. To kiss her hand and ask her to keep it safe for their son.

He chuckled out loud, barely able to recognize himself in his own thoughts.

When he rounded the corner to the dining room, he saw that Rocheforte was already there, his eyes narrowed as he examined the place settings at the table.

"Rocheforte," Bret said in merry greeting.

Rocheforte yanked a hand back. Had he been planning to tamper with the seating arrangements? Bret didn't care, just so long as Catriona was by his side.

"Bretton," Rocheforte said with an uncharacteristically awkward nod.

"Please tell me I'm not next to Miss Marilla," Bret said, coming to the table to see for himself.

"Er . . ." Rocheforte arched his neck as he came around to the other side. "No. You're between Miss Burns and the other Miss Chisholm. The one with the red hair and spectacles."

"And you?" Bret returned. "Please feel free to swap the cards if you need to get away from her. It'd do Oakley good to have to suffer through a meal next to her."

Rocheforte cleared his throat, then offered a lopsided grin. "Precisely, although I will confess that my need *not* to sit with her is greater than my desire that my cousin be forced to do so."

Bret took a moment to follow that statement.

"At any rate," Rocheforte continued, "Miss Marilla was already ensconced between Byron and Taran, so we are both of us safe."

Bret chuckled at that. "You will forgive me if I remain in the dining room until the appointed hour, then. We wouldn't want to fall prey to any switching of the place cards."

"Of course not," Rocheforte replied, "although I don't know that we're meant to gather anywhere else prior to the meal."

"Not in the sitting room?"

"My uncle is hardly that civilized. He'll wish to eat immediately."

As if on cue, they heard Taran crashing through the castle, bellowing something about hunger and nonsense and God only knew what else.

"And there won't be any port after the meal, either," Taran was saying as he tramped into the dining room, followed by an aggrieved Lord Oakley and the four young ladies. Marilla was first, still clad in the gravity-defying red gown she'd worn to breakfast. Lady Cecily followed in her delicate blue evening gown, shivering beneath some odd-looking shawl. Fiona Chisholm and Catriona brought up the rear, both of them wearing the same clothing in which they'd been kidnapped.

Sensible women, the both of them, Bret decided. Although he supposed Lady Cecily hadn't had much choice. She'd been in some wisp of a thing the night before. At least now she wasn't going to freeze to death.

"No after-supper port?" Marilla twittered. "Why, Taran, that is positively heathen of you."

"There's no port in this castle," Taran said proudly. "Not when we can be drinking whiskey in its stead."

Bret caught Catriona's eye. She smiled.

"Eh, and besides," Taran continued, "I didn't bring you here to send you off to the sitting room while the men get drunk." He grinned over at Lady Cecily. "I'm much more sociable than that."

"Of course," Lady Cecily murmured. "I would be delighted to have the gentlemen join us in the sitting room after supper."

"We shall play games," Marilla announced.

Bret thought he heard Oakley groan.

"It shall be grand," Marilla continued, clapping her hands together with enough force to make the ladies gasp and the gentlemen avert their eyes.

Except Taran, who stared at Marilla's quivering bosom with open fascination.

"Shall we dine?" Lord Oakley said with great haste. "Mrs. McVittie has outdone herself, I'm sure."

"Oh look, Lord Oakley," Marilla cooed. "You're next to me." She leaned toward the earl and murmured something Bret could not hear. Oakley didn't flinch, so it couldn't have been that bad, but his response was a stammered collection of barely intelligible phrases.

"Miss Burns," Bret murmured, holding out her chair. "How lovely that we are seated next to one another."

He wasn't positive, but he thought she might have blushed when she said, "It is most fortuitous, Your Grace."

Had she tampered with the seating arrangements? He smiled to himself. He was loving her more by the second.

"Well, this is a boon," Taran announced, grabbing the hands of the ladies on either side of him and giving them a squeeze. "The two loveliest lasses in the Highlands, right here next to me."

Marilla beamed and Lady Cecily winced, presumably in pain. Taran did not appear to have modified his grasp for her delicate hand. Bret glanced at Catriona and Fiona, but neither appeared to have taken any affront at having been excluded from Taran's pronouncement. If anything, Fiona looked relieved.

And Catriona amused.

"It is really too bad the rest of you were not able to watch the caber toss," Marilla said to the other ladies. "It was marvelous. The men were so very, very strong."

"Ach, but the point isn't how far you can throw the thing," Taran reminded her. "It's whether you can land it neatly on its end."

"Yes, yes," Marilla said dismissively, "but surely you must agree, sometimes brute force is preferable to finesse."

"Oh, Marilla," Fiona groaned.

"Lord Oakley took my breath away," Marilla said, laying a hand on the newly horizontal plane of her bosom. "He was so strong."

Oakley's color heightened and Bret almost felt sorry for him . . . but not quite.

"His muscles!" Marilla exclaimed. She laid a hand on Oakley's upper arm in what might have been a squeeze. Or a caress. Bret couldn't tell for sure.

"How are you feeling, Miss Burns?" Oakley asked, politely tugging his arm free of Marilla's grasp.

Catriona blinked several times in complete incomprehension.

"You were feeling faint," Bret reminded her gently.

"Oh! Yes. I'm quite recovered," she answered. "Thank you so much for your concern."

Under the table, Bret placed his hand on hers.

"Are you sure you're well?" Lady Cecily asked with some concern. "Your color is quite high."

"I'm fine," Catriona answered. She tugged on her hand, but Bret held tight, his thumb making lazy circles on her palm.

"Did you also toss the caber, Mr. Rocheforte?" Lady Cecily asked.

Rocheforte jerked a little and said, "Yes." And then, while everyone stared at him for his terse answer, he added, "Thank you for asking."

"Who threw it the farthest?" Fiona asked.

"Byron," Taran answered, jerking his head toward Oakley. "But Robin's attempt wasn't anything shabby." He grinned over at Marilla. "I'm leaving him the castle, you know."

"Uncle," Rocheforte said, "don't."

"Eh, now," Taran grunted, "it's not like anyone thinks ye've got two pennies to rub together. We all know what's what."

Rocheforte said nothing, just sat stiffly in his chair.

"I think Finovair is charming," Lady Cecily said, smiling encouragingly at Rocheforte. "It is a lovely heritage."

"Really?" Taran said, drawing the word out with great interest.

"Yes," Lady Cecily replied, dipping her spoon into the soup that had just been placed before her by one of Taran's ancient retainers. "It's a little cold, but of course it *is* December."

"One doesn't always get to choose *when* to live in one's castle," Rocheforte said brusquely.

"Robin!" Taran said sternly.

But Rocheforte just shrugged and turned to his soup.

"You seem quite unlike yourself," Oakley said to his cousin.

Indeed, Bret thought. Rocheforte's silver tongue and ready smile were legendary. Both seemed to have deserted him.

"It must be the cold," Rocheforte replied.

"The cold certainly wasn't bothering you this afternoon," Marilla said, leaning forward so that she could smile at him. "I was shocked when you removed your coat. But I must confess, it did seem to give you a greater range of movement when you picked up the caber."

"I'm sorry I missed it," Lady Cecily said.

Rocheforte flushed.

"*I* was the only one who landed the bloody thing on its end," Taran said.

Marilla gave him a placating smile, patted him on the hand, and then returned her attention to Oakley, who appeared to have nudged his chair as far as he could in the opposite direction.

"Have you recovered from your exertions?" Marilla asked.

Oakley cleared his throat, adjusted his cravat, and turned toward his soup. Somewhere in the midst of all that, he muttered, "Yes."

But Marilla could not be tamed. "I was so very, very grateful that I had a handkerchief with me this afternoon to wipe the perspiration from your brow."

"It was warm, too," Taran chortled, motioning to his chest. "Pulled it right out from—"

"Uncle!" Oakley cut in.

"Eh, well, she *did*. And don't say you didn't notice."

"There isn't a man alive who could fail to notice her bosom," Fiona muttered under her breath.

Bret had a feeling he wasn't supposed to have heard that, but he smiled at her nonetheless.

"What shall we play after supper?" Marilla asked Oakley.

Oakley was speechless.

"Hide-and-seek?" Taran suggested.

"No," Marilla said, playfully tapping a finger on her chin. "It's not very sociable. And you did wish to be sociable, did you not?"

"I always wish to be sociable," Taran replied.

Rocheforte coughed, loudly.

"The problem with hide-and-seek," Marilla continued, "is that all of the players are separated for the bulk of the game. And we must be so quiet. It's hardly fun when the aim is to become better acquainted."

"Quite right," Taran said vigorously. "What a clever lass you are. I had no idea." He jerked his head toward one nephew, then another. "Take note of that, boys."

Oakley smiled tightly. Even Rocheforte could not manage a response.

"Have I mentioned," Bret murmured to Catriona, "how very grateful I am not to have any blood uncles?"

"You don't?"

"Not a one. My mother had six sisters. Three older, three younger."

"And your father?"

"An only child."

"As am I," Catriona said.

"Really?" The sane and lucid part of his brain reminded him that he had known her only one day, but still, it seemed incomprehensible that he did not know this.

"My parents had me quite late in life," she told him. "I was something of a surprise."

"I am also without siblings," Bret said.

"Really?" She smiled, and then he smiled, and it was the most ridiculous, lovebird-hearts-and-flowers sort of thing, but he almost sighed, because it felt like such an important connection.

And then Fiona Chisholm snorted.

"Oh, Catriona," she said, her innocent voice not quite masking a devilish intent, "do you believe in love at first sight?"

"What?" Catriona asked, dropping her spoon.

"What?" Bret heard himself echo.

"What?" came Lady Cecily's voice from down the table.

"I was only wondering," Fiona murmured.

"Do *you* believe in love at first sight?" Catriona countered.

"I don't think so," Fiona said thoughtfully. "It does seem quite improbable."

"Madness," Rocheforte put in.

"But," Fiona continued, "I don't see why one could not fall in love at one's first meaningful conversation. Do you?"

Bret turned to Catriona. She was swallowing uncomfortably, and her cheeks had gone a particularly dusky shade of pink. He knew that Fiona meant no malice, but all the same, Catriona clearly did not relish having been placed so squarely at the center of attention.

"I believe," Bret announced.

Catriona flashed him a grateful glance.

"You believe in what, Your Grace?" Fiona asked.

"In love at first meaningful conversation. Why not?"

"Why not, indeed?" Marilla exclaimed, clapping her hands together. And then she *beamed* at him.

"Oh dear," Bret whispered.

"Did you say something?" Catriona asked.

He shook his head. But he didn't let go of her hand.

"Blindman's buff!" Marilla cried out. "Oh, it will be perfect."

"Then we must play it," Taran said, smiling at her the way she was smiling at Bret.

Good God.

"I've never been good at games," Oakley said, in what Bret thought was a phenomenally lame attempt to escape the oncoming torture.

"I know," Taran retorted. "It's why you should do it more often. You're playing, and that's final. You too, Your Dukeness," he said, jabbing a gnarled finger in Bret's direction.

Which was how Bret found himself cowering in a corner an hour later, answering Marilla's call with as quiet a voice as he could manage.

"Blindman!" she sang out.

"Buff," he whispered.

"Oooh, I hear someone," she sang out.

Bret looked frantically for Catriona. Hell, he looked frantically for anyone. But Oakley was half out the door, and Rocheforte had disappeared entirely. Lady Cecily was standing on a bloody table.

"Blindman!"

"Buff," he mouthed, but Marilla continued marching toward him with unerring precision. There was no way Marilla couldn't see from underneath her blindfold.

"Oh, I do love a meaningful game," she trilled.

Meaningful? Good God.

He caught Catriona's eyes. She had hopped up onto the table behind Lady Cecily. *Save me*, he implored. Surely she would take pity.

But no, she had her hand over her mouth and was giggling away, the traitor.

"Blindman!" Marilla called out.

Bret didn't even bother mouthing the word this time.

"Oh, I hear someone," Marilla cooed, still walking toward him. She held her hands in front of her, moving them this way and that. "You must warn me if I crash into something," she called out. "But of course not some*one*."

Bret inched to the left. If he timed it just right, he might be able to squeeze behind the grandfather clock. He also might knock over the grandfather clock, but he wasn't so concerned about that at that moment.

Just a little more . . . a little more . . .

Marilla turned, following him like a beacon.

"She's good at this game!" Taran hollered.

"I'm good at many games," Marilla murmured.

That was when her hands found his chest.

It was all very amusing.

Until it wasn't.

Catriona had been standing on the table, clutching on to Lady Cecily's shoulder for balance as she watched Marilla stalk the duke. They'd all been laughing, because it was *funny*, it truly was. Even Lord Oakley had started to chuckle, and he never laughed about anything.

But then Marilla attacked.

"Who could this be?" she asked, placing her hands on Bretton's chest. "Remember, you have to hold still while I guess your identity."

Catriona frowned as she watched Marilla move her hands to Bret's shoulders.

"Someone very athletic," Marilla purred.

Catriona's arms began to tingle. And not in a good way.

"Let me see," Marilla continued. She trailed her fingers up to Bret's face, lightly touching his lips. "It's definitely a man," she said, as if that hadn't already been obvious, "but—"

"Enough!" Catriona roared.

"Miss Burns?" Lady Cecily said.

But Catriona had already vaulted off the table and was halfway across the room. "Unhand him!" she yelled, and before Marilla could make a response, Catriona had grabbed her by the shoulders and wrenched her away.

Marilla let out a shriek of surprise and would have crashed into a table had not Taran leaped forward to save her.

"Here now," Taran said accusingly. "That's not very sporting of you."

"She was mauling him," Catriona growled.

"It was just a game," Marilla sniffed.

"It was—" But then Catriona stopped. Because Marilla *hadn't* been doing anything wrong. She'd been playing the game precisely as it had been meant to be played.

Catriona's stomach clenched, and all of a sudden she realized that everyone was looking at her. With pity. With shock. With—

She looked at Bret's face, terrified at what she might find there.

She looked at Bret's face, and she saw . . .

John.

John Shevington, the man with whom she'd fallen crazily, spectacularly, and apparently quite publicly in love.

He would never be the Duke of Bretton to her again. He would never even be Bret. He would always be John. *Her* John. Even if they never saw each other again, if he left Finovair and refused to ever take another step in Scotland, he would be her John. She would never be able to think of him as anything else.

"I'm sorry," she whispered. Because she'd made such a scene. Because now everyone was looking at him, and he was going to be forced to save the situation, to find a way to laugh it all off.

Because she couldn't. It was taking her every ounce of strength not to burst into tears then and there.

"No," he whispered. "Don't be sorry."

She swallowed, then looked down at their hands. When had he taken her hands in his?

"You are magnificent," he said.

Her lips parted in surprise.

And then he smiled. One corner of his mouth tilted up, and he looked so boyish, so handsome, so just plain wonderful, that she thought her heart might burst.

He dropped to one knee.

Catriona gasped.

Marilla gasped even louder. "He is *not* proposing to her!"

"He is," John said with a smile. And then he looked up, right into Catriona's eyes. "Catriona Burns, will you do me the indescribable honor of becoming my wife?"

Catriona tried to speak, but her words tangled and tumbled in her throat, and finally, all she could do was nod her head. But she nodded with everything she had, and finally, when she realized that tears were running down her face, she whispered, "Yes. Yes, I will."

John reached into his pocket and pulled out an ancient ring. She stared at it for a moment, mesmerized by the delicate etching on its sapphire center. "But this is yours," she finally said. She had seen it on his finger. On his pinkie. She hadn't even realized that she'd noticed this about him.

"I am lending it to you," he said, his voice trembling as he slid it onto her thumb. Then he lifted her hand and kissed it, right where the gold touched her flesh. "So that you may keep it safe for our son."

"Kiss her!" someone yelled.

John smiled and stood.

"Kiss! Kiss! Kiss!"

Catriona's lips parted with shock as he drew her close. "Right here? In front of ev—"

It was the last thing she said for quite some time.

Chapter 9

One could hardly say that there was adequate documentation on the matter, but Byron Wotton had always taken hell to be a fiery proposition.

He was wrong. Hell was obviously freezing, decrepit, and located in the Scottish Highlands. What's more, it was ruled not by Beelzebub, but by an uncle with a fiendish sense of humor and not a single gentlemanly instinct to his name.

Byron had been watching, dumbfounded, as his old friend the Duke of Bretton declared everlasting love for a woman he'd met practically five minutes before, when Taran—alias Chief Tormenter—pulled him to the side.

"I hope ye're taking some lessons from that English booby," his uncle hissed.

Byron was watching the besotted look on his friend's face as he gazed into Catriona Burns's eyes. It gave him a queer feeling. Not that he could imagine himself in the grip of an emotion of that sort.

"What are you talking about?" he said, looking away as the duke drew his new fiancée into his arms. Actually, he could only assume they were affianced; he hadn't heard her whispered answer to Bret's proposal.

Given the way he was embracing Miss Burns, though, it must have been in the affirmative. It was truly odd. Byron knew damned well that the duke hadn't any plans for marriage. Bret had confided only last summer that he planned to marry at the ripe age of thirty-five, and he was still a good six years from that milestone.

But now . . .

"Did you hear me?" Taran barked at his shoulder. "I gave you nevvies a chance to do the wooing that you don't have ballocks to do yourselves, and yet you've let an Englishman steal a march on you."

Byron scowled at him. "I have all the balls needful. And may I point out that you're a single man yourself, Uncle, but you haven't done a bit of wooing in the last decade or so that I've noticed."

"I'm too old to put up with a woman."

"More likely one wouldn't put up with you."

"No man in his fifties should be asked to make the sacrifice!"

"You're only a year or two into that decade," Byron pointed out.

"I'm a widower," Taran said piously. "Kept your aunt's memory in my heart, I have."

Byron snorted. No woman in her right mind would accept the old scoundrel.

"Back to the point," his uncle persisted. "You've lost one heiress already. You know what they say: as you grow older, yer balls grow colder."

"You are being manifestly rude, Uncle." He glanced back over his shoulder. Bret and Catriona were still locked in each other's arms.

"Thank the Lord, he's too much of a fool to realize that Catriona Burns doesn't have tuppence to her name," Taran muttered. "Her da will be kissing my feet for last night's work, I'll tell you. Burns would have danced a jig if she'd landed the second son of a baronet, let alone a duke. And he can't say I didn't try to chaperone the two of them."

"Be quiet!" Byron hissed. He'd known the duke since they were both boys, and though Bret was easygoing to a fault, Byron had the firm conviction that no one would ever be allowed to insult his wife without being beaten within an inch of his life.

"As I was saying before," his uncle said, mercifully abandoning that topic, "I'm giving you two every opportunity to snatch up yer brides, same as that Englishman done. Blindman's buff seems to be working. I'll make certain we play it every night. You lads are so lily-livered that you need the help of a blindfold."

"I do not need help choosing a wife, from you *or* a blindfold," Byron responded, keeping his voice even.

"No, yer problem is keeping her, once you've proposed," his uncle scoffed.

The lovers had finally drawn apart, but Bret still held Catriona's hands in his, and was looking down at her with such an adoring expression that Byron felt a true pulse of envy. He hadn't deluded himself that either he or his former fiancée, Lady Opal Lambert, had felt that sort of feverish entanglement, but it was a bruise to his vanity to think that Opal wanted someone other than himself to the point of not caring about scandal.

"One more round of blindman's buff," his uncle called, surging forward. "Marilla, tie that blindfold back on. Now where's Robin got to?"

"Robin left the room a good hour ago, when the blindfold first made its appearance," Byron pointed out. He was rethinking his lifelong policy of courtesy.

Why shouldn't *he* simply retire to his room and stay out of the fray, the way Robin had done?

"Dang and balderdash," Taran muttered. "How does that lad think he'll catch himself a wife if he can't even stay put for an evening?" He started barking out orders. Bret, Catriona, and the rest of the guests reluctantly, but obediently, gathered around Marilla again.

The lady was looking distinctly irritated. She had made it obvious that she hoped to lure Bret into the parson's mousetrap, so she must be vexed that her overly intimate patting of his chest had led to his marriage proposal—to another woman.

But she smiled prettily enough when Taran handed the blindfold to Catriona so that she could cover Marilla's eyes. "Lord Oakley," she called, "you simply *must* join us. This children's game won't be at all fun without you."

Byron stepped forward and Taran scuttled into place beside him.

"*She's* up for anything," his uncle whispered approvingly. "Blast Robin for leaving the room. Here I got him a lively one with a sweet fortune, and he flees like a sheep at its first shearing."

"She's an impudent baggage," Byron said, taking advantage of the fact that Marilla was surrounded by giggling young ladies adjusting her blindfold and couldn't hear him. "Didn't you see how outrageously she behaved with the duke?"

"You are turning into a proper antidote," his uncle snapped, rounding on him. "A pompous, self-righteous turnip! I heard about what you did to your betrothed, merely because she gave a buss to her dancing master. Likely she meant it no more than as a matter of courtesy, and you ruined her reputation for it."

Rage swelled in Byron's chest. He had found his fiancée bent backward over a sofa, one slender leg wrapped around her dancing master's thigh. If that kiss represented the standard expression of appreciation for a dance, there would be far more men capering about English ballrooms. "I will never allow a strumpet to become Countess of Oakley," he replied frigidly. "As for her reputation, I never mentioned the kiss; it was she who told her father all."

"That's the English for you," his uncle said, looking disgusted. "A Scotswoman knows to keep such matters to herself. Though 'tis true Scotswomen have no need to stray. One kilt can keep a woman warm all winter long."

Byron looked away from his uncle and met the eyes of the girl who wore spectacles. Fiona, he thought her name was. Her disdainful expression implied she'd overheard their conversation. He tightened his jaw; he didn't care what she thought.

He wouldn't choose a wife from this assembly if someone paid him. In fact, he'd just as soon never return to Finovair again. Next week, he would travel back to London, and in time he would marry a woman who possessed the proper respect for both her person and his title.

A second later he came to the discomforting realization that the emotion in Fiona's eyes wasn't disdain. In fact, it looked like pity. Damn.

"Turnip!" his uncle repeated, stamping off to the other side of the circle.

Byron took a deep breath. The game had begun, and one glance told him that the blindfolded girl was heading in his direction, arms outstretched. Presumably, he too was about to be patted down. But in his case, no young lady would leap to his rescue.

Marilla's giggles were breathy and uninhibited. She sounded like the type of woman who would throw herself into the arms of any man with a gift for capering.

But he stood rigidly still. It wouldn't be polite to back away from her; the group was watching and laughing, as always seemed to happen during absurd games like this. Taran, for one, was clapping like an organ-grinder's monkey. She was coming closer and closer . . . He would wager anything that Marilla could see through that blindfold. She was heading straight toward him with as much single-minded purpose as a child who spies a sweetmeat.

He wasn't the only one who had realized that Marilla was cheating. Fiona had a distinct scowl on her face as she watched her sister's antics. Even given her spectacles, he could see that she had eyes the color of a dark Scottish forest, the kind that stretches for miles and miles.

Then a fragrant, soft bundle tumbled against him and began laughingly patting him, not on his chest, but his face.

"Oh, I think I know who this is!" Marilla cooed. "Such a resolute chin and powerful brow could only be one man . . ." She burst into a storm of giggles. "And now I must beg forgiveness from the rest of you. Of course, every one of the gentlemen in the room has a strong chin. But this nose . . .'tis a Roman nose."

Byron clenched his jaw. It wasn't her fault that he had taken a dislike to being touched since his betrothal fell apart. He wasn't the sort of man to keep a mistress, and it was something of a shock to realize that he hadn't been with a woman in months. Not that

Opal had touched him in such an intimate fashion, of course.

Marilla was now stroking his neck, which was only slightly less unpleasant than when she touched his face. His repulsion must be some odd response to the dissolution of his engagement.

"Make your guess, Marilla," her green-eyed sister called, a commanding tone in her voice.

"So who do you think you've caught in your arms, lass?" Taran demanded with obvious glee. "Who do you choose?"

"I choose you," Marilla breathed, so softly that no one except him could have heard her. Then, before he grasped what she meant, she said more loudly, "Of course, we all know there's only one way to be certain," and without pause she rose on her toes and brushed his mouth with hers.

Byron reacted reflexively, thrusting her violently away and stepping back. Then, realizing what he'd done, he lunged forward, catching her in his arms as she toppled. "I beg your forgiveness," he said, carefully placing her back on her feet.

The room had gone silent. Lady Cecily was gazing into a corner, an agonized expression on her face, and the spectacled girl was scowling. Bret had the delighted air of a man realizing that he'd barely escaped a man-eating tiger. Deserting all claims to respectable behavior, the duke dropped a kiss on Catriona's rosy lips with a distinct air of relief.

"So you *should*," Marilla cried with a pout, as she pulled the blindfold from her head. "I could have fallen to the floor and injured myself." She widened her blue eyes. "*Not* the action of an English gentleman, Lord Oakley. Nor a Scotsman, either, I assure you."

She was inarguably right. Byron ground his teeth and swept into an apologetic bow. "I offer my sincere regret. I'm afraid I have had a tendency to startle since I was a boy."

"*This* nephew is a nervy type," Taran said, popping up at his elbow like an evil sprite. "Now, my nephew Robin is a real man, the kind who knows how to keep a woman in his arms, though not on her feet!"

This crude jest was greeted with marked silence by everyone except Marilla, who giggled. Byron held out his arm to her. "May I escort you to the stairs? I'm sure we all feel quite tired after our frivolities." It was just the sort of sticklike comment his father would have made.

"Damned if you don't sound older than me," Taran cackled, as if he'd heard Byron's thought.

Marilla on his arm, Byron followed her sister through the door. Marilla's figure showed to exquisite advantage in her evening gown, the high waistline emphasizing her breasts, which were magnificent by any man's measure.

In contrast, Fiona's gown was conservative. Her evening gown was a sober blue, with long sleeves, and without even the smallest ruffle to relieve its austerity.

Still, you knew with one look that her breasts were luscious as well. And sensual, and feminine, and all the things that he hadn't felt or tasted in months. Just because Marilla's were on display didn't mean that—

With a start, he wrenched his thoughts back into place. "I'm sorry," he said, looking down at the bright curls of the girl at his side. "I didn't hear what you said."

"I *said* that the storm is worsening," Marilla repeated, an edge of disapproval in her voice. Clearly, she was under the impression that he ought to hang on her every word.

He cast her a glance that conveyed a censorious view of her pretensions. That look—he'd been reliably informed—was feared throughout London. Oakley was one of the oldest earldoms in the country, and Byron had learned at his father's knee not to tolerate impudent and overfamiliar mushrooms.

Marilla didn't even flinch. She merely patted his arm and dimpled up at him. "But I will forgive you,

Lord Oakley. I know you must have any number of very, very serious matters on your mind. Men are so given to that sort of thinking."

"I do not think it is necessarily a trait of the sex," came a quiet voice in front of them. Fiona was waiting for her sister at the newel post. "Marilla, it is time that we bid the company good night."

Marilla did have a very pretty pout. "No, don't bow again!" she said gaily to Byron, who had no such intention. "We should not be on such terribly formal terms here, don't you agree?" She pointedly looked behind them. Bret and Miss Burns had made it as far as the drawing room door before they started kissing again. "Obviously," she added, "at Finovair we are not obligated to adhere to the very, very silly rules that London society requires."

"Exactly," Taran chortled, coming up from behind to beam at the girl. "We are all friends here."

Byron shot him a silent snarl.

"I would contest that," Fiona stated, putting a hand under her sister's arm.

Marilla jerked away in a somewhat ill-tempered manner. But her face betrayed nothing but sweetness when she looked back up at Byron. "I think we should all be on familiar terms, don't you?" she asked. "My name is Marilla."

She had melting eyes, the color of cornflowers in spring. Ridiculously, Byron felt an overwhelming urge to flee, but stilled himself. It wasn't her fault that her eyes were the same color as Opal's.

"You're asking the wrong person," Taran said with his usual blustery cheer. "My nephew Robin, now, who will someday own this fine castle, *he* will be on the easiest of terms with a lovely lass such as yourself. Byron here is a bit stuffy. Always has been. He got it from his father. I tell you, I thought I'd seen it all when me other sister got married to a Frenchie, but Byron's da was even worse. When she brought the earl—the old earl, that is—back to Finovair for the first time, I almost fled to the Lowlands. He was a humorless, obstinate old bastard who acted as if every Scotsman should kiss the toes of his withered slippers. I never blamed her when she flew the coop."

Byron gritted his teeth. He'd heard the story a hundred times . . . from both points of view.

"Course, it only took a Scotsman one well-placed blow to lay the earl out flat," Taran said, chortling. "Marilla and Fiona's father did the honors. Took out that Englishman with a doubler to the jaw. No . . ." He paused. "I've got a detail wrong, I do believe."

The company waited, some of them even looking faintly interested.

"It wasn't a doubler," Taran finished triumphantly. "It was a roundhouse. We didn't ever see that pompous fart again in God's green country. The man never met a Scotsman whom he didn't find beneath his touch, and the same went for Englishmen. Didn't have a friend in the world, to my mind."

"My father had numerous friends," Byron stated.

"Not one," Taran contradicted. "Even sadder than that was the fact that Fiona's da took him out with one blow. The man didn't even get his hands in position."

Byron heard a little moan. His eyes met Fiona's. Apparently, he wasn't the only one who was finding Finovair Castle less than idyllic.

"My father was not given to common fisticuffs." But he didn't stop when he should have. "And I am not stuffy," he heard himself saying. "As a matter of fact, I am on familiar terms with my *many* friends. My Christian name is Byron, and I invite you all to use it."

Bret had one eyebrow raised now, and his face radiated compassion. Byron gritted his teeth again.

"As I said before, my name is Marilla," the blonde chirped, patting his arm once more. "Now we will all be comfortable with each other! I shall look forward to seeing you tomorrow morning, *Byron*." She said it with a breathy emphasis that made his jaw tighten.

Don't be narrow-minded, he reminded himself, as Fiona grabbed her sister's arm and hauled her up the stairs with what seemed unnecessarily forceful disapproval. True, Marilla was a lively girl.

His father would reject her on those grounds.

"Good work, boy," Taran said approvingly. "Not that I want you to steal an heiress from under Robin's nose. He needs the blunt more than you do. Pretty as a picture, ain't she? I thought she was best of the bunch. Lady Cecily has a bundle of the ready as well. Why don't you take Marilla, and we'll reserve Cecily for Robin. Dang that lad, he's missed all the fun."

Byron headed up the stairs without taking leave of his uncle. There are limits to a man's patience, and he had reached the limit of his.

He wasn't pompous, he told himself. Or stuffy, or narrow-minded. That was his father.

He was just . . . irritated.

Chapter 10

The following afternoon

"I know it's exciting to find yourself in a household with two eligible bachelors, even after the Duke of Bretton made that surprising proposal to Catriona," Fiona said to Marilla, blocking their bedchamber door so that her sister couldn't push her to the side and rush downstairs in hot pursuit of those very bachelors. "But you *must* play this right, Marilla. Neither of the other two gentlemen would be interested in a minx. Your behavior at blindman's buff last night did you no credit, and you already have a mark against you as a Scotswoman."

Marilla scowled at her. "I'm not the trollop; *you* are."

"Just don't play your hand too obviously."

"If they think I'm a minx, it will be because your reputation ruined my chance at a good marriage before I even left the schoolroom," Marilla said shrilly.

Fiona took a deep breath. "I am not under the impression that my lost reputation has, in fact, affected your eligibility for marriage. Your fortune has outweighed such concerns."

"No one could possibly forget what kind of woman *you* are," Marilla retorted. "I would likely be happily married by now if it weren't for you."

It was certainly true that there are some events from which no woman's reputation can recover. An immodest kiss? Perhaps. A lascivious grope? Perhaps not. A fiancé falling from her bedchamber window to his death? Never.

Fiona had been labeled an uncaring trollop throughout her village by sunset on that fateful day; by week's end, she was known throughout Scotland as a reckless fornicator. If not worse. The mother of her former fiancé spat in her path for a good three years at the merest glimpse of Fiona, and she wasn't the only one.

No one seemed to care that when he fell, the lumbering oaf Dugald Trotter had been climbing up to her window without the slightest encouragement on her part. They were too busy being scandalized by her shameless ways—not to mention the fact that she had, in their version of events, "callously neglected" to inform Dugald that mere ivy cannot hold a man's weight. Even those inclined to excuse frolicsome behavior between betrothed couples couldn't seem to forgive her for not warning him.

Of course, any man with a functioning brain could have taken a look at the ivy below her window and come to his own assessment of its strength. But that was how stupid her fiancé had been, at least in Fiona's uncharitable recollection.

Dugald apparently didn't think of it, and she hadn't warned him because—as she kept trying to point out, to no avail—she never planned to welcome him or anyone else to come through her window.

In the aftermath of the tragedy, she often found herself outraged at the universal rejection of her account of the event. Her own father had racketed about the house for months, moaning about how she had besmirched the family name.

"So *you* say," he would bellow, in response to her protests. "What was poor Dugald doing at your window, then? Sharper than a serpent's tooth is a female child! He wouldna climbed your ivy, you silly goose, if you hadna turned a carnal eye in his direction. Ach, poor Dugald, poor, poor Dugald."

There the argument would stop, because Fiona didn't allow herself to comment whenever the chorus of *poor Dugald* reached deafening proportions. She knew perfectly well that she had not thrown Dugald any come-hither glances. In fact, she wasn't even sure what such a glance would look like.

She wouldn't have learned it from Dugald. He seemed to regard her as a pot of gold rather than a nubile woman, at least until the last evening of his life. In fact, she'd thought him more in pursuit of her fortune than her person.

But that night she had refused to kiss his whiskey-soaked mouth, only to find herself shoved against a brick wall and forcibly dealt a wet kiss accompanied by a rough squeeze to her breast. The very memory made her shudder. She had slapped Dugald so hard that he reeled backward, after which she had run into the ballroom—with every intention of breaking her betrothal on the morning.

As for what he was doing climbing up to her window later that night . . . she could only think that he had decided to take matters into his own hands. Presumably, he had planned to force her to accept the marriage, and the only thing that had saved her virtue was the fragility of the ivy.

She certainly could not suggest such a terrible thing aloud. God forbid she would dishonor a man's name after death by suggesting he might have had something so sordid as rape in mind. *Poor Dugald* had killed himself, to her mind.

Besides, she came to think of herself as lucky. What was ruination compared to being married to a beast of a man? She proceeded to shape a life that was happily husband-free, regularly offering prayerful thanks to her late mother for leaving her the fortune that made such a decision possible.

By five years after the "incident," as her father called it, most people had stopped crossing the street when she approached. The last two seasons she had even ventured to London as Marilla's chaperone; her half sister seemed likely to cause a nasty scandal if she wasn't closely watched.

And though Fiona was not precisely fond of her sister—it was hard to imagine who could be—she did love her. Somewhat.

In short, during the last five years Fiona had arrived at the conclusion that the fatefully flimsy ivy had preserved not only her virtue, but her happiness.

A wealthy, unmarried woman has all the time she likes to read whatever she wishes. She can learn cheese making and experiment with medicinal salves for the pure pleasure of it. She can brew dyes from red currants, and then try making wines from the berries instead.

Freed from the need to hunt and catch a man, she could eschew crimping irons and chilly, yet seductive, gowns. She need not blunder around a ballroom pretending that she has perfect eyesight; instead, she can balance a pair of spectacles on her nose and accept the fact that she resembles someone's maiden aunt.

Which status she would presumably attain, someday. She was *free*.

"Please do not spontaneously offer either gentleman a kiss," she said now. "From where I stood, Oakley looked mortified rather than flattered."

"Kissing means very little." Marilla tossed her curls. "You've been out of society too long, Fiona. I can assure you that *he* understood it as a jest, even if *you* did not."

Fiona silently counted to five. Then: "If kissing means very little, I still think it would nevertheless be better to allow a gentleman to kiss you, if he shows the inclination, rather than chasing him yourself."

"As if I would do something that fast!" Marilla caught a glimpse of herself in the glass and froze for a moment to coax an errant lock into place.

She was extraordinarily beautiful; you had to give her that. Fiona crossed the room and picked up a hairbrush to shape the long lock that fell down Marilla's back. Her sister accepted the attention as her due; she was smiling at herself with a tilt of her head that she likely considered sophisticated.

Indeed, Marilla was so exquisite that men could hardly stop themselves from falling at her feet . . .

Though they seemed to fall out of love just as quickly, once they came to know her. As Fiona had bluntly told their father on Marilla's debut, he should have matched her quickly, before news of her temperament circulated among eligible men.

Regrettably, that hadn't happened, though Marilla was only beginning to notice the lack of offers; her vanity was such that she deemed virtually all potential suitors beneath her notice.

"We have only a few days before the pass is cleared," Fiona told Marilla, giving her hair a little tug to get her attention. "Perhaps three or four . . . five at the outside."

"I know that," her sister said, twitching her curl free.

"I have no doubt but that Rocheforte or Oakley will fall in love with you. But I would suggest that you make sure of the man before the three days are up."

"Rocheforte?" Marilla snorted. "Granted, he is very handsome and he's reputed to have a sportive disposition—in every way. But he could have fled back to France for all I've seen him. He hasn't spent more than five minutes with us. 'Sides, I want a title. A *real* title, not some French sham."

"All right, Oakley will fall in love with you," Fiona said patiently. "But not unless you play your cards right."

"Are you implying that I cannot do so?" Marilla cried. "That nun of an English heiress can't hold a candle to me. Though I was shocked to see the duke fall prey to that dreadful Catriona Burns. I've never liked her."

"I have always liked her," Fiona said. "She's exceedingly nice."

"My point is that Oakley will not pose any particular challenge for me."

"Of course not." There was no point in taking issue with Marilla's overweening self-regard. It was as infinite as a starry night. "Do try to control your temper. Be docile and chaste."

"Why should I be docile? I hate to fawn over an Englishman. I—"

"Because you want to marry into the peerage," Fiona interrupted. "The *English* aristocracy. Though I have to say that Rocheforte's title is an ancient and honored one, not a sham in any sense of the word."

"That's right," Marilla agreed, the little smile coming back to her mouth. "I do want to marry an aristocrat. But I don't care how old Rocheforte's title is. He could crawl on his knees across Scotland begging for my hand, and I wouldn't marry him. The man was too superior to join us for games after supper. I'm sure I don't know what right he has to be so haughty; the duke and the earl are perfectly happy to join us."

"In order to marry the earl, you must be docile, courteous, and *gentle*, as in *gentlewoman*." Fiona felt like a governess reciting the alphabet, but that was the reality of being Marilla's older sister.

"Gentleness doesn't suit me." Marilla's nose wrinkled. One thing you could say about her was that she did not bother to lie to herself.

"Pretend," Fiona said, rather grimly. "No more behavior such as you exhibited last night."

"Blindman's buff invites that sort of playfulness," Marilla said, with an edge to her voice. "You know how much I love frolics of that nature. Every man in the room tried to find *me* as soon as he had a blindfold over his eyes." She squared her shoulders and readjusted the bodice on the ice blue gown she'd chosen from Taran's ancient selection. "I think I would prefer to carry your reticule than mine. It would better suit the color of this gown. Give it to me, please."

"I can't seem to find it," Fiona said. "I must have dropped it during the kidnapping. Or perhaps I left it in the carriage."

Marilla raised an eyebrow. "Careless of you," she drawled. But her eyes returned to the mirror. "These clothes are terribly old-fashioned, but I rather like them."

"I didn't think the neckline would be quite so low on you when I altered the gown," Fiona said, wondering how shocked the room would be if Marilla bared a breast to all and sundry.

"Actually, you didn't do an adequate job altering the dress, so I had to adjust it myself," Marilla replied, carefully arranging a long, silky ringlet so that it lay in the valley between her breasts.

"Be careful with your tone," Fiona warned. "I'm no subservient Cinderella here to do your bidding. I sewed on your gown all morning so that you wouldn't be stalking the castle half-naked, but if you are rude about it, I shan't even thread a needle tomorrow."

Marilla glared back. "You want me to marry, if you remember. It's to your benefit that I leave the house, so that you can have Father all to yourself."

"And I would remind you that you want to be married," Fiona replied. "So kindly remember not to gesture too enthusiastically. Your bodice may well lose its claims to propriety."

"I doubt it."

"From all I've heard, Englishmen like their wives chilly and chaste."

"That puts you out of the hunt," Marilla said with a spiteful giggle. "I'm sure they already know all about you and your infamous bedchamber window."

"Perhaps," Fiona said. "But it would be better for you if the news doesn't leak out."

"You tarnish my reputation just by existing, do you know that?"

"So you have reminded me, many times," Fiona said, adding, "You sound like a shrew, rather than the docile virgin you should be playing."

"I *am* a virgin," Marilla retorted. "Which is more than I can say for you!" She turned up her nose and flew out the door in a flutter of skirts.

Fiona lingered for a moment to look in the glass.

The clothing she'd found in her wardrobe actually flattered her. She had a figure meant for gowns that hugged her curves in a way that current fashion did not; the tiny velvet balls that adorned the snugly fitted bodice and danced along the curve of her breasts were a particularly nice touch. In fact, she looked better in this gown than she did in her usual garments. She fancied it would draw male eyes to her best features. What's more, her skirts were a trifle short and revealed her ankles.

Not that anyone showed an inclination to gape at her ankles.

Fiona sighed and made her way down the wide stone steps leading to the great hall. A fire burned in the huge hearth, but the room was as echoing and cold as it had been the previous night. Even the ancient retainers who were knocking about last night seemed to have disappeared.

She hesitated for a moment, wondering where she might find the others, and was moving toward the drawing room door when she heard Marilla's laughter.

There must be some other room to which she could retreat, perhaps a library or a study; she didn't want to watch Marilla chase the earl around a sofa. Her sister apparently thought a man who displayed that kind of icy precision would make a complacent husband.

Oakley wouldn't.

There was something buried and formidable about him, something that made all his control seem a façade. He would *not* be comfortable. She was sure of that. But she was also sure that if Marilla wanted him, she would take him.

When they were in London, Marilla was hemmed in by society's strictures. But there was nothing to stop her here, in this isolated castle. Ever since she was a little girl, Marilla had taken whatever she wanted—including

Fiona's toys and Fiona's clothing. Faced by a little angel with buttery curls, their father had always given in.

Just then Marilla burst out of the drawing room, but the smile dropped from her face the moment she saw Fiona. "Go away!" she hissed. "You'll ruin everything. This bodice is a trifle chilly, so I'm going to fetch a shawl. Then I'm returning to the card game."

"I'll find the library," Fiona said.

"Just stay in your chamber," Marilla ordered. "The earl hasn't come down since luncheon, but he is obviously very punctilious about his reputation. I don't want him to recall that we're sisters, in case he knows of your disgrace."

The laird's ancient butler emerged from the dining room on the far side of the great hall as Marilla trotted up the stairs. "May I be of assistance, miss?" he asked.

Fiona gave him a warm smile. "Could you advise me as to a room to which I might retire for a spell? The library, perhaps?"

"In there," he said, nodding at a door. "Nobody goes in but the gentlemen after supper, for a smoke and a bit of brandy. If you don't mind the smell of dogs and good tobacco, you'll be comfortable."

"That sounds perfect," Fiona said. "You're my savior, Mr. Garvie, indeed you are."

"I shouldna be doing it," Garvie said. "You're supposed to be marrying the young comte. By all rights, you oughta be in the drawing room with the rest of them. The laird won't be pleased."

"I'm not the right one," she assured him. "Any of the other ladies will make a better mistress of the castle than I. May I beg you to have some tea sent to me, Mr. Garvie?"

Fiona pushed open the door to the library and found it surprisingly cozy, given that the castle ceilings were so high. Its walls were lined with books, and the roaring fire in the fireplace didn't hurt, either.

This was much better than joining the party in the drawing room, playing some sort of game devised by Marilla to throw herself into the arms of the chilly earl.

She wandered along the shelves, trailing a finger over the leather-covered volumes. Books on crop cultivation, on iron working, on terracing . . .

Old plays, poetry . . . and *Persuasion: a Novel by the Author of Sense & Sensibility*! How in the world did such a novel end up in the laird's library? It could not have been published more than a few months ago.

She read the first couple of pages and instantly began smiling. Sir Walter Elliot—he who read no book for amusement but the Baronetage—was surely a parallel

to Lord Oakley. Sir Walter viewed those below his esti-
mation with pity and contempt, which was a fair sum-
mary of the way that the earl looked at lesser beings
such as she.

She threw herself happily onto the sofa before the
fire. It wasn't exactly a comfortable piece of furniture—
more lumpy than soft—but the inimitable Sir Walter
promised to make her forget any discomfort.

It was a good forty minutes before Mrs. McVittie
appeared with a pot of tea, but Fiona was so engrossed
in the novel that she scarcely noticed.

By then she had wriggled into a more comfortable
position: head propped on one arm of the sofa, feet
crossed on the other arm. Marilla would squeal like a
stuck pig if she walked in and saw Fiona's ankles, clad
in pale pink silk, but Marilla was in the drawing room,
presumably chasing a blindfolded peer around the furniture, if they had moved on from cards.

"This is heaven," she said to Mrs. McVittie, swinging her feet to the floor and smiling at her. "Thank you
so much."

"Mr. Garvie's taken a shine to you," Mrs. McVittie
confided, bending over to put another log on the fire.
"He reckons that you're not the sort to marry, so you
might as well be comfortable. The rest of them are all
in the drawing room playing at Pope Joan and the like."

"He's right," Fiona said. "I am not the type of woman who marries." She felt only a tiny pang at that idea, which was quite a triumph.

In no time, she had sunk deeply back into the book and had realized that the prescient Miss Austen had, in addition to creating Sir Walter—who bore such a similarity to the Earl of Oakley—created in Anne Elliot a perfect portrait of her own sister, Marilla, who like Anne was indeed "fully satisfied of being still quite as handsome as ever," but "felt her approach to the years of danger." Granted, Marilla was only twenty-one, but even she had begun to notice the reluctance of English gentlemen to offer for her hand during her three seasons in London.

Englishmen seemed to be remarkably canny. They buzzed about Marilla like flies in honey, but they didn't come up to scratch.

It was much more satisfactory to read about Sir Walter and his daughter than to be trapped in a cold castle with two versions of the same. While the aggravations and extravagances of polite society were funny on the page, they were deeply irritating in real life.

Chapter 11

After luncheon Byron couldn't stop thinking about the way Catriona Burns looked up at Bret, eyes shining, her love obvious. His own expectation of marriage did not include feelings of that nature. His father had taught him well: one's wife should be a chaste woman of good breeding. Passion between a husband and wife was out of the question.

The new Countess of Oakley, as his father had instructed him time out of mind, should be virtuous, well mannered, and above all, show respect if not fawning submission to her husband.

Respect and submission wasn't what Catriona felt for Bret.

Envy was an uncomfortable emotion. It felt like a dark, raging burn in his veins.

Before he chose Opal to wed, he had danced with every maiden on the marriage market who fell into his purview—which left Scottish girls such as Marilla and Fiona to the side—and then he had made what he thought was a reasoned, intelligent decision.

His thought process had been a bit embarrassing, in retrospect. He had decided that Opal would make a good mother. He hadn't known his own mother well, since she had run away with his uncle—his father's younger brother—when he was just a child. They had gone to the Americas, and for all he knew, they were there still.

Still, it didn't help to know that he had a reason to feel unsure of himself around women. His father's freezing tirades, which invariably emphasized female lust, had clearly affected him.

He would have sworn that Opal was chaste; among other signs, he had never detected the faintest shadow of desire when she looked at him. Now he thought back to the docility with which she accepted his compliments, her downturned eyes, and the way she turned her head to the side . . . He had been a fool.

It wasn't that he wanted to make a fast woman his countess. An unblemished reputation was of supreme importance. But . . . he would like to have his wife love him. Enough so that she wouldn't leap to another man's bed.

What's more, if Bret could make a woman love him, Byron damn well could as well. His competitive edge rose to the surface. He could make a woman look at him with wild delight. He could bind her to him so persuasively that she would never look at another.

Marilla Chisholm was an obvious candidate. She was pretty, devastatingly so. Her curls were soft as butter, and her eyes a delightful blue.

And the fact that her youthful spirits led her to behavior that would be classified as outrageous by the strict matrons who ruled the *ton* . . . well, that was all to the better. After all, she was trying to kiss *him*, rather than a dancing master. She was probably just innocent of the ways of the world.

To be fair, his fiancée had not shown any reluctance to accept his kisses, to the best of his recollection. It was he who had thought to protect her maidenly virtue, never venturing more than to give her a chaste buss. If he had kissed Opal more passionately, would she have turned to him, rather than the dancing master?

He rather suspected that might be the case.

One could almost think that she had deliberately planned that he should discover her in a compromising position. When he'd entered the room, she had seemed neither shocked nor dismayed. He had stood there, consumed in an incandescent rage, and Opal watched him as she pushed away her dancing master, smiled prettily, and said, "Well, I suppose our betrothal is at an end."

The more he thought about it . . . the more he was convinced the whole scene was calculated. She probably paid that dancing master for the kiss. That was how much she wanted to get rid of him. Of *him*, the Earl of Oakley.

Yet his figure was agreeable, if not better than that. His nose was Roman, as Marilla had pointed out, but not overly so. He was wealthy and titled.

But he hadn't bothered to woo Opal. In fact, he'd been something of a pompous ass about it, bestowing his hand upon her with the expectation that she would consider it life's greatest blessing.

It wasn't as if he didn't recognize the prototype. His father had judged people solely on their claims to bloodlines and estate. No maid in the late earl's presence raised her eyes above shoulder level unless spoken to. No child, including his own, spoke unless invited to do so. No woman, including his own wife, expressed disagreement with one of Lord Oakley's opinions, at least to the best of Byron's memory.

He took a deep breath and squared his shoulders. He might have inadvertently fallen into some of his father's habits of mind and conduct. But that needn't mean he had to retain them; he was, after all, possessed of a free will. The late earl had been a cold-blooded man whose only deep concern was for his reputation. He had sent Robin to Rugby after the comte died because of what people would say if he didn't; but he wouldn't let Robin come home on holidays because of the French "taint" in his nephew's blood.

He, Byron, didn't have to take after his father. He could be spontaneous and warm. Amusing, even. *Charming.* All those things that Robin was and he wasn't . . . but only because he hadn't ever really tried.

He couldn't imagine himself in love—but he could damn well make a woman fall in love with him. For a moment he considered Fiona Chisholm, but there was something in her gaze that suggested she was unlikely to succumb to tender feelings. Some sort of reserve that echoed his own.

Lady Cecily was pretty as a picture, but his friend Burbett had mentioned that he was as good as betrothed to her, so there was no point looking in her direction.

That left Marilla. She was lively, beautiful, and— for the most part—well mannered. Her joie de vivre would keep him young. He could play blindman's buff with his children someday.

Byron took himself downstairs that afternoon resolved to win Marilla's heart. He would begin by reiterating the request he had made to her to address him by his Christian name.

If he married someone like Marilla, it would prove to Taran that he wasn't stuffy, like his father. The more he thought on it, Marilla was practically perfect. The other young ladies seemed to regard her as something of a leader: witness the way that they followed her suggestion of blindman's buff.

Leadership was a good attribute for a countess.

He reached the bottom of the stairs, hesitated, and then turned into the library rather than the drawing room. Even given his new determination to consider Marilla as a countess, it was something of a relief to find that she wasn't in the room.

In fact, the library's only occupant was Marilla's sister, Fiona. She lay on a sofa before the fire, reading a book, dark red curls tumbling down one shoulder. Her spectacles were surprisingly winsome, he thought. Really, it was enough to make one think that they might become fashionable.

As he walked over to the fireplace, she looked up from her book, and her brow creased for a moment. He could tell perfectly well that she had momentarily forgotten who he was. This was a woman truly unimpressed by his consequence.

"Lord Oakley," he prompted, adding, "but please call me Byron; we are all on terms of the greatest familiarity at Finovair." It wasn't at all hard to ask her that. In fact, he would rather like to hear his name on her lips.

She swung down her legs, rose, and dropped a curtsy. "Lord Oakley," she said, her eyes shadowed by curling eyelashes.

Byron bowed to the young lady and then walked over to stand in front of the sofa. He nearly sat down without being invited to do so, because that was the way people on easy terms behaved. Or at least, so he thought. But his breeding got the better of him and he remained on his feet. "We all agreed to address each other by our Christian names," he informed her, hating the hectoring tone of his voice even as he spoke. "Mine is Byron."

She regarded him silently for a moment. Her eyes were just as green as they had appeared last night, and her spectacles perched on a delightfully pert nose.

"In fact, you and my sister made that agreement between you, though I must presume that the Duke of Bretton and Catriona have agreed to the same informality. Does all this lack of ceremony distress you?" she asked, avoiding use of his name, he noticed. *And not offering to allow him to use her own.*

"I am not accustomed to it," he admitted. "Do I remember that your name is Fiona?"

"Yes," she confirmed, again not granting him permission to address her as such.

Despite himself, he felt a little stung. "I apologize for interrupting your reading," he said, making up his mind not to leave the room directly, because it was *good* for him, one might say *instructive*, to remain with people who took no account of his importance. Fiona certainly fell into that category. "May I ask what volume has caught your interest?"

The earl was dangerously beautiful, Fiona thought. But so controlled. Did he even perspire when he made love? Did his face turn red, did he make inelegant noises, did he . . .

"I am reading a novel called *Persuasion*," she said, jerking her mind from that disgraceful (though interesting) subject. As it happened, she had not personally acquired information about intimate encounters of that nature, but she had heard all about them. Nothing she had heard about grunting, sweaty encounters sounded terribly appealing.

"You have found your way into the wrong room, Lord Oakley," she said, tucking herself back into a corner of the sofa. Her finger marked her place in her novel. When he first entered the room, the pompous Sir Walter of the novel and the pompous earl in front of her were confused in her mind; she had blinked at Byron as if he had somehow materialized out of the book's pages.

In reality, her comparison wasn't fair in the least. Oakley was young and remarkably good-looking, with white-blond hair clipped very short, and winged black eyebrows. He reminded her of a medieval saint carved from ivory: all dignity, virtue, and pale skin.

But he was still Sir Walter, under that lovely exterior. A man who could not conceivably feel other than disgust for her.

"Everyone is doubtless having a wonderful time in the drawing room. They will be missing you," she said encouragingly.

"I am too old to play games," he countered, as if she'd shown the faintest interest in his age.

"Does that mean you actually played games as a child?" she asked, with a queer mix of genuine curiosity and a strong wish to puncture his rigid control. He looked as if he had been born in an immaculately pressed—and elegantly tied—silk neck cloth.

"Certainly, I did."

Frankly, while the man might be an exceptional physical specimen, he was not a very captivating conversationalist. All the same, it would be rude to simply resume reading in front of him. "Is there something I might help you find in the library?" she asked, her tone once more implying that he should take himself elsewhere.

Instead, he sat down beside her.

Fiona took a deep breath, and then wished she hadn't. He even *smelled* good, like starched linen and manly soap. She didn't like English earls. In fact, she didn't like Englishmen in general. This one was distracting her from her book. He made her . . . he made her think about things she had given up.

Men, for example.

She had agreed to marry once, and that was enough. Though, of course, her betrothed had been nothing like Oakley. Dugald had been an oaf—and a violent, drunken one at that. The earl didn't look as though he ever relaxed enough to drink spirits.

"Lord Oakley," she said, rather less than patiently, "would it bother you greatly if I continued to read my book?"

"May I ask you a blunt question before you recommence, Miss Chisholm?"

"If you must," she replied. "But only if you give me the same courtesy. What on earth are you doing here? You should be in the drawing room being wooed by adoring young ladies."

"Adoring young ladies?" He seemed genuinely confused.

"I hope you are not wounded by Catriona's defection to the duke. Either my sister or Lady Cecily would be a splendid countess, and I'm certain they are waiting with bated breath for your return to the drawing room." A less severe man might have been thought to smile, she noticed. Perhaps he did smile, with his eyes, though not with his lips.

"I gather that you deem Miss Burns and yourself as birds of a feather."

"You wouldn't want me to adore you," Fiona assured him. "I have a ruined reputation. That being the case, I think we could simply skip the part where I try to entice you into an unwise marriage based on our unexpected propinquity, don't you?"

"That was a very long sentence." Yes, he was smiling. Amazing.

"I can translate it, if you'd like," she offered.

"I cannot decide how I am to take your wit. I seem to be the target of it, so presumably, I should not laugh. But if I am not to laugh, then who is the recipient?"

Fiona took a swift breath. "You have put me in my place. And," she admitted reluctantly, "I deserved it. I should not have made fun at your expense, particularly since my jests were weak. But, in truth, Lord Oakley, I'm certain everyone is awaiting your return to the drawing room. I mustn't keep you with this foolish babble."

He was silent for a moment. "I suppose I *am* looking for someone to adore me. Though it sounds remarkably arrogant, put so."

Fiona winced. "I have offended you again. I am truly sorry. I have no right to judge your demeanor, and I would never consider you in such a light." She didn't know where to look, so she glanced back at her book.

"I'll leave you to your reading. If I might ask a question first?"

"Absolutely," she said, and then, unable to stop herself: "Though I'm positively dying to finish this novel, so I would be grateful if you would ask your question immediately." It wasn't the book, not really. There was something very dangerous about the earl, doubly so because he was so domineering and arrogant—and yet at this moment there was also something slightly uncertain about him.

It made no sense that a pang of faint anxiety should overrule her dislike of arrogant men, but there it was. She didn't even want to meet his eyes again, for fear she would see that utterly disarming note of uncertainty.

"My question is in reference to your sister."

At that, Fiona lifted her head and gave him a judicious smile. "You couldn't do better than to choose Marilla as your countess," she cooed. It was manifestly false, but family loyalty is surely a greater good than truthfulness.

"I was wondering whether her affections were otherwise engaged. A woman so beautiful must have many local admirers."

"Not at all! That is," she added, "of course Marilla is much adored. But she has not yet settled on the man to whom she would like to bestow her hand."

He appeared to be brooding over something, so Fiona said mendaciously, "And I'm sure I need not tell you how admired she is. She has a very lively personality."

"Too much so, some might say."

Fiona stiffened. Marilla was objectionable, but nevertheless was still her sister. "What precisely do you mean by that?" she inquired, her voice as chilly as she could make it.

"Merely foolishness," the earl said. He stood, and gave her a slight bow. "I will give your best to everyone in the drawing room."

She felt a pang of guilt. Something like disappointment clouded his eyes. Though that was ridiculous. It was as if she caught a flash of a lonely boy, but looking at the magnificently dressed, handsome aristocrat before her, she was obviously mistaken.

"I would greatly prefer that you did not," she told him. "They may feel the need to gather me into the game-playing fracas on the other side of the wall."

When the oh-so-severe earl smiled, which he did now, his face was transformed. His eyes could make a woman into a drunk who lived for those moments alone. She hastily returned her gaze to her book.

He paused for a moment, and then she saw his boots receding and heard the door to the library quietly closing.

Fiona sat still, biting her lip, not reading. She was reconciled to her lot in life, truly she was. But there were times when she felt a stab of anger at Dugald, anger so potent that it burned the back of her throat. What right had he to take away her chance to marry a man like the earl?

The absurdity of that thought jerked her out of her self-pity. She had attended Marilla in two of her last three seasons in London. Though she stayed, appropriately, at the fringes with the chaperones, she had nonetheless spied Oakley from afar. Dugald or no Dugald, she would never have had the slightest contact with a man such as the earl under any other circumstances.

She opened *Persuasion* again and pushed away the pulse of sadness. What was she thinking? That implacable look in his eyes would make him a terrible—

What *was* she thinking? Even if she wasn't known the length and breadth of Scotland as a hussy of the worst order, she was a mere Scottish miss.

Noblemen such as Oakley did not deign to look at lowly beings such as she.

Her fingers curled more tightly around the volume as a sudden image of Marilla as Countess of Oakley flashed through her mind. Byron as her brother-in-law. Seated across from her at the supper table before retiring upstairs with Marilla.

She'd move to Spain.

No, that wasn't far enough.

Chapter 12

Two hours later

Fiona was firmly under the spell of the cheerful but slightly battered heroine of *Persuasion*—not to mention Sir Walter and his daughter—when she heard the door to the library open and then quickly shut again.

She was curled up under a toasty red blanket with a comforting doggy smell, and felt vastly disinclined to move.

"Hello?" she asked reluctantly, sitting up.

The earl was standing against the door, finger on his lips. She nodded and lay back onto the sofa.

She had decided to keep her distance from the earl. She could not allow herself to be enticed by that air of confidence and power that he wore like an invisible cloak. It had probably been bestowed in the cradle along with his insignia or crest or however it was that earls distinguished themselves from mere mortals.

She read the next paragraph three times, trying to fix her attention on the words, even though every fiber of her being was dying to know what Byron was doing. Against her better judgment, she had started to think of him as Byron, an inappropriate intimacy, if ever there was one.

When she'd read the paragraph for the fourth time, and still had no idea what it said, she conceded defeat. She sat up again to confront Byron just as the door was slammed open and Marilla appeared, flushed and radiant. If Marilla was exquisite at the best of times, when she was rosy and excited, she was terrifying. "Oh, Byron! I'm very, very sure you're here!" she caroled.

The moment she noticed Fiona, her eyes narrowed, and her voice lost all claim to charm. "I'm looking for the earl. Has he entered?"

Marilla's quarry had flattened himself against the wall behind the door. His lips were moving, perhaps in prayer or entreaty; either way, he had the look of a hunted animal. Marilla had obviously overplayed her hand again, but Fiona couldn't bring herself to care very much.

She quickly looked back to her sister so as not to betray his presence. "No, but I think I heard someone running up the stairs."

The sparks in Marilla's eyes faded as she contemplated the significance of this. "Of course! He's hidden in his bedchamber or mine, so that we may enjoy a moment or two of privacy once I find him."

Fiona frowned, and Marilla added irritably, "High-society games are little more than opportunities for dalliance, which is something *you* could never understand. The forfeit is a kiss. We've been playing hide-and-seek all afternoon, but the duke and Catriona insist on finding no one but each other, which is tiresome for the rest of us."

"In that case," Fiona said, "perhaps you'd better find the earl before Lady Cecily steals a kiss."

Marilla smirked. "She's proved to be a regular sobersides. We're *all* playing, even Taran, and—"

"*Taran* ran off and hid?"

"I found him in the back of the kitchens! He's surprisingly fit for a man on the edge of the grave. He actually insisted on the forfeit."

"Taran is hardly on the edge of the grave," Fiona pointed out.

Reputation—as distinguished from virtue—seemed to have been declared irrelevant for the duration of the storm-imposed confinement. Fiona was fairly certain that the Duke of Bretton and Miss Burns were not worrying about reputation . . . well, now she thought about it, Catriona's virtue as well as her reputation might be at risk. But that was hardly Fiona's problem, and besides, they were betrothed.

"Don't you dare return upstairs or come to the drawing room," Marilla ordered. "Our bedchamber may be occupied for some time." Her smile was more predatory than sweet.

"I'm getting hungry," Fiona protested. "It's teatime."

"You're plump enough. You could go a whole day without eating, and it would be the better for your waist."

Fiona's eyes must have narrowed, because Marilla suddenly looked a bit cautious. "I suppose if you must eat, you could ring for something. I am certainly not the person to wait on you hand and foot."

"The library has no bell," Fiona pointed out. "In fact, I doubt the castle has a system to summon the help."

Marilla sighed. "I'll have one of those disgusting old fools send you some seedcakes, I suppose."

"I would like a hot drink as well."

"Very well," Marilla said with a flounce. "Just remain in this room. As I said, I do not want the earl to associate the two of us in any way. It's better that you stay tucked out of sight."

"I shan't leave," Fiona promised.

Characteristically, Marilla slammed the door behind her.

The library fell silent again. Fiona could hear Marilla impatiently delivering orders on the other side of the door, and then the patter of her slippers as she left in hot pursuit of her prey.

"Ignominious and yet fascinating," Fiona remarked, as soon as the sound of her sister's footsteps had faded completely. Against all reason, she found herself unable to suppress her laughter. "The fabulously rich and powerful Earl of Oakley cowering behind a door, as if the hounds of hell were in hot pursuit. I thought this kind of scene happened only in French farces. And in *those*, the main characters are already married."

He strolled forward, his eyes glittering with less-than-suppressed anger. "Your sister," he stated, "is a threat to every unmarried man in Great Britain."

"Oh, I doubt that."

When the earl had first been pointed out to her in a ballroom two years before, she had thought him utterly aloof, in the way of men who are so consumed by their own consequence that they were like ice statues: rigid and cold.

But now his color was heightened. In a man less ferocious, his expression could be deemed an insulted pout.

"Marilla has strong opinions about titles," Fiona
said. "She thinks they improve a man immensely,
rather as a vintage does a wine. What did she do to give
you such a fright?"

The way Byron glared at her suggested he was prone
to murder; she parried it with an even more lavish
smile, because it would never do to let him know that
all that glowering menace was effective. "One would
think that such a big, strong earl as yourself wouldn't
be overcome by fear," she cooed, "but there's nothing
to be ashamed of. Fear is a natural human emotion."

One more furious stride, and he was glowering down
at her.

He didn't look frightened: more the opposite. He
looked like an enraged beast, roused from a peaceful
den by an impudent intruder. Fiona loved it. Her heart
sped up, which was utterly perverse.

"Your sister is a menace," he spat. "Do you have any
idea what she did to me? Any idea?"

"No," Fiona said, tipping back her head in order
to see his expression. "I've been right here all along.
Something lacking sense, no doubt."

He bared his teeth at her. "I am a calm man."

"Oh, I can see *that*," she said with some enjoyment.

"And I can see that you merely pretend to be a quiet, bookish young lady."

"Well, I did tell you that I had a bad reputation," she said, grinning at him the way she smiled only at her closest friends because . . . well . . . this was just so much fun. "But since we both seem to have a hidden dark side, may I say that yours is more interesting? I judged you a chilly aristocrat to the bone, but now you more resemble a barbarian." She frowned. "Perhaps a barbarian chased by a rhinoceros. Really, what's the worst Marilla can do to you? There's no chaperone here to force the two of you to wed simply because of a rash kiss."

"You think I'm boring and predictable. The sort who would prefer respect to love in matters of marriage."

Her mouth fell open.

"Don't you?" He braced his arms on the back of the sofa and leaned over her. The flush of anger in his face was fading, but his eyes were still hawklike. Fiona frowned at him, not sure what she was seeing. Hawklike and *wounded*?

"Yet even the most liberal gentleman would think it reasonable to avoid a woman who, when her bodice slips to her waist, merely giggles. And what happened thereafter—" He broke off, obviously remembering he was speaking to Marilla's sister.

"Given our constrained circumstances, we cannot be criticized for wearing ill-fitting garments," Fiona said, coming to Marilla's rescue. "Lady Cecily's clothing is hanging from her like drapes from a narrow window."

"At least Lady Cecily manages to remain decently covered," Byron retorted.

"Yet more surprising information about the male sex," Fiona said. "*I* was always under the impression that men quite liked a risqué glimpse of an ankle and the like."

"You mock me."

Fiona couldn't help it: laughter bubbled out of her, and when he scowled, she found herself practically rolling on the sofa, gasping with laughter until he gave a reluctant smile.

"I'm sorry," she said, giggling. "I really am. I've been indoors too long, obviously. No fresh air."

"I wish to ask you a question," Byron said, interrupting. He moved around the sofa to stand in front of the fire, the better to glower at her.

"What happened to the icy earl?" she asked, a last giggle escaping. "I feel as if the fairies stole you and returned with a hot-tempered . . ." She eyed him.

"Hot-tempered what?"

Backlit by the fire, his muscled legs showed to remarkable advantage. Suddenly, he didn't look like an aristocrat, like an English aristocrat. It was as if he shifted before her eyes, replaced by a big, muscled man emanating a sort of primal heat. And . . .

She wrenched her eyes away. Wonderful. Now she was ogling him with as much fervor as her sister probably had done.

"Hot-tempered giant," she said quickly, sobered by that thought. "What was it you wanted to ask me, Lord Oakley?" Her book had slipped to the floor; she picked it up and smoothed the pages. She had a third of it left. She should bury herself in the plot, and stop thinking about Byron altogether. He was too male, too beautiful . . . too volatile. And he was obviously in the grip of some fierce, barely contained emotion.

It couldn't be that Marilla had roused all that passion.

Or perhaps she had.

He glanced down at the book in her hand. "I see you are still reading. What is the title again?"

"*Persuasion*, by Miss Jane Austen."

"And are you enjoying it?"

She looked at him and hardened her heart. Men as beautiful as he were surely accustomed to fighting off the advances of young ladies. "Yes," she said shortly. "I am. But surely, Lord Oakley, that is not the question you wished to ask me."

"It's not a question, precisely. I was hoping that you could inform your sister that I am an unlikely focus for her attentions."

"Everyone knows that you are looking for a bride," Fiona said, feeling her way into a further defense of Marilla. "News of your broken betrothal traveled before you. I'm afraid that I cannot alter the tide of public opinion. Every unmarried young lady considers you a suitable focus for her attentions. *More* than suitable."

His brows drew together. "Perhaps you might tell her that I have determined not to marry."

Fiona rolled her eyes. "Please. Marilla will no more believe that than I would. You still need a wife; you merely need to find a woman who isn't interested in kissing other men. Marilla, for one, would never kiss a footman. As I told you, she's mad about titles."

"My fiancée was not kissing a footman," he said, giving the distinct impression that his teeth were clenched together. "It was her dancing master." To her shock, he strode over to the sofa, pushed her legs aside, and sat down.

Then he folded his arms and looked at her challengingly. "It's not a matter of my being overly punctilious, either. Do you see what I just did? *Where* I am? I pushed you aside and sat down without being asked. I'm sitting in this room with a young lady who has identified herself as having a less-than-perfect reputation."

Another giggle broke from Fiona's lips before she could suppress it. Was she supposed to congratulate him on his bravery? Or his finesse?

He gave her a narrow-eyed glance. "I may be a dunce, but I'm not a self-righteous turnip."

"I would never think of you in terms of a garden vegetable," she said encouragingly.

"At any rate, a dancing master is not precisely a servant." He paused. "Although lately I begin to think that she set up the entire event so that I would break off the engagement."

Fiona reached over and patted his knee. The stuffy earl was obviously having some sort of stuffy person's crisis, and she was thoroughly enjoying watching it, even though such pleasure cast a dubious light on her own claims to being a kindly soul. "Oh, don't underestimate the allure of a dancing master. *So* much more understandable than a footman. Was he French?"

"If you are warming up to casting aspersions on my ability to dance, as has my cousin, I would prefer that you refrain."

Fiona had been planning to do just that, so she started over. "Marilla hasn't the faintest interest in kissing anyone—except, of course, her husband, once she has one. And she would *never* kiss a commoner; she has very high standards. Therefore, she will be a perfect match for you."

"Your sister has already kissed me," he stated. "I played only a passive role in the incident. I am well aware that my uncle's foolishness has thrown us all together without a chaperone, but—"

"Exactly!" Fiona said, grasping thankfully on to that excuse. "Marilla is overcome by a heady sense of freedom."

"Then *you* should act as her chaperone."

"Unfortunately, my sister pays me no mind," Fiona said, more honestly than was perhaps advisable.

"I had given her hardly any encouragement," the earl said, a heavy frown indicating something that she had long suspected. Men liked to seduce, rather than be seduced.

"You're very attractive," Fiona said, silently cursing Marilla's propensity to overplay her hand. "She was overcome by your . . . your . . ." To her horror, her mind went blank; the only thing she could think of was his thighs and that ferocious maleness about him. "Your *charm*," she cried. "Overcome by your charm, she has temporarily forsaken her maidenly modesty."

A smile curled one side of his mouth. Really, a man shouldn't have such a full lower lip. It wasn't fair to the female sex. "I feel a bit wounded that it took you such a time to come up with a single attribute about me that might attract a young lady such as your sister, apart from my title, of course."

Fiona ignored this. "Marilla would make a perfect countess."

"I beg to disagree."

She persisted. "Yes, she would." She raised a finger to enumerate. "She's an heiress. You do know that land isn't entailed here in Scotland, don't you? She will inherit my father's entire estate, and it is considerable."

"Your father bequeathed her everything? What about you? Don't you have a dowry?"

"I have my own fortune from my mother," Fiona said. "My father had no need to provide a dowry."

There was a gleam in his eye that made her frown.

"Money is not everything," she pointed out. "I'm not eligible for marriage, at least not to anyone like yourself. I have already told you of my reputation, though Taran must have forgotten about it when he scooped up his potential brides. To return to the matter at hand." She raised a second finger. "Marilla is not only an heiress, but she's very beautiful."

"Beauty is in the eye of the beholder," the earl said promptly.

She cast him a glance. She couldn't imagine the person who would judge *him* less than beautiful, and that went double for Marilla.

"Don't you agree, Miss Chisholm, or may I call you Fiona?" the earl said, leaning toward her. His eyes were rather warm. "I think Fiona is a lovely name."

"I wouldn't know about beauty," she said with some severity. "I wear spectacles, as you see. That keeps me from drawing conclusions about people based on something as shallow as their appearance. But I am aware that a gentleman would like to take that into account, and I can assure you that Marilla is one of the most beautiful young ladies in all Scotland. And England as well, from what I've seen," she added, somewhat recklessly.

"Your sister is like a hound in full-blooded chase after a fox. In that metaphor, I am the fox," he stated.

Fiona shut her eyes for a moment. "She is young. And as I said, she's wild about titles. Just *wild* about them."

"*Wild?*" His face said it all.

"I assure you that the phrase is used in the most polite households. Miss Austen uses it several times."

She opened the book and found the relevant paragraph in a moment. " 'The girls were wild for dancing.' "

"Wildness is not a trait I am looking for in my bride."

"I expect you are not looking for a wild girl," Fiona said, trying to sound conciliatory. "But if you wouldn't mind a bit of plain speaking, after the unfortunate affair of the dancing master, the trait that you truly want is an understanding of propriety. Marilla wouldn't kiss a servant if she were at the point of death. She understands her own worth. I'm her sister, and I should know. That is, I *do* know."

"I am not interested in her behavior once married."

Fiona nodded. There was no hope for Marilla; one had only to take a look at Byron's stony countenance to know that. "I will tell her." Honesty compelled her to reiterate, "But she won't listen to me."

"Why not? In the absence of your parents, she should pay respect to you."

"You have no siblings, so I gather you have no idea how ignorant that assumption is."

"I do not wish to quell her natural spirits. She is quite beautiful, sportive, and charming."

Fiona flipped open her book. She'd had enough talking about Marilla for the day, and besides, if the earl thought her sister was that charming, he'd probably end up married to her, whether he wished to or no. "I completely understand," she said, glancing down. "I will inform her that you prefer that she offer no more kisses, and that she keep her bodice firmly in place."

A moment later she was immersed again in the story, bent on ignoring the man sitting at the other end of the sofa . . . except he did not stir. "I thought you were leaving," she said finally, peering at him over her spectacles.

"I have been watching you instead."

"A tiresome occupation," Fiona observed.

"You mean it, don't you? Your sister will pay no heed to an admonishment from you."

Having already been unduly honest, Fiona saw no reason to prevaricate now. "It could be that your absence from the drawing room has turned her attention to someone else . . . the Comte de Rocheforte, perhaps."

"It is my impression that Rocheforte is looking elsewhere."

Fiona raised an eyebrow. "Really? That's quite interesting."

"He's my cousin," Byron explained. "I know him better than any other person in the world. He pretends to be a care-for-nothing, but in fact, he has a great affection for this place. However, without an estate, he cannot afford it, so he acts as if it is not important to him."

"I've seen people act in that manner before," Fiona said, thinking that she did it herself.

At that moment the door opened behind them. Byron froze and then he turned slowly, his eyes bright and wary.

Chapter 13

Fiona had been looking forward to the next act in the French farce that their kidnapping had become, but rather than Marilla, one of the laird's men pushed his way through the door, a tray balanced on his shoulder.

"Brought you buttered crumpets," he said with a grunt. "And mulled cider." He walked over to the fire and put the tray down on a hassock. Then he set a lidded silver pitcher on the floor close to the hearth. "Leave it here so it'll stay hot," he ordered.

"Thank you," Fiona said. "We will."

He straightened, caught sight of Byron, and scowled. "Does the laird know that you're in here?"

"No, and you'll not tell him." The words were delivered with a hard tone that seemed to make an impression on the man.

"Wooing!" he said, and turned and spat into the fire. "Time was a man dinna have to do this kind of wooing. Groveling for money, more like." His gaze moved to Fiona. "Begging from women who has the money. It's unnatural." He collected her cold teapot and headed for the door.

Byron strode after him. "You didn't see me here," he stated.

The old Scotsman snorted and stomped off.

Oddly enough, that snort made Byron smile. Fiona decided that she didn't understand him. He was unnerved by Marilla's advances, but amused by a retainer's flat rudeness. As she watched, he not only closed the door but turned the key.

"Is that truly necessary?" Fiona inquired.

"If you're asking whether I'd prefer to avoid the experience of having another strange breast fall into my hand like an overripe plum, the answer is yes."

Perhaps she should say something to defend her sister. But an overripe plum didn't sound very nice.

"What if it weren't a *strange* breast?" she asked, unable to resist.

"I am not familiar with any woman's breasts," Byron replied, walking back to the sofa. "At the moment the world is full of strange breasts. Though I must say, this is a very improper subject."

"You *do* need to marry," Fiona pointed out, struck by his observation. "You should be out there groveling at someone's feet—Lady Cecily's for example—in the hopes of gaining an intimate acquaintance with body parts other than her feet."

"There are better things a man could do with his time than grovel at a woman's feet," Byron remarked.

With a start, Fiona realized that he was looking at *her* as he sat back down. With a lazy smile.

A dangerous smile.

For a moment her heart hiccupped, but she got hold of herself. "Right," she said briskly. "You may have one of my crumpets, and then I would ask to be left in peace. I don't have much left to read in this novel, and I'm keen to finish it."

"If you force me to leave now, I shall starve," he complained, picking up a linen napkin from the tray.

"Only because you're afraid to go into the drawing room for tea."

He reached a powerful hand toward the crumpets. Devil take the man, his limbs were probably as beautifully knit as his fingers. "More cautious than afraid," he said. "Have you noticed how much worse the storm has grown today?"

She didn't even glance at the windows. She'd lived in the Highlands all her life, and she knew the howl of the wind. "It will worsen through tomorrow evening, I should guess. You are now in the Highlands proper, Lord Oakley."

"My name is Byron," he said, for the third or fourth time, as he handed her the napkin and a crumpet.

The incongruity of this man being named Byron flashed across her mind. Byron was a poet, a man who wrote of love, midnight, and a woman's smile. The earl, though, was of a different character altogether.

He obviously read her expression. "I have no connection whatsoever to that paltry rhymester Lord Byron. The name has been in my family for generations."

"You're not a poet, then?" She smiled at him, acknowledging that the mere notion was ridiculous. In fact, his christening had to be some sort of jest on destiny's part. *This* Byron was the least poetic man she'd ever met.

On the other hand, his person could easily be the subject of poetry. From the top of his ice-blond head to the toes of his perfectly shined boots, he was flawless. Even in the width of his shoulders and the clear blue of his eyes.

He had finished his crumpet, so he picked up the pitcher and poured hot cider into her empty teacup.

"Brandied cider," she said happily. "What a perfect drink for an afternoon such as this."

"It's not afternoon; it must be going on six in the evening," Byron said, pouring himself a mug. "At any rate, I could write poetry if I wished." Stubbornness echoed in every word.

She eyed him. "Are you this competitive in every aspect of your life?"

"It is not competitive to understand that poetry presents very little challenge. A rhyme here or there is hardly problematical." He tossed back his cider.

Fiona thought precisely the opposite, but she kept prudently silent. It had just occurred to her that he might have had a rather sad childhood. Still, thinking that an earl—a man immersed in privilege and luxury—could have been neglected was absurd. She was mistaking innate arrogance for something else.

"Did your governess teach you the fine art of writing lyrics?" he asked, reaching past her toward the plate of crumpets. "Or were you sent to school?" His lips had taken on a buttery shine. If she had the nerve—and life were completely different—she would kiss him just there, on the bow of his lower lip.

Snow was dashing itself against the windows, and the library felt like a very warm, very snug nest. "We were largely raised by a nanny and a governess," she told him. "We had different mothers, but unfortunately, neither survived past our early years. My governess was not poetical, to the best of my memory."

"Mine felt that nursery rhymes were poor substitutes for biblical verses," the earl said.

"That sounds . . . tedious," Fiona said honestly.

He nodded. "I think it would have been better had I a sibling. I would have guessed that Marilla was spoiled. 'Too pretty for her own good,' my nanny would have said."

"Did your nanny say that of you?"

"I'm not pretty," he said, reaching for the last crumpet.

"Please save at least *one* crumpet for me," she asked pointedly.

"Oh, I don't know," he replied. To her surprise, there was a wicked amusement in his eyes. "I'm sure Marilla would say I should eat them all, the better to protect your waistline."

"Beast," she said, but without heat. His gaze made it perfectly clear that he thought her waistline was fine as it was. In fact, that was probably the kind of carnal look that her father thought she'd given Dugald. She hadn't. Ever.

"I wouldn't want us to quarrel over crumpets," Bryon said, a glimmer of a smile at one corner of his mouth. Then he did something that she would never in a million years have expected: he held the crumpet up to her lips.

She looked at him.

"Open your mouth and take a bite," he ordered.

He watched her lips so intently that she felt a curl of heat in her stomach. He couldn't truly be attracted to her.

Not that it mattered. At the moment he knew next to nothing about her past, yet all too soon he would. But then . . . his eyes met hers as she took the bite, and the curl of heat grew a little more intense.

It was as though they were having two completely distinct, yet simultaneous conversations. It was most disconcerting.

"Marilla was a beautiful infant," she told him, unable to think what else to say. He took a bite of her crumpet, still watching her intently. "The adoration her curls inspired wasn't terribly good for her."

"I suppose it led her to believe that she was the most endearing child in the Highlands, as opposed to the most willful." He held out the crumpet again.

"Lord Oakley," she asked with some curiosity, "do you feel that you might have a fever?"

"Absolutely not."

"You seem to be acting out of character. Do you think your friends would recognize you if they could see you now?"

"Of course they would."

She hesitated. "You do know that Marilla and I attended the London season the last two years?"

A slight frown creased his brow. "Will you eat this crumpet, or shall I finish it?"

She accepted what little remained of the crumpet and finished it in two bites. Butter dripped onto the back of her hand, and without thinking she licked it off. Their eyes met again, and the warmth in her stomach spread to her legs.

"I glimpsed you at two balls in the last season," she said, straightening her back. "You were pointed out to me as one of the most eligible men in London—that was before you asked for Lady Opal's hand in marriage, of course."

"But we were not introduced." He frowned in a rather irresistible way. "I would have remembered you."

"Of course we were not introduced," she said, almost laughing at him. "Marilla and I are as far beneath your notice as butterflies are to a . . . a . . ."

"Hawk?" he suggested.

"Elephant?"

The right side of his mouth hitched up in an enchantingly hesitant smile.

"At any rate," she said hastily, reminding herself that this flirtation had no future, "I rather think your friends might believe you'd lost your mind if they could spy on you."

"I would like to know what it was like to grow up with a sibling," he said, ignoring her comment. "Did she steal your toys? I believe that is common behavior."

"Surely Rocheforte stole your things when you were boys?"

"My father did not consider Robin suitable company for his heir," the earl said. "A matter of his French blood, you understand. We met only as adults, so I did not share my nursery with anyone."

Her hunch had been right, then: his had indeed been a lonely childhood. "Marilla did borrow my things occasionally," Fiona admitted. She took a sip of the cider and broke into a fit of coughing.

He leaned over, slipped a hand behind her, and gave her a gentle clap on her shoulder. "Are you all right?"

Excepting the fact that she could feel the touch of his fingers all the way through ancient velvet, two chemises, and a corset, she was fine. Just fine. "Your uncle's cider is a trifle stronger than I'm used to."

Byron poured himself a new cup, and took a healthy swallow. "Brandy with a touch of cider, rather than the reverse," he said with obvious pleasure. "It isn't as though we have to do anything requiring coordination."

Fiona took another sip. The drink burned on the way down to her stomach, reminding her that one crumpet, plus two bites of another, wasn't much of a meal.

"Let's return to the subject of your childhood," Byron said, settling into his corner of the sofa.

"Let's not," Fiona said. "We ought to join the others in the drawing room. It must be nearly time for supper."

There was something wild and boyish about the earl's face, as if he'd thrown his entire personality—at least, what she'd seen of it in London—out the window. "Not after I went to all that trouble to sneak in here," he said. "Besides, I'm enjoying this. Very much."

Fiona felt a blush creep up her neck.

"Lord Oakley," she said cautiously, "did you take anything to drink before that cider?"

"No," he said, tipping his head against the back of the sofa. "I did not. But I might drink that whole pitcher; I may never return to the drawing room." He turned his head and looked into her eyes. "I don't want to be kissed by your sister again. And that's even though I gave some thought to marrying her."

Fiona cleared her throat. "I can understand that."

He leaned toward her. "But I wouldn't mind if you kissed me. If you address me as Oakley once again, I shall kiss *you*. There: I've given you fair warning."

"I shall not kiss you," Fiona exclaimed, drawing back. "I don't kiss anyone."

"And your reason for such abstinence?"

"That's none of your business."

He settled back into his corner, nodding. "You would probably share such information only with your intimates. Friends."

Fiona glanced at him, feeling shy, but she couldn't bring herself to tell him about Dugald. Not yet. "Marilla and I didn't fight over toys," she said, looking back to the fire. "I didn't mind sharing. But when we were growing up, my sister always wanted a portrait frame that I owned."

He stretched out an arm along the back of the sofa; it was amazing how a person could not touch you . . . and still touch you. "Did she take it from you?"

She nodded. "I always got it back, though."

"And that frame held a portrait of your dead mother." She felt him pick up a lock of her hair.

"How on earth did you guess that?" She turned to face him again, and her hair slid from his fingers. Her toes were a little chilly; she pulled up her legs and wrapped her arms around her knees.

"Power of deduction," he answered, shrugging. "I suspect that you have always given Marilla what she wants, because I doubt there are many material objects you hold dear. I could think of only one thing that you wouldn't give up. She would want it all the more because it was important to you."

She stole another look at him, and realized that there was one other thing that she would never willingly give to Marilla . . . but *he* wasn't hers to keep. It was a horrifying thought. It was hard enough to recover from the emotional morass caused by Dugald's death. She didn't need to fall in love with an improbably beautiful and thorny lord as well.

"It was a *very, very* pretty frame," she said, realizing she had adopted Marilla's favorite phrase only as she said it. "Silver worked with pearl, and of course my sister was quite young when she first saw it."

Byron stood and moved to the fire, onto which he carefully placed two more logs. As she watched him, it occurred to Fiona that he probably did everything carefully. He returned to the sofa, but somehow ended up seated not at one end, but in the middle.

His hip touched her slippers, in fact. Once again, he slung his arm along the sofa and picked up a lock of her hair. Unsure how to react to this, Fiona pretended not to notice.

"What happened to the frame?" he asked.

"She began stealing the portrait and hiding it, after which I would tear apart her bedchamber looking for it. Eventually, my father heard of our battles, and he sent off to London to have a precise duplicate made, but with a portrait of Marilla's mother rather than mine. She was, you understand, very beautiful."

"Your mother must have been extraordinarily lovely as well. What was your father's secret?" His eyes held an expression she recognized, though it wasn't often directed at her. She'd seen it too often in the eyes of men looking at her sister to mistake it. He must be drunk to feel lust for her. Quite drunk.

"In fact, my mother was an ordinary woman," she said, hugging her knees.

"I doubt that." He paused, then: "How did she die?"

"She caught pneumonia one particularly cold winter. I was quite young, so I haven't many memories of her, but she was motherly, if you know what I mean."

"Dark red hair like yours?"

She nodded.

"Your hair has all the colors of the fire in it, like banked logs that might burst into flame any moment. And it curls around my finger like a molten wire." Without stopping, he asked: "What happened when the portrait arrived?"

"Nothing," Fiona said, rather sadly. Her sister had tossed the portrait—painted by Sir Thomas Lawrence from an earlier likeness—to the side as if it had cost mere pennies. She could still picture her father's crushed expression. "Pearls are old fashioned, Papa," Marilla had snapped. "Don't you know *anything*? I swear I don't belong in this mud hole. I belong in London."

The earl tugged the lock of her hair that he held, rather as she had tugged Marilla's that morning. "Lord Oak—"

He tugged harder.

"Byron," she said, reluctantly. "This conversation isn't at all proper. Not at all. I don't wish to call you by your given name."

"And why is that?"

"Because this is some strange fairy-tale moment, and tomorrow, or possibly the next day, the snow will stop and then the pass will open, and you will return to your life. And I will return to mine."

"Will you come to London for the season this March?"

"No," she said swiftly, knowing instantly that she would rather die than sit on the edge of a ballroom and watch the Earl of Oakley waltz with another woman as everyone attempted to decipher his haughty expression. "I didn't like you very much when I saw you there."

He nodded, seeming to understand. "You wouldn't like me this time, either. But couldn't we pretend that I'm someone different? Likable? After all, we're buried." He gestured toward the windows. They were encrusted with snow and ice.

"I'm not very imaginative," she said apologetically. "All I can see is an earl who is well-known as a most punctilious man, but has apparently lost his head. It would be one thing if I were Marilla. But you're not struck mad by my nonexistent beauty, so the only way I can explain your flirtation is to believe that you do so in order to avoid my sister. And that doesn't make me feel very flattered."

"Why couldn't I be enthralled by your face? Because, as it happens, I am." He reached over and poured more cider into both of their cups.

She frowned at him. "How strong is that cider?"

"You are very beautiful, in a quiet way. You're like a flower that one sees only after wandering away from the coach into a field. And then, behind a rock, one finds a tiny blue flower, like a drop of the ocean in the midst of a brown field."

"Goodness," she said, startled by this flight of lyricism. "Perhaps you do have something in common with Lord Byron."

"Absolutely not," he said, his lip curling. "The man leads a licentious life and deserves every drop of notoriety he's earned."

"Reputation is tremendously important to you by all accounts."

"An excellent character is a person's greatest blessing," he replied. It sounded as if he was repeating a sentence he'd heard many times.

"It's far more complicated than that. The public nature of one's character can differ from the nature of one's intrinsic self," she answered, feeling her heart ache. Surely she wasn't falling in love with a man she hardly knew. Clearly, she was feeling *too much.* More than she'd allowed herself to feel in years, since the wrenching horrible days when she realized that her father didn't, and never would, believe her about Dugald.

Byron stretched his feet out toward the fire. A log cracked in half and sent a shower of sparks like live bits of gold up the chimney.

"My father believed that nothing mattered except for one's reputation," he said, staring into his mug.

"He would have approved, then, of your broken betrothal?"

"Without question. Though I should say that, in point of fact, *she* broke the engagement after . . . after the incident."

"Did you love her?" Speaking the words sent a little pulse of savage longing down her neck. Why would his fiancée kiss a dancing master when she could have kissed this complex, beautiful man? It was inconceivable.

"No," he said morosely. "And obviously, she didn't love me, either. But I didn't ask for love." His expression made it clear that was an important distinction. "I never asked for that."

"You should have," Fiona exclaimed, before she could catch herself.

He pushed to his feet and squatted before the fire, using the poker to move a half-burnt log closer to its heart. He moved with a powerful grace that belied his large physique. "I begin to share your opinion."

She raised an eyebrow, but he didn't look back at her. "Neither love nor affection is a prerequisite for marriage amongst the nobility," he continued. "But faithfulness is. That's what a woman's reputation means: that she won't sleep with another man, and leave a cuckoo to inherit one's estate."

"I think kindness is important," Fiona said, thinking of Dugald and his lack thereof.

"Of course. Sanity is also a good attribute in a spouse." Humor laced his words again, albeit humor with a dark edge.

"You've omitted physical attractiveness," Fiona offered. "From what I've seen during the season, gentlemen find beauty tremendously important."

He was placing another log on the fire, but he half turned in order to see her face. "Why do you single out my sex? Don't ladies feel the same about their future husband's appearance?"

She thought about it. Dugald hadn't been handsome, not in the least. Of course she would have preferred a good-looking man, but when her father had presented her with the marriage, it never occurred to her to say no for that reason. "We generally don't have the freedom to choose on that basis."

He looked back at the fire. "The dancing master was going bald. That's what I remember most: the way his head shone in the back."

Without conscious volition, Fiona rose and walked a step to his side. But once there, she was at a loss. Obviously, he had cared about his faithless fiancée, no matter how much he protested to the contrary. She put a hand tentatively on his shoulder. Her velvet sleeve was a little too long; its folds fell over the arm of his coat. "I'm sorry," she said.

He got to his feet. "I didn't care about her overmuch." Perhaps he was telling the truth, but she knew instinctively that he would never admit it if Lady Opal had broken his heart.

Byron was a stubborn, stubborn man. That square chin conveyed a level of obstinate, masculine strength that a woman could lean against—and battle—for the whole of her life.

Fiona found herself smiling at him as if he were a true friend, as if genuine affection flowed between them. Somehow, beyond all reason, she felt as if she had just become friends with a pompous, irascible turnip of an English lord.

From the look in his eyes, he had come to the same realization at the same moment.

Then his eyes fell to her lips. She licked them nervously. "Of course," she said, her voice coming out in a breathy tone that reminded her uncomfortably of Marilla, "of course you didn't love her!" Somehow she managed to give the sentence a perky tone that was utterly inappropriate.

His eyebrow shot up. He was mocking her, and yet . . . yet there was sensual promise there as well.

"No," she whispered.

He didn't answer, at least not directly. Instead, he reached over and pulled one of her hairpins and, before she could stop him, another. Without pins to hold it up, her heavy hair tumbled down over her shoulders.

Byron made a sound in the back of his throat that sounded like a hum.

"What are you doing?" Fiona said, stepping back and frowning. Her spectacles had slid down her nose;

she pushed them back up. "I have already informed you that I am not an appropriate person with whom to conduct a flirtation, Lord Oakley."

"And I have already warned *you* about using my title," he said, his voice throaty, and just as she remembered his threat of a kiss, his arms came around her and his mouth descended on hers.

It was not her first kiss. In the heady days before her father matched her with Dugald, she had kissed two boys. For years afterward, she had remembered one of those kisses in particular. She could even remember the sharp smell of the pine needles that crackled under their feet as she and Carrick Farquharson stood in the shade of a garden wall. There had been no second kiss. Carrick had left to fight in His Majesty's army, and never returned; his body lay in a grave somewhere in France.

Byron's mouth brushed across hers, and she smelled pine needles, like a ghost of a promise. It was awkward. She didn't know what to do with her arms, or her spectacles.

The only thing she felt was a deep sense of rightness . . . and an equally powerful sense of wrongness. "We mustn't do this," she whispered.

He eased back enough to remove her spectacles. Holding her gaze, he carefully put them on the mantelpiece.

That just meant that Fiona could see his face even more closely. Her brows drew together as she tried to make sense of what was happening. "Why are you kissing me?" she said, keeping her back straight, so that she didn't relax against him like the veriest trollop. And then, fiercely, "Is it because you know of my reputation?"

"Have you kissed a dancing master as well?" His voice was threaded with a lazy sensuality that made her step back, though his face blurred when she did it.

She shook her head. "No."

"Then what spurred your lost repute? Not that I would believe such a rumor, because any fool could see that you're not the one in your family handing out kisses like bonbons."

"My fiancé's name was Dugald," she began. She took a deep breath, but he interrupted.

"A terrible name."

Words bubbled up in her chest, but she didn't open her mouth to blurt out the story of ivy, and windows, and a reputation so blackened that she was infamous throughout the Highlands. The truth was that she longed for another kiss, just one, before he learned the truth and turned his back in disgust.

When she didn't speak, Byron cupped her face with his long fingers, carefully—as carefully as he did anything else. Yet when he put his mouth to hers, there was nothing sensible about his kiss. She opened her mouth to his without thinking, wrapping her arms around his neck and standing on her tiptoes.

It was a wicked kiss, deep and wild and *glad*. She could taste it in his mouth, that sudden, vivid delight, as clearly as if he had said so aloud.

The knowledge of his pleasure curled in her stomach, flared into an odd heat that made her shiver against him, and then he was kissing her so fiercely that her head tilted back.

It was dark behind her closed eyelids. She concentrated on the taste of him and the smell of him, and the way one kiss melted into another, kisses that made her ache and breathe as if she were running, but not away—toward him, closer to him.

Her arms curled more tightly around his neck; then his hands slid to her back and he pulled her against his body. As if it mattered to him that she feel all that hardness and strength.

Their tongues tangled and she slid her fingers into his short hair. Part of her was frozen in stark disbelief that an English earl with white-blond hair and a muscled body was kissing her. Making her feel meltingly soft, and impatient. Making her long for more.

That thought was instantly followed by a rush of panic. She—*Fiona*—didn't allow herself to long for anything. She never had. That way was madness. She kept herself sane by never wishing for what she could not have, by recognizing that life had sensible boundaries.

Longing would mean acknowledging that she wished that her mother hadn't died, that her father cared about her more, that she had never met Dugald, that people had believed her . . . It meant the heartbreak and desperation of knowing that she wanted children, that she wanted a husband, that she . . .

Her panic was as chilling and as overwhelming as an ice-cold wave breaking over her head. She pulled back. "I can't do this," she said, her voice rising to a squeak when she looked up at Byron and understood that *longing* wasn't strong enough to describe what she was feeling. She seemed to have succumbed to a kind of madness, though she hardly knew him.

In an impulse for self-preservation, she reached out, put her hands on his chest, and pushed at him. She felt hard planes of muscle under her fingers as she pushed, which merely increased her alarm. He didn't even fall back a step.

"I'm not like this," she said, her breath sounding harsh in her ears. "I don't do this. I know I have a terrible reputation, but I'm not . . . I'm not a whore."

"I would never think that!" he said, quick and fast, and some errant part of her saw his chest rising and falling as fast as hers and was triumphant and glad. He wasn't unmoved by her, by plain Fiona Chisholm.

Even so, she fell back another step. She would *not* allow herself to want him. He wasn't hers. He could never be hers.

"No," she repeated. But there was something uncertain in her voice, and his eyes flared, hot and feverish.

It didn't matter that he couldn't be hers; clearly, he was thinking that she could be . . .

"No," she said with a gasp, and she almost spoke aloud, but it was too foolish to even think that the Earl of Oakley would consider a mere Scottish lass to be his. The possessiveness in his eyes probably meant he was considering making her his mistress. "I am not a strumpet," she said, stronger now. "I'm *not*. Even if I am Scottish, and . . . and not beautiful."

"You *are* beautiful."

She stared at him blankly for a second, because she had always trusted herself and her judgment. All her life. She had been a mere six years old when she discovered that her father was weak. All of ten years old when she realized that Marilla was always angry—too angry to be a loving sister. Sixteen when she learned that Dugald was a bully. And what she saw in this man's face, this almost-stranger's face, was trust, desire, and longing. For *her*.

"No," she whispered. "You mustn't."

He reached out for her again. "I already do." His voice was sure and confident.

Fiona struggled free before his lips could again touch hers and make her fall into that pool of hot, wild desperation. "This is madness," she said, putting her hands on her hips. "You, sir, should have better control of yourself than to exert your seductive wiles on a—a maiden like myself." Because she was a maiden, even if no one believed her. "I am not available to slake your lust," she added.

"*Slake?*" Laughter shone in his eyes along with that deeply unsettling gleam that spoke of lust.

She waved her hand impatiently. "Whatever you wish to call it. I am not a strumpet whom one can tumble just because the door is locked. You are not the first to try to take advantage of me, you know. And you shall not succeed!"

It was all different from Dugald trying to climb in her window, but it felt good to shout at him.

The startled look on his face was worth it, too.

"I would not have taken advantage of you," he said, his brow darkening.

"Then why is the door locked?" she challenged.

"To keep your bloody sister out," he snapped back. "It had nothing to do with the two of us being inside." He walked over to the door and unlocked it.

But when he turned around, he wasn't irritated any longer. He looked like a gleeful boy. "Thanks to that lock, I've just realized that I *have* ruined your reputation," he said, sounding pleased with himself. "We've been locked in a room together. We'll have to marry. It's what a gentleman would do." He walked toward her, his eyes intent.

"Oh!" she cried in frustration, stepping backward. "Why have you changed like this? I don't understand you!"

"I decided this afternoon that I wish to make a woman fall in love with me."

Fiona glared at him. "So I am the subject of an experiment? Are you planning to accost young ladies on a regular basis?"

He shook his head. "No."

"Then what on earth are you doing?" she cried, exasperated. "I don't believe for a moment that you plan to ruin my reputation and marry me, if only because it's already ruined. It's very unkind of you to make jokes of this sort to a woman like myself, who has no prospect of marriage."

"I suspect I have gone a little mad." Byron lunged and scooped her into his arms. "Whenever I touch you," he whispered against her lips, "I feel as if you are the woman I have been looking for my whole life, though I have denied, even to myself, that I was looking."

Despite herself, her lips softened and he took her invitation, embroiling her in a kiss that made her feel soft and feminine, all those things that she *wasn't.*

More than anything, it was a possessive kiss, the kind of kiss a man gives a woman whom he is determined to make his, to have and to hold . . . Madness or no, her every instinct told her that Byron was telling the truth: he wanted to marry her. And he wanted to bed her. Craving swept her body like a drug, making her sway against him. He groaned deep in his chest, and pulled her still closer.

"We can't," she said, the words emerging in a little sob. "I haven't told you . . ."

"You will be a wonderful countess." His hands stroked slowly down her back, leaving her feeling as if her skin woke only after he touched it.

"No, no, I will not," she gasped, unable to believe that they were having this discussion. "We don't know each other."

"I didn't know Opal, either, as is manifestly clear," he offered, his eyes hot with desire. His hands—

"You shouldn't touch me there," Fiona managed.

His hands tightened on her bottom, and then slid upward to her hips. "I love your curves," he said thickly. "I promise to spend at least forty years getting to know you."

"I know why you are saying this," she said, trying to ignore his touch, though she couldn't make herself move away from him.

"Because you are delectable?"

"Because you have decided that Lady Opal only staged her affection for the dancing master. You could tolerate her betrayal when you thought she was in love with another man, but now you feel bruised."

"You taste like apples," he said, ignoring her comment and taking her mouth again.

She allowed the pure pleasure of his kiss to sweep her under. It was bliss, this kissing, the way their tongues played together, the way he held her, as if she were shy and precious and beautiful, when she was none of those things.

This time it was he who pulled back. "I know enough about you, Fiona."

"You know nothing," she said shakily.

"You are very intelligent and you love to read." He dropped a kiss on her left eyebrow. "You are extremely kind, even to your sister, who would strain anyone's generosity. You love deeply and you're very loyal. You don't suffer fools gladly, but you are instinctively polite."

He kissed her right eyebrow, and his hands tightened on her hips. "You have beautiful curves," he said, his voice darkening a trifle. "Your hair has red tones that look like the most precious jewel in the world. I want to drape you in rubies. I want to see you lying on my bed, wearing nothing but a ruby necklace."

Fiona felt as if she were caught in some sort of dream. Byron's eyes were fervent. He meant every word. And he had no idea, none at all, of what had happened to her.

She squared her shoulders, summoning the courage to crack open the little enchantment that had bewitched them both, when the library door suddenly opened.

They swung about to find Mr. Garvie standing on the threshold. "Supper is in an hour," he told them in his usual surly tone. "So if you two mean to dress, you'd better get at it."

"If you'll excuse me," Fiona said, and like the coward she was, she fled. She could feel tears coming as she ran up the stairs. It was so—so unfair. Byron was undoubtedly suffering from some sort of temporary madness. But he looked at her in such a way . . . and said those things . . . things she never thought she'd hear from anyone.

It was cruel that she couldn't marry him. She caught herself thinking a hateful thought about Dugald before she pulled herself together.

Her chest felt hollow, as if there was a physical reason for the ache there. It was absurd. She didn't even know Byron. He may have decided that he knew *her*, but all she knew was that he was an absurdly beautiful man, an English earl who'd been thrown over by his fiancée, and for some fairly inexplicable reason had decided on her as a replacement, even though she'd told him at least three times that her reputation was ruined.

"I'd like a bath, if you please," she told a stray retainer she encountered in the hallway.

He put up a protest, but she fixed him with a tiger's eye and he backed down. "You'll miss supper," he said in a parting shot.

Hopefully, he would be right.

Chapter 14

Taran was not employing the great hall for dining; a storm this fierce sneaked in through windows and took over the larger rooms. The wind howled as it rounded the corners, scouring under the doors, keeping the air frigid and moving.

Instead, supper was to be served in the antechamber where they'd taken all their meals. It was small and cheery; a boy had been assigned to keep a fire burning there all day. Its small mullioned windows were so crusted with snow and ice that the wind couldn't even make them rattle.

Byron changed into an evening coat and returned downstairs far faster than his usual wont. He walked over to one window and stared at the snowdrift blocking any view of the storm. He had been making an annual winter trek to Finovair for a decade or more, and he could not remember seeing the snow piled quite so high in the courtyard before.

Fiona was so different from Opal. She didn't look away from him; she laughed straight to his face. She never seemed to be at a loss for words. She just said what she was thinking. He had a tremendous feeling of *rightness*, even thinking of the way her eyes shone with mischief.

She wouldn't lie to him. She would mock him, and argue with him, and probably infuriate him, but she would never lie to him.

And she had told him about Marilla's theft of her mother's portrait. Perhaps if Opal and he had talked, really talked, she would have told him that she didn't care to marry him. She wouldn't have had to stage that scene with the balding dancing master.

If, instead, it had been Fiona who had decided she didn't care to marry him, she would tell him face-to-face. Let's say they were betrothed—a funny shot of heat came under his breastbone at the notion. He would like to put a ring on her finger. A ring that would tell other men that everything about her—from her sweet little nose, to those curved hips, to the perplexed look in her gorgeous eyes—it was all *his*.

Just hypothetically, if he were betrothed to Fiona, and she decided to throw him over, she wouldn't do it through a dramatic scene. She would probably glare at him, and then she would tell him that he was a stupid, jealous . . .

Jealous?

He had never been jealous. Marriage wasn't about jealousy. It was about respect and promises. But then he thought for a moment and realized that a seething cauldron lit in his chest at the very idea of a dancing master approaching Fiona.

This train of thought was insanity.

He leaned his forehead against the icy window, just to see whether he was dreaming. The glass was just as cold to his forehead as to his fingertips. A feeling of profound calm cut through with elation swept through him. He would do it: he would marry Fiona Chisholm, and have a bespectacled, honest, beautiful countess. She would probably be a good mother, but honestly, he didn't give a damn.

If she was a bad mother, they could get a nanny. Well, of course they would have a nanny. He wanted her for *himself.* So he could . . .

So he wouldn't be alone. So he would have a friend, and a lover, and a wife, all in one. The elation spread. How could he be so lucky?

He was never lucky.

The door opened and he turned, heart thumping. Not Fiona. It was Marilla, her breasts barely kept in check by an edging of lace, her eyes lighting up at the sight of him.

"You disappeared this afternoon!" she chided, disapproval softened by forgiving laughter.

"I spent the afternoon in the library," he said, watching her closely.

She was approaching him, her hips swaying, but she froze for a second. Then her smile grew wider. "But wasn't my sister, Fiona, hiding there? She's *so* reluctant to be in company, you know. I promised her I would have someone send her tea so that she need not be embarrassed by her lack of social skills."

He held out a chair for her and then said, "I didn't notice any shyness." Happiness thrummed low in his chest simply because he was talking about Fiona.

This was ridiculous. Preposterous. Like the sort of lovesickness that is visited on mere boys. He thought he wanted a woman to fall in love with him, but instead he was the one infected. Just like a giddy boy, he discovered he was grinning at Marilla.

"Fiona has no friends," Marilla said, waving at the seat beside her. "Since we do sit on consequence, Byron, I certainly hope that you will remain at my side." Her smile was lavish, but then, all of Marilla's smiles were lavish.

He sat, thinking about what she just said. It didn't make sense to him. Fiona was funny and wry and altogether delightful. Of course she had friends. But then, perhaps she didn't have friends . . . perhaps she was as profoundly alone as he was.

"Where *is* your sister?" he asked, keeping his tone casual.

"Fiona has little regard for the servants. She asked for a bath not long ago, even though it's not easy for those old men to carry hot water up the stairs." Marilla slid her hand over his, and frowned with a kind of dewy earnestness. "She has no idea how to run a large household. My father made certain that I was trained in a chatelaine's arts. One of the most important rules is that the lady of the household must respect those in her service. Yet Fiona asks for separate meals, as she did this luncheon, and baths!" She rolled her eyes. "She bathes every day, and never mind how much work it is to haul pails of hot water up and down the stairs."

Byron thought with some satisfaction of the new-fangled pipes he'd added to his house two years ago. And then he thought of Fiona sitting in his bath, steam rising around her, all that glorious hair curling into smaller ringlets, her creamy skin flushing . . . He hastily put his napkin in his lap.

The door opened and Bret and his betrothed entered, laughing. He had his hand on Catriona's back, and the way he looked down at her was so resonant with desire that . . . well, the couple was just as improperly intimate as they had been the night before, but now Byron saw it with a different eye, looking not at Catriona's face, but at Bret's.

He wanted to put his hand on the small of Fiona's back. He'd never thought about the gesture, but now he perceived the possessiveness in that light touch. He wanted to hand Fiona into a chair and then sit beside her, a bit too close, and hold hands under the table, the way Bret and Catriona now were. He wanted to escort her to supper with lips that had been kissed the color of dark cherries, as Bret had.

Hell, he wanted to join her in the bath and . . .

After making her his bride, of course.

Marilla's voice cut into his thoughts again. She had curled her fingers around his forearm, and was leaning forward, saying something to Catriona. "Oh, we feel the same," she cooed. "Byron and I were just talking about the arduous duties of running a large household. This strange little interlude at Finovair has done so much to bring us all close! I'm thrilled to know that I was there when the Duke and Duchess of Bretton fell in love. I cannot wait to tell my friends."

Byron drew his arm away, while Bret threw him a look that said, clear as day, that Marilla wasn't going within two miles of the duchy of Bretton. Byron grinned back and then watched the puzzlement grow in Bret's eyes.

His old friend hadn't figured it out yet. Hell, *he* had hardly figured it out. All he knew was that his entire being was tense, waiting for Fiona to get out of that bath and join them at the supper table.

Taran blew in the door, followed by a train of his retainers carrying platters. "Lady Cecily dines in her room," he said briskly. Robin was nowhere in evidence: he was probably hiding in his room as well. And still there was no Fiona.

The laird sat down and scowled rather unexpectedly at Marilla. "Keep your hands to yourself, lass. Your father wouldn't approve."

Byron realized that Marilla had once again curled her hand around his forearm. She gave Taran a lofty smile and didn't move a finger. Instead, she moved even closer and said in a breathy voice, "Byron, do tell me about your castle."

"I don't have one," he said calmly.

"What a pity," Marilla said. "But I suppose you could always buy one if you wished."

"No," Byron said, catching Bret's eye. Bret was trying not to laugh and not succeeding very well. "I could not. Castles are far and few between in England."

Without even glancing at Marilla, he knew she was pouting. "Such a pity! This is the first time I've stayed in a castle and I find it very, very charming. It's so grand . . . so much bigger than most houses."

Naturally, it's all about size, Byron thought uncharitably.

"My sister is very retiring," Marilla informed the company when they reached the second course and the plate to his left was still empty. "She likely lost her courage, and will eat in our bedchamber. Of course we must continue without her. In our household, my father and I often forget that she's there at all."

Byron was contemplating what Fiona's life had been like in company with her relatives, when she walked into the room and began heading around the table to the open chair.

She looked a bit pale, but her greeting was cordial enough. But he didn't care for "Good evening, Lord Oakley."

He stood and pulled the chair out for her. "I thought we agreed that you would not address me as Oakley," he said to her, ignoring the conversations that had started around the table.

Not that anyone ignored his statement. Even Marilla's semiflirtatious conversation with Taran—the woman seemed incapable of conversation that was not suggestive—halted in mid-sentence.

Fiona had just seated herself; she froze and turned a little pink. Her hair was slightly damp from her bath, and enchanting pin curls framed her face. Bret looked swiftly from her face to Byron's and then leaned over to whisper something to Catriona. There was a huge grin on his face.

Byron just wanted to make it all clear. He was possessed of the happiest emotions of his life, and even though the object of his happiness looked stunned, he was bent on sharing them. Could she really believe that he would kiss her—the way he had kissed her—and mean nothing by it?

He bent down and dropped a swift kiss on her lips, and then another on her damp curls for good measure. She sat as rigid as a statue, not seeming to draw a breath, looking . . . stricken?

"Well, the tone of this gathering has lowered, has it not?" Marilla said shrilly on the other side of Byron. Her voice trembled with fury.

"Marilla," Fiona whispered.

"I gather I have to protect my sister once again from the illicit lust of ne'er-do-well gentlemen," Marilla cried, ignoring her plea. "Isn't it enough that she is branded a whore the length of all Scotland? Must *you*,

Lord Oakley, who has some claim to being a model of propriety, show your contempt for her so openly? Kissing her in an open gathering? When you know perfectly well that a man of your noble heritage would never make her his countess? Shame on you, Lord Oakley, shame on you!"

Byron was so stunned that he stared at Marilla for a moment, registering the cruel gleam of rage in her eyes.

Then he turned, slowly, back to Fiona. Branded a whore? *Fiona?*

She had turned the color of parchment. As their eyes met, she raised her chin. "I told you repeatedly that I had a reputation. Apparently, you did not believe me."

"Yes, but did you tell him that your fiancé fell to his death from your bedchamber window?" Marilla shrilled.

At this, Taran threw back his chair and stumped around the table. He reached out a hand and jerked Marilla to her feet. "You and I, lassie, are going to have a good talk, because it's obvious to all of us that the beauty in your face doesn't match your heart. You're acting like a mean-spirited little horror, you are."

Before Marilla could say another word, he pulled her over to the door, pushed it open, and slammed out into the corridor.

"I'm sorry," Fiona said to Byron, her beautiful green eyes as grave as a monk's. "I kept trying to tell you what happened."

"He fell from your window?" Byron echoed, finally sitting down himself.

He could feel all the joy draining from his body. It felt as if he had turned back to a brass automaton, to the half-dead man he'd been when he arrived in Scotland. His father's double. Obviously, women were as lustful as his father had warned, even sweet ones from Scotland who smelled like fresh bread and innocence.

There was dead silence around the table. Fiona nodded. "Yes. My fiancé, Dugald, lost his life in a fall. All Scotland knows it. I am sure that our friends at the table will be gracious enough to forget the implications of what you said a moment ago."

Bending her head, she spread her napkin in her lap.

"I never believed it," Catriona said with a note of ferocity in her voice, "and neither did my mother. She should know, since she was godmother to Dugald himself. How could a man who was as fat as a distillery pig think to climb a strand of ivy?"

"The window was there, as was the ivy, and unfortunately, so was Dugald," Fiona said. "Yes, I would like some roast, if you please. Catriona, what games did you play this afternoon?"

Catriona looked as if she wanted to continue her defense, but she succumbed to the pleading expression on Fiona's face.

Byron endured three more courses without saying another word. Taran strolled back in at length, looking pleased with himself, but Marilla never reappeared. Byron was aware of the warmth of Fiona's arm next to his, though they never touched, even accidentally. The conversation stumbled along until finally the subject of Robert Burns's poetry was brought up, which provoked a spirited dispute.

"As full of air as a piper's bag," Taran shouted, in response to Catriona's praise of the poet.

"I rather like the poem about how he'll love his betrothed until the rocks melt into the sun," Bretton murmured, looking (of course) at Catriona.

"Until the sands of life run dry," she whispered back to him, but Byron heard her.

After that, he just sat still, thinking. Really thinking.

If his father weren't already dead, the thought of a notorious woman becoming the Countess of Oakley would have killed him.

He didn't know what his mother would think, because after she ran away with his uncle, he never heard from her again.

But the question, obviously, was what did *he* think?

Fiona was still pale, but she had joined the conversation about Burns. He watched her talk and even laugh when Taran said something particularly outrageous, without ever glancing at him.

He felt as if he'd been given a glimpse of heaven, only to have it torn from his hands. How could he dishonor his ancient name? Breach his father's memory in such a fashion?

This had been a momentary madness, that's all.

"You're mad as May butter!" Taran shouted at Catriona, who was thoroughly enjoying sparring with him, to all appearances.

Not Catriona: him.

He was as mad as May butter.

Chapter 15

Fiona had been humiliated before. Having to sit through a homily on the evils of lust, read at Dugald's funeral, came to mind. But in its own way, this was worse. She had been in shock during the funeral, and she had gone through it as if in a trance, still not understanding that no one believed her, and that no one ever would.

Now she was older, and thoroughly clearheaded. She would never be able to forget the moment when Byron's eyes turned cold. His face had gone completely blank, and stayed that way. It was as if he put on a mask, and all there was to be seen was the arrogant, haughty Earl of Oakley, the man whom she saw from afar in English ballrooms.

When supper finally, mercifully, ended, Fiona excused herself and ran up the stairs. She opened the door to the bedchamber to find Marilla sitting on the bed. Acid rose in Fiona's throat. She couldn't—she really *couldn't*—bear to speak to her sister at the moment.

Without a word, she headed directly for the ancient wardrobe and pulled out the fur-lined cloak she'd worn for the caber-throwing contest. It appeared to be as old as the wardrobe, and could have belonged to Queen Elizabeth herself, but it would keep her warm.

"I'm to apologize," Marilla said, her voice scratchy from crying. "Taran insists."

Fiona didn't even glance over her shoulder. "I accept. I'm going to the carriage to find my reticule. I'm sure it must be there."

"What are you talking about? You're going out in the snow?"

"The carriage is in the stables."

"Just tell a footman to fetch it for you!"

"I would welcome some fresh air. Do go to sleep without me."

"You cannot do such a stupid thing as walk out into this storm! You're pouting, Fiona, and it's a very unpleasant, childish thing to do. I *have* apologized."

"There's a cord that leads from the kitchen to the stables. Mr. Garvie told me about it the first night." She almost added, *So don't worry about me,* but the words died in her mouth. She was tired of pretending that there was something more between them than the potent reek of Marilla's dislike.

"I truly am sorry I told the earl about Dugald's death," her sister said.

Fiona had discovered a pair of gloves that, although ancient and cracked, were lined with fur like the cloak. All that remained was to find something warmer than her slippers to put on her feet. She began poking at the bottom of the wardrobe.

"Are you ignoring what I just said?" Marilla's voice rose a bit.

Fiona had exhumed something that felt like a sturdy pair of boots; she backed out of the cupboard, straightened, and turned around. Her sister was looking at her with tearstained defiance. "No," she stated. "It will never be all right with me. Once this accursed storm ends, I shall move to my own house. It will be easier for all of us. Papa can hire a chaperone for your next season."

Marilla stared at her, her jaw dropped.

Fiona pulled the boots on, and then the gloves. She probably looked like an ancient crone wearing a bear costume inside out. But when she glanced at the mirror, she didn't even see her own reflection: instead, she saw Oakley's blue eyes. They were an extraordinary color, the color of the sky on a summer day, when one lay on one's back in a meadow.

"Good-bye," she said, walking out and closing the door behind her.

"I didn't mean it!" Marilla called shrilly. Fiona pretended that she hadn't heard, and kept walking, down the stairs, through the baize door, and into the kitchen.

She stopped only to grab a bag of apples and a bottle of wine from the kitchen staff. The apples were for the horses, and the wine was for her. She'd never drunk to excess before. Ladies never became inebriated. But she wasn't a lady. She was ruined, ruined, *ruined.*

The blowing snow was like a slap to her face, like a scream turned into material fact. Walking away from the warmth of the kitchen and into the howling wind felt like a punishment, but she didn't mind.

She couldn't bear to sleep in the room with her sister that night. Nor to be down the corridor from a man who actually thought—howsoever briefly—that she was worth making his countess. Who had kissed her like . . . like that. And then regarded her with no expression at all in his eyes, as if she were no more than a strange, distasteful woman, who happened to be seated beside him at supper.

She bent her head down and kept her hand tight on the cord. Luckily, the wind was scouring the courtyard and driving the snow around the other side, so drifts of snow hadn't been able to settle the way they would when the wind died down. A wooden wall loomed out of the moving wall of snow before her so suddenly that she bumped into the door.

A second later she was tumbling into the warm, dim stable. "Who's there?" came a cracked voice. And then, "Ye're a woman!"

She nodded, throwing back the hood on her cape and shaking herself to remove some of the snow. "Mr. Garvie said you could return to the castle for the night if you wished. I shall remain just long enough to look for my reticule in the carriage, and then I'll follow you."

"I ain't leaving any *woman* alone with my horses," the old man cried.

"Away wit' ye!" she barked, her voice emerging in a perfect Scottish burr.

She reached out and took the lantern from his hand. "Get off with ye, then," she commanded, with a jerk of her head.

"What are ye doing here?" he demanded. "This ain't no place for ladies. You won't have a bit of yer reputation left."

That did it. "I'm not a lady," she shrieked. "I'm Fiona Chisholm." She saw his eyes widen and felt a primitive surge of pleasure at the fact that he recognized her by name. "I've got no reputation, and I'll do whatever in the bloody hell I choose to do. I might stay here all night. You have got no say in it!"

"Ye're off yer onion," the man grumbled, moving backward. "There's no call to scream at me like a banshee. Ye be careful with that lamp, you hear? I don't want to find my stable on fire."

"I'll be careful."

The moment the door closed behind him, Fiona heaved a sob. But she refused to let herself be dragged into that morass of self-pity. Never again. Instead, she walked down the center aisle of the tiny stable.

The four horses that had drawn the Duke of Bretton's carriage put their heads over their stalls' doors and nickered at her when she began offering apples. They were beautiful, with soft noses and shining eyes.

After the four of them came a pretty mare, and finally a gelding who took his apple carefully from her flattened hand, his lips curling as if with disdain.

"They should call you Byron," she told him, stroking the star on his forehead. His black ears flicked back and forth, and then, as if in sympathy, he rested his chin on her shoulder. His apple-breath was sweet.

"You just want another apple," Fiona said, choking back tears. She gave him one and realized she'd come to the end of the horse stalls.

The Duke of Bretton's carriage had been pulled in through wide doors at the opposite end of the stable. It was so large that the shining black end of the vehicle loomed in the dusky light. She walked around, opened the door, and listlessly held up the lamp, but no reticule was visible.

Another row of stalls, mostly empty, lay opposite those she had just visited. The last, back where she had started, contained an ancient pony. The pony lumbered to her feet as Fiona approached, her belly almost as round as she was long.

A tear slid down Fiona's cheek, because the self-pity she had sworn not to allow herself wasn't easily vanquished. She would never have a child, and so never have a pony . . . Still, she made herself stop after one quivering sob. She slipped into the stall with the pony, who ate an apple and promptly lay down in the straw once again.

She hung the lantern safely from a hook on the wall, and then removed her cloak and dropped it in the straw. Finally she sat down and, leaning against the pony's fat tummy, pulled the cork from her bottle of wine.

The wine was rich and fruity, like the earth in the springtime, if dirt was good to eat. She took another swig. It was peppery too, like . . . like pepper. She peered at the label. It was quite dim in the stable even with the lantern, but she could make out that the wine had come from Italy.

As she upended the bottle again, it came to her: she needn't stay in Scotland with a father who didn't care very much for her, and a sister who cared not at all. She had money. No—she had a *fortune*. She could leave Scotland.

She slowly put down the bottle, the happiness caused by this epiphany exploding in her heart. She would go to Italy and travel to the vineyards. She would buy a little house in the countryside . . . or in Venice . . . or Rome. She needn't even stay in Italy; she would travel wherever she wished. She need never see an English earl again in her life.

Idea after idea came to her: she would like to see the Parthenon, and a camel, though she had the vague sense they weren't to be found together. A camel had come through the village in a fair when she was a child. She had never forgotten his long, curled eyelashes, and the way he chewed, thoughtfully, as if he were solving the world's problems and just not bothering to share the solutions.

Lying there, drinking as she considered the adventures she would have, she began to feel chilled. A bit of a search turned up some horse blankets, and she made a nest with these. Then she curled up and pulled her cloak over herself, fur side down, and resumed her reverie. Only when the bottle was nearly half gone did she come to another epiphany.

She could take a lover. An Italian lover. A man with loopy black curls and golden skin, as far from a pallid, blond earl as could be imagined. "I don't have any reputation anyway," she told the pony. "Everybody thinks I did all . . . all *that* with Dugald. I didn't. But that doesn't mean I can't do as I wish. Maybe I'll have a child after all."

The pony twitched her ears encouragingly.

"I *will* have a child," Fiona decided, taking another drink. "I'll tell people I'm a widow. I have more than enough money for the two of us. Who needs Scotland anyway? My father won't even notice I'm gone."

Her tiresome conscience had just reminded her that her father likely would notice if his elder daughter never returned, when she became aware of a banging noise coming from the wall next to her stall.

"What's that?" she asked the pony, who didn't seem to have an answer. Fiona balled up her fist and thumped back on the wall.

No one answered. "I won't ever think about him," Fiona told the pony. "Never, ever, ever." She looked at her bottle. It was dangerously close to half empty. Tomorrow she'd probably have a "head," as her father called it.

Never mind; it would pass. Tomorrow she would be planning her trip. There were likely travel guides in Taran's library. She'd be halfway to Italy before anyone noticed she was gone.

"An' I'll never even think of him," she said, hiccupping as she put the bottle down.

There was a crash as the stable door flew open and bounced off the wall.

"Lords a mercy," Fiona murmured, huddling deeper into her furry nest. She had just begun to feel sleepy.

Then the door slammed shut, and footsteps stamped down the corridor to the accompaniment of someone cursing a blue streak. An Englishman, she thought, not caring much. Probably the duke's coachman, coming to check on his horses.

"*Fiona!*" Her name emerged from the Englishman's lips in a dark growl that had her eyes springing open.

It wasn't the coachman.

"What in the bloody hell are you doing here?"

"We say *bloudy 'ell* in Scotland," Fiona told him, pulling her fur a little higher around her shoulders. "When in Scotland, do as the Scots." And, because she really didn't want to see those blue eyes ever again, she closed her own.

Chapter 16

Byron could not believe what he was seeing. After Fiona's hell-born sister had blurted out where she had gone, he had risked his life making his way to the stable, stumbling around the side of the castle in the storm, sick with fear that he was about to walk over Fiona's fallen body . . . only to find her tucked down in a stall nestled against a fat old pony, the two of them peacefully asleep.

He pulled off his gloves with a muttered curse. Thank God the stable was so small, and preserved heat so well. His fingers burned with the cold, and his toes felt as if they might fall off. He took another irritable look at the sleeping girl at his feet.

Her hair had fallen out of its bun. Tousled strands of it curled around her face and unfurled over the pony's rough winter coat.

He squatted down and put a hand on her cheek. The skin burned hot under his fingers, and her eyes flew open on a little shriek. "Take your hand off me!"

"You're warm. And," he said, catching sight of a bottle of wine, "you're drunk."

"I am not drunk," she told him, tilting her little nose in the air. "Though I may as well point out, since you do not know me, it could be that I am an invet— an inveterate inebriate." She said the last two words carefully.

He bent down and pulled off his boots, which were covered with snow. That strange joy that Fiona Chisholm seemed to inspire in him was spreading through him again like liquid gold. Like the kind of dizzy, silly joy he distantly remembered experiencing as a child.

"What are you doing here?" Her eyes were suspicious.

"I came to rescue you."

"*What?*"

"I thought I would find you dead in the snow," he said conversationally, knocking snow from his hat before hanging it on a hook. "I think it was a near go myself, in truth. I kept losing the castle as I was trying to get around to the stable. I was completely blinded by the snow. Needless to say, we don't have storms like this in London."

She sat up, a molting fur cape slipping from her shoulder. "Didn't you follow the rope from the kitchen door?"

"The kitchen?" He shook his head. "I knew nothing about that, so I went out the front door. Your sister said you went to the stable; I looked out the window and thought it was a damned foolish and dangerous thing to do. So I followed the castle around to the stable, but I kept losing touch of the walls. Blasted amount of snow out there."

"You could have died!" Her voice cut straight through the muffled sound of the wind howling outside.

"Would you have cared?"

She lay back down. "It doesn't matter what I think."

But Byron heard her voice wobble. "I couldn't stay away," he said, staring down at her. "I know your reputation is . . . whatever it is—"

"Stupid Englishman," she said, opening her eyes again. "I know you heard what Marilla said. Every word of it is true."

He took off his greatcoat and shook the snow off in the corridor before he came back into the stall. "Your fiancé, Dugald, had the brains of a gnat, if he thought ivy would bear the weight of a grown man. You're better off without him."

"I won't be your mistress just because everyone thinks that of me!" she said, her voice very sharp, wrapping her arms tight around herself. "Believe me, I've had plenty of offers, especially in the first year after Dugald's death."

Byron froze as a hot wave of anger rushed to his head. "They talked of climbing up to your window, I suppose?"

"I've heard all the sallies you can think of involving ivy," she said, obviously trying for a careless tone but not succeeding. But her voice strengthened. "I'm a ruined woman. But that doesn't mean that you can simply take advantage of me."

Byron managed to shove all his rage back into a little box, with the silent promise that he would wring the names of every one of those damned Scotsmen out of her.

He came down on his heels in order to be at Fiona's level. The old pony raised her head sleepily, and he scratched her between the ears. "I told myself to go to my room, and then I tried to find you anyway. I wandered around and talked to Lady Cecily for a time."

"She's very nice. You should marry her." She said it flatly.

"I don't want to," Byron said, as flatly as she.

"You can't have everything you want in life," she said, looking at him with an expression of mingled rage and pain. "Haven't you learned *anything*, Byron? Not even that?"

"There have been many things I've wanted." He gently stroked the pony's ears so she twitched in her sleep. "I wanted my father to care for me. I wanted my mother to come home. I wanted to be less alone."

Fiona pointed to a bottle of wine. "Have a drink."

"I wanted a wife who would never play me false, or break my heart, the way my father's heart was broken."

"I never considered it before, but I'm finding wine is quite good at soothing a broken heart," Fiona offered.

"Is your heart broken?" His whole body froze, waiting for her answer. He didn't know what he was doing, what he was saying. But he was caught up in madness.

"What did you talk to Lady Cecily about?" Fiona said, ignoring his question, her eyes sliding away from his.

"We talked about the difference between what the world thinks of a person . . . and who that person may truly be." Byron rather thought that the one sentence—that one thought—had changed the course of his life forever.

Fiona snorted. "The world thinks Cecily is tremendously nice, if a little boring, and from what I have seen in the last few days, she is."

"I don't think she's boring."

"Wonderful. Marry her. Her reputation is undoubtedly snow white and deserved."

"Do you think that I am precisely what the world thinks me to be?"

She looked at him, and for a moment there was something raw and intense and full of longing in her eyes. Then she blinked. "Likely not," she said, her voice disinterested.

She settled back against the pony's stomach. "I'm leaving the country," she announced.

"*What?*"

"I'm leaving Scotland. I can't think why I didn't have the idea before."

"Of course," he said, calming instantly. "You're coming to England." *With me,* he thought, feeling the truth of it in his bones. "Move a bit, would you? I'm going to put this animal in the stall next door. There's not room enough for three of us."

"No, no, not England," she said, far too cheerfully, though she did sit up so that he could coax the pony to her feet. "I mean to live in Italy. The vineyards, the sunshine, the ancient Roman ruins . . . It will be wonderful! And when I've tired of gondolas, I'll just move on. I'd like to see a camel. I'd like to *ride* a camel!"

"Hell no, you're not," Byron growled. He kicked open the door and led the pony through, glancing over his shoulder.

Fiona reached for the half-full bottle of wine leaning against the wall, but she paused. "Did you just swear at me?"

"No." He opened the stall next door; the old pony ambled in and collapsed in the pile of straw.

He walked back to her, closing the stall door behind him.

"I'm glad that you didn't swear at me." She smiled in a way that showed pretty white teeth. "Because you have nothing to say about what I do with my life."

Byron grinned back at her, enjoying the rebellion in her eyes. Not to mention the way her cloak had slid down to her waist so he could see the luscious curve of a shadowed breast.

"How will you finance these travels?" he asked, sitting down on a pile of straw opposite her.

Fiona took a swig from the bottle. "Oh, I inherited my mother's fortune," she said. "Didn't I mention that? I reckon I have the edge on Marilla, if you add it all together. I have quite a bit of land."

Byron reached out, took the bottle, and held it up to the oil lamp. "This half must be mine."

"Actually, it's all mine," Fiona said, a little owlishly. "Though you may have a sip if you like. I'll have plenty of wine once I move to Italy. Did I tell you that I'm moving to Italy?"

He just looked at her.

"I suppose I did," she said thoughtfully. "Well, since you don't seem to like that topic of conversation, let's discuss something else. Why on earth did you try to save my sorry self from gracefully falling asleep in a snowdrift? Didn't you tell me this very afternoon that a chaste reputation was the greatest possible blessing? I don't have one, in case you missed the announcement."

"I suppose I did say something of that nature."

"Dugald's mother has stopped spitting when she sees me." She paused. "You know how people say there's a silver lining to a dark cloud? I hate to say it, but not having that woman as my mother-in-law is something of a blessing."

Byron took another gulp of wine, and placed the bottle to the side. Then he reached out, tossed the fur cape to the side, and crawled forward until his hands were on either side of her shoulders.

She frowned up at him. "You're not the lord of the manor, you know." She hiccupped. "The lord of the stable. Don't think I will kiss you again, because I will not. I'm done with kissing."

He gazed down at the rose flush in her cheeks, her liquid, slightly hazy eyes, her plump lips, and felt that surge of gladness again. "You're done with kissing forever?"

"Oh no," she said, her forehead wrinkling in thought. "I've decided to make exceptions."

"Good," he said silkily. "You can make one for me."

"No." She shook her head. "Only for my Italian lover."

The hiss that came from between his teeth wasn't a noise a civilized man would make. "Dugald wasn't Italian, was he?"

"What? No." She frowned at him. "Would you mind not crouching over me like some sort of demented housecat grown large?"

Byron dropped to his elbows and, very deliberately, lowered his body onto hers. There was a gasp from her, and a barely stifled groan from him. "There will be no Italian lover," he said, clenching his teeth so that he didn't resort to a ridiculous, primitive display of manhood.

"Who are you to say that?" she demanded, her eyes darkening, even as her arms looped around his neck. "You are not my fiancé."

"I know; he's dead."

"And ruined me in the process," she pointed out, yet again.

"Right." Byron had already decided that he didn't give a damn about Dugald. If he, the Earl of Oakley, was going to throw over his father's principles, he was going to do it in style. In other words, he would not only marry the most notorious woman in Scotland (if she was to be believed), but he would never tax his wife with the fact that she came to their bed less than innocent, tarnished by a blackguard fiancé with the stupidity to compromise her as he plummeted to his death.

"You really must stop flirting with me." She scowled at him. "Though this can hardly be called flirting."

"What is it?" Byron asked, settling his body a bit more firmly on top of hers. All the right parts of him were pressing against the right parts of her.

"Something worse," she said darkly.

"Or better," he said, leaning down so he could give her earlobe a little nip.

"I know it doesn't matter to you, but I'd rather not have everyone think that I've dallied with you as well as with Dugald. I'm already next thing to a Babylonian scarlet woman. A Highlands version, of course."

"That bad?" Her ear was delightful: small and round and feminine.

"I told you that Dugald's mother crosses the street when she sees me. After spitting."

"What about the Italian lover?"

"What about him?"

"What's his name?" Byron asked, keeping his tone easy. He didn't want her to know that the Italian was about to plunge from his own metaphoric ivy.

"Well, how should I know? I haven't met him yet."

A great burst of joy spread through Byron's chest, so he bent his head to her mouth. She tasted like wine and Fiona, a combination more potent than the strongest whiskey.

"Ach, man," she whispered, when he slipped away from her lips and kissed a path along her jaw. "Ye do drive me mad, ye truly do."

"Your burr comes out when you're drunk," he whispered back.

"I'm not drunk! I'm a little tipsy, that's all."

"And you've decided to take an Italian lover?"

She nodded. She seemed not to notice that her hands were exploring his back, each touch making him press more firmly into the cradle of her legs.

"*Ti amo, amore mia.*"

"I suppose you're trying to make me think that you're Italian, rather than the most punctilious earl in all London?"

Byron dropped a careful line of kisses down her neck. "I'm not your Italian lover. I'm your Italian husband."

Her eyes were closed, but at that she opened one and squinted at him. "Don't you understand who I am?"

He smiled down at her. "Most scandalous woman in all Scotland. Seducer and killer of an idiot by the name of Dugald. Have I missed anything?"

"Probably not."

"Future countess," he added calmly.

A crease appeared between her brows, and he kissed it.

"You've gone mad." She seemed quite convinced of it.

"I don't care." He caught her mouth again and plunged into a craving, demanding, all-consuming kiss. One hand found its way to her breast, and with a little sigh, she arched toward him, sending a rush of fire to his loins.

"What if you change your mind?" she whispered, a while later. There was just the tiniest quaver in her voice.

"In my family, we never change our minds. That was my father's problem, you know."

"He had a problem?"

"My mother left when I was a boy," Byron said. He rolled off her body and pulled the cape over her again.

Then he ran a finger down her delicate nose. "One day I realized that she hadn't summoned me to her room in some days. I finally concluded that she must have died, if only because my father was so obviously affected."

Fiona came up on one elbow, her beautiful eyes fixed on his face. "You grew up without a mother."

"As did you." He dropped a kiss on the end of her nose. "That's why I knew the one thing you wouldn't allow Marilla to take from you must be a portrait of your mother."

Her eyes softened. "I'm so sorry, Byron."

The pang was hardly more than a pinprick. "My mother was not very motherly. I thought . . . I thought if I could find a wife who showed no signs of passion that she wouldn't think of leaving our children for another man."

She nodded. "You must have been devastated when she left."

"I didn't know her well enough to be devastated. But my father was. He grew harsh and rather brittle. Even after I was grown, I didn't question him about what happened. I had the feeling he might break."

"What would happen if he had broken?"

He considered. "I suppose all that pent-up emotion would have rushed out . . . It would have been embarrassing for both of us."

"So you never asked him where she was?"

"I pieced it together slowly, mostly from things I overheard. She ran away with my father's brother. His younger brother."

Fiona gasped. "That must have been so awful for your father!"

"Yes. He always talked of his brother as a man led astray by an evil woman. For a long time, I had no idea that my mother was the evil woman in question."

"That's dreadfully sad. No wonder you were taught such concern about your reputation."

"It's not my reputation that's at the heart of it." He moved a little closer, just enough that he could put an arm around her waist. "I like touching you."

She frowned at him. "If not your reputation, then what?"

"I couldn't bear to become like him," Byron explained. "I thought if I didn't fall in love, and I chose a woman who was utterly chaste, I could avoid the possibility."

"Lady Opal . . ."

"I didn't know her at all. But she seemed like the driven snow."

Fiona giggled. "She obviously got to know you well enough to guess precisely what would drive you away."

"I might kill a dancing master you kissed." His voice came out hard, all the sheen of a civilized Englishman stripped away, leaving a blazingly possessive man. Just a man. It felt as if his heart stopped as he waited for her to answer, his breath clenched in his chest.

The sharp pain there eased only when she leaned closer to him and said, "You don't have me, so you'd have no right to raise an eyebrow." There was a promise in her voice, a daring, silky promise.

Byron took a deep breath, threw a silent prayer of thanks to whatever deity happened to be listening, and began nimbly undoing the lacing on her velvet bodice.

"What are you doing?" she yelped.

His fingers stilled. "How drunk are you?"

Her eyes were clear. "I seem to have grown quite sober. But perhaps you should give me the bottle. I'm pretty sure that I'm hallucinating, and I don't want it to stop."

"It won't," he said. He slowly pulled her jacket wide open. Of course, she was wearing layers . . . a blouse, a corset, a chemise.

He had her out of the blouse and was unlacing the corset before she asked, "Byron, why are you doing this?"

"Because I'm marrying you."

She was silent, and then: "Did I miss the moment when you asked me?"

"Yes. You must have had too much to drink." He threw her corset to the side.

But she shook her head when he reached toward her chemise. "Byron. No."

"I want you," he said, his voice dismayingly like a growl. "I've never wanted anyone the way I want you. I . . . I think I—"

But she interrupted before he could finish that sentence. "You want to marry me, even given my reputation."

"You're the one for me," he said, giving up on her chemise and cupping her face in his hands instead. "I don't know why. All I know is that the moment I saw you, my life changed. What I wanted from life changed. I don't want to marry a woman who dislikes me enough to stage a performance with a dancing master. I don't want to be safe and prudent. It's true that if you leave me, I'll turn into my father and stalk around being horrible and brokenhearted. I'd rather risk it than not be with you."

"But you're beautiful. You're an earl, you're brilliant, and if you stop being so frighteningly distant, ladies will fall at your feet. You needn't marry me merely to prove that you're a changed man." She gently pulled his hands down from her face.

"Would you marry me if your fiancé hadn't died falling from your window?" Byron asked. "Not just because I'm an earl, but . . . for me?"

Chapter 17

Fiona's heart was pounding so loudly in her ears that she hardly heard his quiet question.

She'd always told herself not to *want* anything. Now she was breaking all her own rules. It was strange and rather terrifying to discover just how much she wanted to catch Byron in her arms, to kiss him, to reassure him, to make that tiny gleam of uncertainty in his eyes disappear.

"I would," she said, her voice ringing out in the stables. "I would want you if you were one of Taran's men, if you were a stable boy, if you were merely an Italian lover."

"But I'm not," he said. "I'm the man who is going to be your husband." Their eyes met, and then he leaned toward her. She closed her eyes, falling into that dark sweep of emotion and desire that came with the touch of his lips.

After that, there wasn't any fighting over her chemise. A short time later, he stood before her, skin the color of cream, dappled with flecks of shadow by the oil lamp, the powerful muscles in his buttocks leading to muscled thighs, lean calves . . . "I even like your ankles," she murmured, devouring him with her eyes. His body was heavy and aroused, like nothing she'd imagined.

He didn't answer, but dropped to his knees before her, his eyes ravishing her, his hands sliding up her legs slowly, seductively. Where his fingers trailed, hot, eager kisses followed.

Fiona writhed on the old blankets, arching her hips instinctively toward him, crying out when his lips moved on to torment yet another part of her.

"I—I—" she cried, meaning to say that she'd never heard of people, respectable people, doing things like this.

But he just nudged her legs farther apart. There was a hum of pleasure in the back of his throat.

He was as careful in this as he was in everything: now delicate, now rough, experimenting to see what made her cry out, alternating with . . . She couldn't find words because she was too busy trying to draw air into her lungs, and then her mind went black, and she was twisting against his hand, trying, trying . . . and then he finally slipped a broad finger inside her and she nearly screamed.

She did scream, at last, when the world broke around her into tiny shards of light that were somehow flashes of feeling at the same time. They swept over her body in wave after wave.

Byron laughed, and then lowered his head again. She reached down just in time and grabbed his hand. "Don't touch!"

"Why not?"

She could hear the laughter in his voice, but she ignored it. The air still felt harsh in her lungs, as if she'd stopped breathing for a time. "I'm—I'm—just don't. It's too much. Too intense."

Byron frowned to himself. Obviously, Dugald had been stupid in more ways than one. A silent shrug. If the idiot Scotsman had been too much of an idiot to please his fiancée, that was all to Byron's advantage.

Fiona lay before him like a dish of strawberries and cream, her skin flushed with pleasure, her dark red hair strands of rubies against the rough woolen blankets. Too harsh for her back, he thought. There was no question but that their joining would make him lose control. He could feel crazed lust possessing him, like a kind of madness.

He had never lost control during a sexual act. Yet with Fiona, the slightest kiss brought him close to the limit of that control. She made him feel like a madman, crazed with the wish to possess her, to make her *his*. Knowing that was stupid didn't help.

She would end up with abrasions on her back, and he had just enough control left to want to avoid that. He picked up her soft body and rolled backward, letting her down on top of him.

She balanced her weight by catching herself on his chest and then pursed her lips in the most carnal pout he'd ever seen. "What are you doing?"

Byron traced the line of her deep bottom lip with a finger. "I thought we'd try it this way for our first time," he said, trying to disguise the keen ache that he felt at the mere sight of her breasts . . . and utterly failing. They were ripe and full, the perfect size to drive a man to his knees with lust. The groan that broke from his throat was more like a growl as he curled up to draw one pink nipple into his mouth, pleasuring first it and then the other.

She liked it. Her fingers clenched in his hair and broken cries flew from her mouth. Through the roaring fog of lust, he spared a thought about his good fortune to find a woman who was not afraid of marital congress. Who wasn't pushing him away and shuddering in disgust the way most virgins did, or so he had been reliably informed.

When he could hardly breathe, and his loins were on fire, he said in a gravelly voice, "*Now!*"

Her head was thrown back, all that gorgeous hair tumbling to her bottom, but at his command she straightened and braced herself on his chest.

There was something odd and tentative about her expression, and Byron realized in a blinding flash that dim-witted Dugald had not only denied his ostensible beloved an orgasm of her own, but that he had apparently made love to her only in the most conventional of ways.

Which left more for the two of them to discover together, he thought with a rocketing streak of pleasure, his tool hardening even more at the thought.

He put his hands on Fiona's lush hips and lifted her up, positioning her carefully, and then let her go.

He was desperate with need, mad to be inside her. Her mouth formed a perfect circle as he thrust upward. She felt like liquid silk, hot and tight.

She was so tight that his vision went white as a voluptuous fog of pleasure enclosed him. He threw his head back, his fingers flexing on her hips and arched so that this time, this first time, he was surrounded by her. A groan burst from his throat as he withdrew and thrust upward again, even the tiniest movement sending a blast of pleasure down his limbs. She was so tight. *Very* tight.

Byron's eyes flew open.

Fiona was leaning forward, braced against his chest. She didn't look precisely as if she was in pain, but her face was tentative.

He froze, his back still arched, his hands gripping the curve of her hips. A good old-fashioned Anglo-Saxon curse erupted from his lips.

Fiona blinked and said, "There's no need to speak in such a fashion."

"You . . . You . . ." The word came out strangled, harsh and dark.

"I'm a virgin," she said helpfully. "Or perhaps I should say that I *was* a virgin." She wiggled her hips, and he swallowed a groan, his fingers tightening on her hips again. "It doesn't feel terrible."

"The window," he gasped. "The—the *ivy?*"

"Do you really believe that I would be stupid enough to invite a lover to enter my bedroom by horticultural means?"

Her eyes were sparkling, although a tightness around her jaw told him that the snug fit that was making him tremble from head to foot was not as delicious for her. He began to lift her away from him, but she curled her fingers against his chest and said, "No!"

He stopped instantly.

She slipped back down until he was snugly hilted inside her. Byron couldn't help it: his hips arched and he gasped her name.

"Did you like that?" she asked, her voice changing from its usual calm, dry amusement with the world to something different. Nearly a purr. She braced herself against his chest and lifted herself a bit and then slammed back down.

A ragged cry broke from his lips and he thrust into her again, taking that last millimeter, burying himself in her slick heat.

Fiona laughed, and the sound fell on him like a blessing. She leaned forward and did it again, and he finally regained enough control to release her hips, though he was pretty sure he'd left bruises on her skin. His hands free, they went naturally to her breasts.

He had his control back now, even if it was held by a thread so delicate it might as well be a strand of her hair. She had to come with him into the intoxicating, ravenous pleasure that beckoned.

She had her eyes closed, swaying a little on top of him, her hands covering his as he shaped her breasts, rubbing those beautiful nipples again and again. Every time, he felt a delicate little shudder go through her body.

Fiona was in the grip of a feeling so sensual that she didn't even know how to name it. It was like the storm outside, as if she'd been caught up in something so powerful that the essential her was lost in the middle of a whirl of wind. Where there had been nothing, there was suddenly this hard, hot . . . this . . . She couldn't think of the word.

And Byron was caressing her breasts, and every time he rubbed a thumb past her nipples, he would nudge upward, just the smallest amount, just enough to remind her that he was there.

Part of her.

The very thought ran like liquid gold over her skin. She, Fiona, was finally not alone any longer. Even though they'd known each other for almost no time at all, she knew it with a certainty that flooded her whole body. His face, that beautiful, beautiful face, was contorted, savage, not graceful . . . because of *her.*

"You will always love me, won't you?" she asked, the words coming out with a gasp. Every time he moved, it made spirals of heat shoot through her legs.

He opened his eyes at that. She knew instinctively that there wasn't a woman in London who would recognize, who had ever seen, the look of savage possession that she saw now on the face of the cultured and urbane Earl of Oakley. "Always. You are mine," he snarled, thrusting up again. Her body had adjusted now, accepted him.

More than that, it welcomed him, sent a shudder of heat through her. She swayed, caught herself on his chest, her fingers curling against hard muscle.

Her eyelids dropped closed. It felt as if her body was narrowing to one point, to this—

His big hands caught her hips and lifted her easily in the air, away from him, into unwelcome coolness. She let out a sobbing cry, but he was moving like a whirlwind, throwing down the fur cape, laying her gently on her back, bracing himself over her.

"I have to have you," he said, his mouth just touching hers, his voice strained but gentle. "It's this bloody possessive side of me, Fiona. I need to—I need to—"

She looked up at him, feeling the fever race through her blood as he started to come to her, and knew that this would always be their fulcrum point.

He would *need* to possess her, to know that she would never leave him, to believe it with every speck of his soul. And she would *need* just as desperately to know that he loved her. That he would be tender, and stand between her and the world's opinion, and always defend her.

It was the blazing truth in his eyes, clear in the way his huge body was frozen over hers, even as he obviously struggled to control himself. He was braced on his elbows, his hands clenched beside her head.

Fiona drew her fingers voluptuously down his back, all the way to the hard muscles of his buttocks. "I want you," she whispered, her voice aching with the truth of it. "I am not complete without you."

The hunger in her voice was matched by the rumbling groan that broke from his throat. He stretched her, and completed her. And then they were both lost in the storm, his head bent so that he could dust her with sweet kisses, catch her panting breaths, lick the line of her lips . . .

While he ravished her.

And she ravished him.

They spoke to each other without words, made promises without words, loved each other without words.

Chapter 18

Earlier that evening, shortly after supper

"Well, Taran, you found me a perfect woman, I'll grant you that." Robin lifted his glass in a mock salute before tossing back the contents.

He'd absented himself from yet another dinner. Absented? Fled, pure and simple. Not that anyone cared except Oakley, and that only because it reflected poorly on the family. *She* certainly wouldn't object to the absence of a known libertine. He narrowed his eyes against the embers glowing in the library hearth. "Damn you to hell, Taran," he muttered.

"Oh! That's a very, very bad word, isn't it?"

Robin swung around. Marilla Chisholm stood artfully arranged in the doorway, leaning against the jamb in such a way that her breasts jutted out like the prow of a ship. Three of her little fingers covered the "O" formed by her lips.

"My pardon, Miss Chisholm," Robin said. "I did not realize I had company."

"Oh!" Marilla repeated, shoving off the doorjamb and mincing toward him. "You mean . . . we are alone?"

She stopped within easy hand's reach and tipped her head up, blinking rapidly. She put him in mind of a myopic spaniel, making up in eagerness what she lacked in discernment.

"Hardly alone," Robin assured her. "Not only is the library door wide open but there's all of Taran's retainers lurking about, eavesdropping. Shouldn't be surprised to find some old man huddled under the cushions over there." He pointed at the library's lumpy old sofa standing before the hearth, its back turned toward them.

Marilla gave the sofa a suspicious glance. "Your uncle is not in my good graces right now. He had the nerve to drag me from the dinner table and *lecture* me on nice behavior."

Robin was frankly astonished because Taran was the last person to whom one would apply the definition of "nice behavior."

"He was most unpleasant to me."

"That's because he is most unpleasant," Robin said. "But what are you doing here, Miss Marilla? Looking for your sister?"

"Good heavens, no. She's off somewhere in a snit," Marilla said dismissively then smiled, sidling closer. "You aren't offended by my concern for my reputation, are you? A lady is nothing without her reputation. Take Fiona—" She stopped suddenly, her hand once more flying to cover her mouth, feigning shock at her near indiscretion.

"Alas, tempting as that is, I must decline," Robin said.

"Oh." Marilla frowned, her hand falling away. "Oh! That was a very naughty thing to say, wasn't it?"

"Again, my pardon."

Marilla tapped his chest playfully, then let the tap become a caress, pleating his shirt's placket between her fingers. "But then, you are a very, very naughty man, aren't you?" Her fingers snuck beneath his buttons to find bare flesh beneath.

The poor thing was so obvious it was almost endearing. Almost. Clearly, Marilla must be doubting her ability to bring Byron to heel and was hedging her bets. He supposed he ought to be flattered she even considered him a possible matrimonial candidate.

"My dear Miss Chisholm," he said, clasping her busy hand and pulling it away from his person, " 'naughty' though I undoubtedly am, I am not so far gone to propriety that I would take advantage of you or in any manner *whatsoever* importune you." He smiled to take the sting out of his next words. "Let alone compromise you."

She had been in the process of working her free hand back beneath his shirt but now she froze, pouting. "You wouldn't?"

Trying to maintain a grave countenance, he shook his head.

"*Why not?*" she burst out, her expression clouding with vexation.

"Because then I would be obliged to wed you."

"Well, yes. Of course," she said, rolling her eyes. "That's how this sort of thing works. What of it?"

Good God, had she an ounce of intelligence the girl would be terrifying. "You don't want to marry me."

"Well, not initially," she admitted. "You weren't my first choice. You haven't any money and you aren't even a real count, being only a *French* comte—and I must say I think it most shoddy that you go about letting decent people labor under the assumption that you are a real count, but I shall let that pass."

"I appreciate your forbearance."

She sniffed. "I mean, really, how could you be my or anyone's first choice, especially since there's both a real duke and a real earl available?"

"But of course, I couldn't be."

A sly look came into her round blue eyes. "But then I realized how much I would like being chatelaine of my very own castle, especially one I could redecorate to my very own liking. So . . . I have the money; you have the castle. And we are in Scotland. All we are in want of is a pair of witnesses."

He took it back. Even without intelligence, she was terrifying.

"What can I possibly say? You honor me unduly." And in truth, she did. He really ought to consider what was being offered. She was a better match than any to which he had the right to aspire. But then, he remembered with heartfelt relief, he had no aspirations. "Am I to take it neither Bretton nor Byron have come up to scratch?"

She eyed him, clearly considering whether to lie, but apparently decided that either he would not be gulled or it wasn't worth her effort. "Yes. I mean no. Not yet."

By God, he should marry her if only because such indiscriminate ambition surely deserved to be rewarded. Except . . . except . . . *Cecily*. What a fool he was. What a ridiculous, pathetic creature. He burst out laughing.

She scowled. "Are you laughing at *me?*"

"No. I am laughing at myself. Though I am flattered by your kind interest, I am afraid I cannot make you the sort of offer you want."

At this, she drew back, and for a moment, Robin was afraid he was about to be slapped. It had happened a few times before under similar circumstances—young virgins with a fancy to taste some forbidden fruit—so he recognized the signs: her beautiful face grew thunderous; her brows snapped together; her lower lip thrust out. But then, abruptly, the anger vanished and she shrugged. She edged closer, her hands once more dancing up his chest. "How do you know?" she purred. "I may be more open to suggestions than you expect."

And with that, she lifted herself up on her tiptoes and planted a kiss full on his lips.

She took Robin so by surprise that for a moment he did not react. Part of him was appalled at her boldness, a greater part of him was amused at his being appalled by her boldness, but the greatest part of all felt only a sort of reluctant sympathy for her. And so, because at heart Robin had a kind nature, he carefully, with chastely closed lips, returned her kiss and then, before she could deepen it, set her gently aside. "And that, my dear, is that."

"But . . . but *why?*"

"Because I have never fancied myself a consolation prize," he said, still gentle.

"Oh . . . ballocks!" Marilla said, and with a huff of annoyance, turned and stomped angrily out of the library.

Casually, Robin retrieved the glass of port he'd set down when she'd entered. He refilled, saying as he did so, "You can get up off the floor now, Uncle."

"Nae, I canna," came a querulous reply from the vicinity of the sofa. "I be felled by amazement. You had an heiress right there in your arms and you turned her aside. I may die of pure horror."

"Don't make promises you have no intention of keeping."

Taran's grizzled head popped up over the back of the sofa behind which he'd thrown himself upon Marilla's arrival. "Are you out of yer bleedin' mind, lad? She's got a fortune and she's the prettiest one amongst the lot of them and she's hot-blooded. True, she's a hellion, but a strong man could tame her. And, most important of all, she wants you." His tone held a hint of jealousy. "You best take what's freely offered."

"She doesn't want me; she wants a castle."

"Same thing." With a click and rattle of knee joints, Taran hauled himself upright. "Besides, ye got no choices left."

"Really?" Robin drawled. "How is that?"

"Well, the duke is offered for Catriona Burns, and Oakley has himself all in a lather over Fiona Chisholm, and I know you ain't man enough to encroach on your cousin's claim."

"And here I'd thought of it as being honorable all these years," Robin murmured.

"Da ye no have an ounce of Scottish blood in yer veins? A Ferguson takes what he wants no matter what the law says."

"Ah," Robin said, nodding sagely. "Suddenly, all the abrupt termini on the family tree make sense. They were decorating another tree entirely. The Tyburn tree."

"Ach," Taran spat in disgust.

"But you said I have no other choice," Robin said, returning to the prior subject. "What of Lady Cecily?" He was gratified by how indifferent he sounded.

"No hope there. Not anymore," Taran snapped.

"And why is that?"

"Because no woman with an ounce of pride would have you after witnessing Marilla rubbing all over you like a tabby in heat."

Robin checked. "What do you mean?"

"Lady Cecily was out in the hall just now. She was aboot to come in but then she saw the two of you locked together at the lips. Stopped her dead in her tracks, it did. No great loss if you ask me. In spite of her great dower."

"Taran—" Robin's voice held a note of warning few had ever heard.

"Oh, she be pretty enough," Taran admitted, unfazed, "but prissy. She jerked back like the pair of you were naked and on the floor."

Robin took a breath and squared his shoulders. What matter? As Marilla had so succinctly pointed out, he was a very, very bad man, and if Lady Cecily hadn't known it before, she did now.

Very calmly, very carefully, he lifted his drink and in one long, slow draught drained the glass.

Chapter 19

Lady Cecily Tarleton was not only lovely, well connected and due to have an unimaginably large sum settled on her upon her marriage, but she respected her elders and never put herself forward. And if some people thought her a bit of a cipher, and others opined her too good to be true, and a few old tabbies purred that a statue had more animation, they were deemed to be jealous sorts. The vast majority of society mamas considered Lady Cecily to have all the makings of a perfect daughter-in-law.

Which made the fact that she was not yet *anyone's* daughter-in-law extremely vexing.

What on earth was wrong with Maycott? Why did he not approve some fellow's suit and get on with it?

It never occurred to anyone that Maycott was not at the bottom of the mystery and that the unfailingly demure Lady Cecily was neither so demure nor so tractable as they assumed, and that she had been encouraged since birth to follow her heart. When it came to choosing a husband, she'd been told to wait for "someone special," and when she'd asked how she would know who that was, had been assured by her mother that "when you meet him, you will know."

Unfortunately, the only sort of men she attracted were somber, dignified fellows who mistakenly thought they'd found in her a matching gravitas, and after three seasons, Lady Cecily had begun to fear she would never meet the man her mother had promised she would know on sight, and end up a spinster. With this specter in the forefront of her mind, this past season Lady Cecily had decided to put aside dreams of heated kisses, easy laughter, and passionate nights and concentrate on achieving more realistic goals: a nursery full of beloved children, and earnest conversations with a . . . a really very nice man.

So she'd told her father to give his consent to the man he liked best of those who'd asked for her hand. At which point, her father had whisked her and the rest of the family off to Scotland, where, away from the distractions of London, she could "make your own drat choice."

Which is how Cecily came to be standing in Bellemere's newly refurbished ballroom when a group of large, gray-bearded men clad in none-too-clean kilts burst in and tossed her and some other young ladies over their shoulders and carried them off to the appreciative applause of the other guests, who'd assumed it was all part of the entertainment.

Though Cecily well knew being kidnapped had not been part of the entertainment, she had not been particularly frightened. First, because one of her fellow kidnappees, Catriona Burns, obviously knew the men and had declared them harmless; second, because the Duke of Bretton was soon discovered to be sharing their—or rather his—well-sprung carriage; and finally, because upon their arrival at Finovair Castle, a scandalously handsome man with a head of loose black curls and a wicked smile had taken her hand and looked down at her with beautiful, black-lashed, laughing eyes, and she had realized, *Mama was right.*

For in that moment, an odd welling had arisen from deep within Lady Cecily's heart alongside a bone-deep sense of rightness, of finally having arrived at a destination she hadn't even known she'd been journeying toward. So it was that Lady Cecily Tarleton, the dutiful, proper daughter of the Earl of Maycott, recognized with absolute certainty that she'd found in Robin,

Comte de Rocheforte, unapologetic scoundrel, self-proclaimed pauper, the scandalous Prince of Rakes, the man she would marry.

She'd known who he was and all about his reputation, of course. He had been pointed out to her on the streets of London. It didn't matter. The only question was what she was to do about it.

It was a question that had her hourly more anxious, especially since Robin had spent the last two days as conspicuous in his absence as, well, Marilla was conspicuous in her availability. In point of fact, his determined nonappearance was beginning to substantially threaten her plan to marry him. Which is what she planned to do, because having finally found love, she saw no reason to relinquish it.

However, she couldn't just tell him that she loved him. Since birth, it had been deeply ingrained in her that a lady *waited* for a gentleman to notice her and then commence his courtship. That wasn't going to work here. Time was of the essence. Soon the storm would end, the passes clear, and her father arrive.

So when Robin had once more failed to appear for dinner, she'd gone looking for him and now stood in a dark hall outside the castle library, her cheeks scalding and tears welling in her eyes. It had taken all her self-control to keep from stomping back into the library, shoving Marilla Chisholm out of Robin's arms, and taking her place.

Only one thing had kept her from doing so: what if Robin did not *want* her to take Marilla's place?

She had no reason to believe he did. She had nothing on which to base her certainty that he felt this . . . this *connection*, too, other than the way he'd looked at her outside Byron's carriage, the profound awareness that had penetrated his amusement and left him, for one telling instant, looking staggered and vulnerable.

She edged away from the doorway and began walking, her thoughts floundering between hope and despair. She didn't note the direction her feet took until she heard a masculine voice hailing her.

"Lady Cecily. Are you all right?"

She turned to find Lord Oakley striding toward her. He looked anything but pleased to see her.

"Did you take a wrong turn? Are you lost?"

"Pardon?" She glanced about and realized that in her distraction she'd wandered into a part of the castle she didn't recognize. The hallway was unlit and uncarpeted and chilly. "I may be."

"You must be near frozen," he said.

"No. I'm quite comfortable," she said, which was true. The velvet material she'd scavenged from her room to act as a shawl was warm if not fashionable.

Beneath the shawl she'd once more donned the dimity blue ball gown in which she'd arrived, the black morning dress having fallen apart at the seams earlier in the day.

"I doubt that," Oakley said, recalling her attention. "Allow me to see you back to a warmer part of the castle."

His attitude was impatient, and clearly, his thoughts were on other matters.

"Thank you," she said, turning in the direction he indicated.

Though she'd never met Oakley in London, she knew his reputation as a stickler of the highest order. She had seen him several times in the company of Lord Burbett, her most solemn suitor, but had never asked for an introduction. He seemed the sort of man who would always find fault with a person, and she never purposely courted self-doubt.

Now Oakley was scowling deeply, his hands behind his back as he walked alongside her. "I am sorry about all this," he finally said. "Burbett will have my head when he hears about it."

She frowned. Apparently, Oakley thought Burbett entertained a position of greater importance in her life than he did. She could hardly inform Oakley that she had turned down his friend's offer. It was Burbett's place to reveal that information in whatever light he chose.

Taking her ensuing silence for a rebuke against over-familiarity, Oakley flushed. "And now I must apologize again."

"Good heavens, m'lord," she said, "this is the eighth or ninth time you've apologized for something or other. You can't possibly blame yourself for *everything*. I assure you, I do not."

"As no one else in my family seems to comprehend the gravity of the situation or claim culpability in bringing it about, if only for pride's sake, I must."

"You do not consider your uncle or . . ." She hesitated. " . . . your cousin to be properly conscience-stricken?"

"Uncle Taran has no conscience," Oakley muttered.

"And your cousin?" she prodded.

For a moment she thought he might rebuff this overture but then the stiffness that seemed an essential part of his demeanor dissolved. He smiled rather ruefully.

"I suppose in all fairness if you are going to acquit me of blame, you must do the same for Robin," he said. "Though it is nigh well impossible to tell from outward appearances, I suspect he is as shocked as I am by Taran's fool antics."

"*Is* he?" Now *here* was a topic far more interesting than Burbett.

Again that unexpected—and unexpectedly charming—smile. "One can but hope."

The opportunity to learn more about Robin was irresistible. "For a gentleman noted for his, ah, appreciation of young ladies, the comte certainly makes himself absent a great deal of the time." It was an appallingly bold thing to say and she could scarce believe she'd uttered it.

Oakley glanced at her in some surprise, but answered nonetheless, "My cousin prefers to give his *appreciation* only to ladies who are no longer young misses."

Ha! Cecily thought grimly, not if Marilla Chisholm had her way.

"Well, it isn't very polite," she said.

"You mustn't take it personally," Oakley said. The earl must be distracted by something—or someone—indeed, to forget his legendary reserve. "I suspect that Robin is trying to ensure that no one's reputation suffers through association with him."

"Or he is simply bound and determined not to fall in with your uncle's matrimonial plans for him?" she suggested.

"It is, of course, possible, but I doubt it."

"Why is that?"

"Because I don't think Robin believes any reputable young lady would consider him a viable matrimonial candidate. No, something else is making him act strangely, and his concern for your reputations is the best reason I can deduce."

"You sound vexed," she said lightly.

"That's because Robin is vexing. And aggravating. And wholly a dunderhead."

"By all appearances, he is quite your opposite, m'lord," she retorted icily, unable to refrain from coming to Robin's defense. "One could see how so congenial a gentleman might try the patience of someone who appears so sober."

His lips tightened. "Who a person appears to be to the world and who that person knows himself to be are not always the same thing."

She understood better than most. She knew society considered her insipid, but as long as her family and intimate friends knew better, she didn't care. But looking at Oakley, a thought occurred to her. "Of whom are you speaking?" she asked. "Yourself or the comte?"

"Perhaps both of us. Even you, Lady Cecily. Burbett proclaimed you to be the most circumspect young lady of his acquaintance and yet here you are interrogating me about my cousin."

Heat flooded up her neck and into her cheeks.

"But then, what do I know of ladies?" he continued on a note of savagery that surprised her. "*Nothing.*

Forgive me. I didn't mean to chastise you. Fool that I am, I insist on seeing things through society's eye and not my own." His jaw tensed. "As it were, I was speaking of Robin's insouciance. It's a pose he's adopted."

She waited, hoping he would elaborate, and after a moment, her silence was rewarded.

"Robin's willingness—or one ought to say *willfulness*—to undervalue himself invites others to do the same. He inherited a vineyard from his father and through sheer determination he's wrested it back from the brink of ruination. Within a decade or so it will be producing some of the finest Bordeaux in the world.

"The *gossips*"—he spat the word—"and tattle tellers and daily rags never mention *that*, however. The fools only speak of his expertise in other areas. And he encourages it." He ground out this last bit. "He readily admits not only to those things he has done, but to crimes he has not even committed. Can you think why anyone would do such a thing?"

Good heavens, whatever had become of the ironclad reserve of London's most famous stone face? She had the odd feeling he was no longer speaking of Robin but something, or someone, else entirely.

She answered, nonetheless. "Perhaps he hopes to preempt the gossips by getting there first, and in doing so at least have the satisfaction of stealing their thunder and, perhaps, avoiding the sting unfounded accusations can bring."

He regarded her sharply. "You may be right," he murmured. "Robin is in many ways as fine a man as I would hope to know. But I would be a poor host indeed were I to allow my guests to unintentionally expose themselves to gossip.

"Be careful, Lady Cecily," he added roughly, but not unkindly. "We have a mutual friend who would never allow his name to be associated, even tangentially, with anything remotely inappropriate. "

He was talking about Burbett again, warning her that if she dallied with Robin, Burbett would break off his courtship. "You needn't concern yourself, Lord Oakley. I have no intention of entering into a flirtation with your cousin."

No. She had other ideas altogether.

"I would never presume such a thing, Lady Cecily," Oakley said, stiffening once more. "You are obviously not the sort of woman who encourages men to . . ." His lips curled in a snarl that looked more frustrated than enraged. " . . . to climb the ivy outside their bedchambers."

She had no idea what he meant by this last, but clearly, it meant something important. She did not wonder for long, however, being wholly caught up in an idea that had taken root with his words.

"Ivy," she muttered, her brow furrowed in concentration. What man could possibly mistake the intentions of a lady driven to such an act? He couldn't.

She was thinking metaphorically, of course, but if Robin would not pursue her, then she would simply have to seduce the Prince of Rakes.

Chapter 20

Very early the next morning

The sky was still a deep cobalt paling to orchid on the horizons when Robin began prowling Finovair's long-abandoned portrait gallery. The storm had passed, and Finovair stood cloaked in heavy white robes, her turrets and tumbled curtain wall shimmering with ice. It was as pretty now as ever it would be or, in all likelihood, ever had been. But Robin barely noted its beauty. His imagination was fixed on quite a different kind of beauty.

Who would have guessed that Lady Cecily Tarleton would prove to be the most dangerous woman in Great Britain? Oh, not to the world at large, but to a very small population of one, she most decidedly was that.

"Were it not so amusing, it would be pathetic," he murmured, his breath turning to a cloud in the unheated corridor's frigid air, glad to find his humor restored.

It had gone mostly missing since he'd first seen her, standing before Bretton's carriage in a pool of torchlight. Snow caught in her lashes, spangled her rich, dark hair like the diadems in fairy queen's veil, and melted on her rosy cheeks. Subtle bemusement had flickered over the cameo smoothness of her face, a sense of wonder growing in her amber-colored eyes as she looked around for all the world as if abduction were a regular occurrence, and she needed merely to enjoy the interim between theft and rescue.

Having been thrown at birth on the mercy of Fate and Fortune—and having discovered therefore that amused acceptance was the best ally against despair—Robin appreciated the same attitude in another. Especially such a lovely "other."

When Byron had taken her hand, Robin had realized *he* had wanted to be the one taking her hand, and since Robin rarely denied himself anything he wanted, especially as he *always* made certain his wants were well within his means, he had fairly shoved Oakley aside and presented himself. As expected of a rake, he'd made some slightly outré comment and grinned wickedly, anticipating her gasp—de rigueur in such situations—or, possibly, if she was a rompish miss, a snicker.

She hadn't done either.

She'd looked up at him. A strange, heart-stealing expression of recognition had arisen in her honeyed eyes, and her ripe, luscious lips had parted but not a word escaped them, and he had been stunned by the force of a yearning so unexpected it had nearly brought him to his knees. And it was at that precise instance he'd realized how very, very dangerous Lady Cecily was. Because against all reason, when he should have been proof against such nonsense, he had done the unthinkable and fallen in love.

And love at first sight, at that.

Robin had never been in love before, which is precisely how he recognized the sensation with such absolute certainty. Shortly thereafter, he had fled—and no, he would not appease his vanity by calling it anything else—from the more habitable portions of Finovair to those parts falling to ruin, which, he thought ruefully, looking around, was most of it. Because while Robin might be in love, he was not insane, and it would be insanity indeed to pursue that which he had no possibility of attaining.

He had learned that lesson early in life when he'd arrived in London as a young man. Society's mamas wasted no time in cautioning their daughters against the son of an impecunious French count. And their papas had been just as quick to take Robin aside—accompanied by their more brawny retainers—to make *very* sure he understood the warning.

Thereafter, Robin had kept his liaisons strictly to the ranks of ladies who did not require marriage as a prerequisite to bed sport. And while his conquests were not nearly so legion as Byron assumed—and Robin let him assume—they were plentiful enough to keep a fellow from deploring his lot in life.

And why should he deplore his lot? he asked himself, stopping to stare sightlessly at the snowy courtyard below. He had health, good friends, a few acres of vines he still managed to keep a working concern, and—he cast a jaundiced eye down a hall of fallen plaster rubble and pockmarked walls—someday would inherit a Scottish castle. What more could he want?

Her.

He scowled at the betraying thought.

Irritably, he pivoted to leave, and as he did so, he heard the unmistakable if faint sound of a female cursing. Relieved by the distraction, he smiled, wondering if along with all the rest of the unwelcome bequests with which Taran—damn his unfruitful loins—intended to saddle him, he would also inherit a ghost. Though he thought even ghosts had more sense than to haunt so inhospitable a place.

He looked down the hall toward where the sound had come just as a pile of russet-colored rags topped by a head emerged from a doorway.

A particularly dark and lovely head.

Lady Cecily.

It appeared he was to be haunted, after all.

Chapter 21

For a second, Robin considered pretending he hadn't seen her—again—and bolt down the adjacent corridor. By avoiding her thus far, he had avoided sampling what he could never wholly have.

True, manners had demanded that he make an appearance at dinner the first night, but he'd seated himself at the opposite end of the table from her and escaped as soon as Marilla had commenced her campaign to win Bretton's . . . Well, if she won anything of Bretton's, it certainly wasn't ever going to be his heart. But, then, any fool watching her manhandle the duke would soon realize that Bretton's heart was never her objective.

But now Robin found he could not resist the opportunity to spend some time alone with Lady Cecily before her rescuers came thundering through the passes. When they arrived, he would be gone. He had no intention of standing by while Marilla Chisholm convinced her father that events had occurred that could only be satisfied with a wedding. Particularly if it was his own.

Besides, perhaps if he spent some time with Lady Cecily, he would discover that she was not what every fiber in his heart declared her to be but simply a young lady whose lovely visage and pretty manners summed up the total of what she was or aspired to become. At least, he thought as he strode toward her, he could hope.

"Lady Cecily," Robin hailed her, his amusement growing with each step.

She'd exchanged yesterday's antique morning weeds for an even older ball gown, dating from an era when women would have had to turn sideways to enter through a door. But without the support of the underlying panniers that would have once jutted out from her hips, the heavy skirts dragged along the ground on either side of her like two broken wings.

The once rich ruby red silk had turned a dull rusty color, and the heavy application of silver thread embroidering the sleeves and hem had become green with age. Huge silk cabbage roses, once white but now dingy and yellowed, hung disconsolately from her elbows, waist, and hips.

Even during the height of George VII's reign, when low-cut dresses were in vogue, the décolletage would have been indecent, but on Lady Cecily's slight frame it hung so loosely that she'd been forced to wrap some sort of velvet shawl around her neck like a muffler before stuffing the ends down the bodice to preserve her modesty. The effort had apparently caused her hair to fall from its neat knot, and it, too, lay tucked beneath the velvet wrapping.

An image of how she'd look had she not been so enterprising with that damned shawl beset his imagination; her hair rippling over her naked shoulders, loose curls playing at her cleavage. Heated desire quickened his body. Ruthlessly, he vanquished the taunting vision.

"Heavens, Comte, whatever are you doing here?" Lady Cecily asked.

Avoiding you, my love. "Taking my morning constitutional. My doctor prescribes clambering over rubble in frigid temperatures at least thrice daily," he said, and she gratified him by laughing at his absurdity. "Might I inquire the same?"

She glanced down at her bedraggled skirts and gave an unexpectedly gamine grin. "One can only wear a gown twice before retiring it. Surely you know that, Comte? I found this in the trunk Mr. Hamish brought to the room and as for this . . ." She grimaced, plucking at the shawl.

His eyes widened. By God, it wasn't a shawl she'd wrapped around her shoulders, but an old velvet bed curtain. He recognized it as coming from a room he'd once occupied as a child! Apparently, she'd ripped it from its moorings.

"I will, of course, make restitution," she added.

"My dear," he said, shaking his head mournfully, "I hardly know what to say. One doesn't find relics like that just lying about, you know."

"No," she answered. "One finds them *hanging* about."

He stifled a chuckle, trying to look stern. "What is even more distressing than your pillaging my uncle's home is that having torn the family tapestry from its rods to decorate yourself, you are now on the hunt for more things to loot."

"Terrible, I know," she admitted, her gaze unsettlingly direct. "I am afraid that when I find something I want, I will fight to the end for it."

He looked at her with renewed appreciation. Those had hardly been the words of a model of propriety. And her gaze was too direct and her expression filled with delight and naughtiness. Indeed, her ripe lips trembled with ill-suppressed merriment.

Damn it.

"How rapacious of you," he said, realizing he'd been staring. "But then, how can I find fault with that? Especially as I have been accused of similar failings."

"Oh. Is it a failing?" she asked innocently, glancing at him out of the corner of her remarkable eyes. With each word and glance, she delighted him more.

This was far worse—and so much better—than he'd expected. The conversations he'd had with young ladies during his first season had been unremarkable exchanges: bland pleasantries, light chat about the latest play, the weather, the most recent exhibitions. There'd been no repartee, no subtext, no—God help him—flirtation.

He must leave Finovair before lunch.

"Besides," she said, "your cousin claims that you are the very model of restraint."

Once more, she'd caught him off-guard. He burst out laughing. "Either you are twitting me, Lady Cecily, or you have discovered a cousin who is entirely unknown to me and who, obviously, knows just as little about me in return."

"He seemed quite confident. But then, you never know with men, do you?" she said. "They always appear to be certain of everything. It must be exhausting. Is it?"

"As I am not certain of anything, particularly this conversation, I dare not answer."

"Oh, I believe you think yourself very certain of who and what you are, Comte."

There was amusement in her voice and he didn't quite know what to make of that. He smiled to cover his discomfort and said, "Please, the title is less than a courtesy. You must call me Robin, especially as Marilla has announced that we are all on first-name terms."

Some of the light faded in her extraordinary eyes. "I should have liked to call you Robin at your own behest, not someone else's."

"It *is* my request. I should like you to call me Robin." He heard the slight imploring note in his voice, but could do nothing to prevent it. He wanted to hear her say his name in every mood: shouted in glee, whispered in intimacy, spoken with easy familiarity.

"Only if you will call me Cecily."

"Your father would hardly approve." The words slipped out unintended. When had he turned into such a pedant? But she really shouldn't be giving the use of her Christian name to a rake.

"But he is not here, and I would never presume to know of what he would approve or disapprove," she said with feigned haughtiness. "I find it rather audacious that you do."

Her sophistry delighted him almost as much as her mental adroitness. Besides, what harm if they played at friendship . . . or even something more, for a few short hours?

"I see I have no choice but to cede to your greater knowledge, La— Cecily. Until I have been told otherwise by the gentleman himself, I will be ruled by your superior understanding. Now, whatever are you doing in these inhospitable climes so early in the morning?"

"As I told you, I am looking for something to wear. Something that fits better than this," she said, tugging at the sagging skirts. "The hunt has led me here."

"I'm afraid you'll be disappointed," Robin said. "This part of the castle has been uninhabited for generations. Anything worth keeping was removed long ago."

"Drat."

He grinned at this small imprecation. "Exactly. I'm sorry."

"No matter. I'll just look elsewhere. There must be something somewhere."

He doubted it, but why dampen her spirits when she was so obviously enjoying her treasure hunt?

"Did you have in mind somewhere particular to look?" he asked.

"Not really. I've already been in every room in this corridor."

"Then perhaps you'd allow me to escort you back to a more likely hunting ground? Finovair might not be very large but it can be confusing. Purposely so."

"Why is that?"

"It's all part of our national heritage. All those Jacobites and Hanoverians littering the countryside, plotting and counterplotting, ferreting out secrets and squirreling others away. Small wonder Scottish castles tend to be warrens of secret passages and blind ends, priest bolts and lovers' cupboards. And the Fergusons were the worst of the lot. As such it only stands to reason their stronghold would be one of the most abstruse. Yes. You really had best let me accompany you—"

She held up her hand, laughing. "Have done, Robin! I am convinced."

Had he sounded so eager? He must indeed be bewitched. His sangfroid was legendary.

"And by all means, I accept," she went on. "I should hate to end up lost in these walls for eternity. Take me where you will. I am yours!"

His heart lurched at her words and he glanced at her to see if she understood what she'd offered, but not a bit of caution clouded her face. She smiled sunnily up at him, sovereign in her consequence. No one would dare assail her. After all, she was an earl's daughter.

Foolish girl, she was far too lovely to make such assumptions. After all, she'd been abducted, hadn't she? Kidnapped and dragged through a storm to a heathen-ish, frozen castle for the express purpose of becoming its heir's bride.

His bride.

The thought hovered with tantalizing effect in the foreground of his imagination. What if he stayed and wooed her? Seduced her? Used all his much-vaunted skill to try to win her for his own? Would she succumb?

Would *he*?

She tucked her hand into the crook of his arm, unaware of the profligate impulses shivering through him.

"I admit," she said, "the idea of being lost here does conjure an amusing image: my poor spirit moaning dolefully through the walls at your descendants, only to have them shout back that I deserve my fate for not accepting your escort. " She peeked up at him through sooty lashes. "At least I assume that any descendants of yours would have scant pity for fools who don't know enough to take what was offered."

He checked, startled by an interpretation of her words that she could not possibly have meant. She gazed at him, all innocence and trust. He swallowed. "You think you know me well enough to predict my unborn descendants' dispositions?" he asked, discovering that he *liked* the idea that she knew him; he even liked the idea that she thought she knew him. Though, of course she couldn't. His lovers had often complained that his laughter and wit deflected any hope of achieving any intimacy that didn't involve the flesh.

But here, at this moment, with this girl in her oversized dress and bed-hanging shawl, looking like a child who had raided her grandmother's wardrobe to play dress-up, walking along a hall where frost rimed the windows and crept like silvery lichen along the ceiling as their breath made little shrouds in the air, in this strange fairy-tale land of predawn glitter and soft, frosted sheen, Cecily's assumption of familiarity felt warm and companionable and . . . *right*.

Perhaps he needn't avoid her after all. Perhaps they really could just be friends . . .

But then he glanced at her, just a glance, and noted the way the angled light limned her full lower lip, the elegant line of her nose, the glossy sheen of her rich dark locks, and the small shadowed vale just visible above where she'd tucked the velvet material into her bodice and realized, no, they could not just be friends.

"Am I presumptuous?" she asked, not looking the least abashed. "I'm sorry."

"Not at all," he said easily. "I am just appalled that my predictability is so blatant you can foretell what traits my descendants will inherit."

"You are kind, Robin," she said, studying him.

Her words made him uneasy. He was a rake and a ne'er-do-well. And a pauper. She must know that.

He drew her back to his side and they proceeded at a leisurely pace, as if they were strolling in St. James Park during the height of the season, not a frozen corridor in a ruined castle in the dead of winter.

"You might well be correct about my presumed offspring," he said. "*If* future Comtes de Rocheforte were to be found lounging about the castle. But I doubt they will be."

"How so?" she asked. "The older gentleman gave me to understand that you will inherit Finovair."

"The older gentleman? Oh. You mean Taran. Hardly a gentleman, though definitely older. And yes, my mother having been so shortsighted as to have given birth to me prematurely, and thus two weeks before Byron's mother bore him, Taran has deemed me next in line to have this great pile foisted upon."

He spoke with a great show of amused indifference. "But even I at my most persuasive—and I can be most persuasive"—he angled an amused glance at her, and was rewarded with a faint blush—"even I would be hard-pressed to talk any lady into living here, let alone raising her children in such a place."

"Why?" She stopped and looked up at him, by all appearances sincerely confused.

Why? His gaze swept down the length of ruined gallery. A vine had crept through a crack in one of the windows and hung bare and twisted as a witch's finger from the ceiling, pointing accusingly at a broken chair tipping woozily against a water-stained wall. She was being disingenuous. She had to be.

"The latest fashions," he said with supreme insouciance, "eschew blue lips. Or so I am told. And I refuse to have an unfashionable wife."

She burst into laughter and he could not help but notice that her lips were, indeed, touched with a violet hue. Wordlessly, he shrugged out of his jacket and, without asking permission, draped it over her shoulders.

She backed away a step as he performed this unasked-for service, clearly startled by the liberties he'd taken. He took the opportunity for even more, tucking the collar around her neck and gently teasing a tress of hair free from under his jacket. Then he smoothed it along her shoulder, smiling down at her as he slowly followed her retreat, step by step. Her shoulders bumped into the wall behind her.

"My pardon, Lady Cecily," he said, coming to his senses. "I am simply doing my part to see that Scotland stays au courant with London. Your lips were turning blue, m'dear."

He didn't mean to do anything more. But her golden eyes trapped him in time, and all he was aware of was the beating of his heart, the sound of his own labored breathing, and then, amazingly, impossibly, she leaned forward, tipping her head back, her eyelids slipping shut, and her lips pursed in a delicious invitation.

A kiss. Something to remember her by. What harm a kiss?

He could no more have declined that wordless offer than he could refuse to breathe. He lowered his head and carefully, gently pressed his lips to hers.

Chapter 22

Desire exploded at the instant of contact, shooting like lightning through Robin. He stepped closer, keeping his hands knotted in fists at his sides, wanting more but certain that if he reached for her, she would bolt.

More kisses. That was all he sought. It was hardly anything, nothing at all, really, just . . . everything.

She made some lovely, half-surprised, half-ravished sound, a sigh and gasp all at once, and reached up, steadying herself with a hand flattened against his chest.

He edged closer still, his legs entangling in her heavy skirts, but trying not to startle her. In an effort to restrain himself, he braced his forearm on the wall above her head, angling his own to better access the perfect ripeness of her lips, to flick his tongue along the sweet seam until—mercy!—her mouth opened and her tongue found his own.

He groaned, surrendering to the pleasure of her untutored exploration. For long, glorious moments he kissed her until he felt her hand creep up his chest and she linked her arms around his neck, her fingers sifting through his hair. In reply, his body turned rock-hard. Only a few inches separated her from becoming manifestly aware of his state of arousal. He wanted to kiss her, not shock her. His jaw tightening with frustration, he stepped back, releasing her mouth.

She blinked, startled by his sudden desertion. He looked away, taking a deep, steadying breath. His emotions were chaotic and unfamiliar, an uncomfortable mix of desire and the desire to protect. She shouldn't be here with him. This was a mistake. A foolish, masochistic indulgence.

"Good heavens, you *are* adroit at this seduction thing, aren't you?" she whispered breathlessly.

"You didn't know? Of course I am. My dear, I am the Prince of Rakes." He glanced back at her sardonically, the once amusing sobriquet coming like a curse to his lips.

Her arms slipped from around his shoulders. He looked down at her, prepared to offer an arrogant curl of the lip, but the sight of her ruined the attempt. She looked puzzled and somber, her cheeks flushed, her eyes bright and unnervingly candid.

"Of course you are," she said. "I mean, I had *heard* that. You do have a far-ranging reputation. But one hears so much about so many people, and then when one meets the individual, one realizes that rumors have simply exaggerated what is, in fact, not all that extraordinary."

He laughed, startled out of his dark mood. She confounded him, robbed him of his intent, his sangfroid, his reputation. She stripped away all his preconceptions about young ladies, leaving him without a clue to guide him. She fascinated and mystified him. What was she doing? What was she about?

"I see," he said. "Rather a letdown, am I?"

"Oh no! Not at all. You *quite* exceed expectations," she hastened to reassure him with such artlessness, such solicitous concern for his rakish reputation, that he could not help but laugh again. "I have never been kissed so . . . so *convincingly.*"

"Now 'tis you who are kind, Lady Cecily," he said, though something about her use of the word "convincingly" nettled him. She thought he'd been playing a role. In truth, he had never before been so lost in a simple kiss and it annoyed him that she did not realize it.

"But then, perhaps you should ask Miss Marilla's opinion," she said. "She may have a different judgment."

He started and stared, stunned she had alluded to the kiss she'd witnessed. A little ember glowed in the depths of her amber-colored eyes. *Jealousy?*

Then she smiled at him with such dazzling unaffectedness that his breath caught in his throat and he lifted his hand to touch her, but she'd already turned away and started down the gallery. He hastened to her side, once more offering his arm. She took it with a nonchalance that startled him, coming so close on the heels of their heated kiss. At least, he thought in growing consternation, *he'd* considered it heated . . .

"Truth be told," she continued as if there had been no break in the conversation, "I don't know many rakes."

"I should hope not," he said, once again caught off-balance by the turn of the conversation. She should be blushing or berating him for taking advantage of her, or perhaps enticing him to try his luck again, responses he was used to and expected. She should *not* be acting as if the preceding moments hadn't happened, as if their kiss were insignificant. It was significant to him!

He'd never been in such a situation before. She had him at sixes and sevens, his assumptions challenged, his body taut with desire, his aplomb all but vanished, and his heart thundering with something that could only be described as a mad craving . . . to touch her, to kiss her.

"In fact," she went on, "I've only known two bona fide rakes: you and a far-removed cousin whose exploits we only speak of sotto voce."

"Do not tell me there is a rival for my crown?" he said, struggling to match her insouciance. "Surely his reputation does not equal mine?"

"Oh, it is far worse than yours," she said comfortably. "I have it on good authority—those being the miscreant's own words—that he has seduced upwards of eighty of the *ton*'s most well-respected ladies."

"He *told* you this?" Robin asked, surprised she had been allowed to converse with a known rake, let alone that the conversation had been on such a subject.

"Yes," she said. "Though not when anyone else was about to hear. Certainly not within earshot of my parents. Oh no," she said, surprising him by chuckling, "they would not have been happy to hear about *that* conversation. Not at all."

Nor was Robin. Acid-bright jealousy curled in his belly. Had this unknown libertine kissed her? And, afterward, had she been this cavalier?

"No," she continued, "he waited until he had me all to himself at my parents' country ball in Surrey last year. They were occupied with greeting their guests when Marmeduke convinced me to walk out onto the terrace with him."

Marmeduke? She was on such intimate terms with this blackguard she called by his Christian name?

"There was no one else about and he took ruthless advantage of our unexpected privacy." She darted a glance at him. "I suspect I should have left at once. We were absent from the ballroom for far too long. But his stories were so fascinating that I couldn't resist staying to listen. I am sure our guests must have begun wondering what had become of us," she finished.

He doubted this, if only for one compelling reason: had Lady Cecily disappeared onto a terrace with a known debauchee long enough to provoke questions, her reputation would never have survived. Yet, apparently, it had.

He'd made a mistake. He had misjudged her. He'd thought her awake to all suits, an uncommonly sophisticated ingénue, but she seemed as unaware of how close she had skirted disaster as a toddler hurtling by a steep flight of stairs. She was a danger to herself. Someone should have been guarding her reputation, and clearly, no one had been.

Far be it from him to interfere, but he could not allow her to go careering about society with no one to guide or protect her. When her father showed up to collect her, Robin would see to it that they had a chat wherein he outlined the gentleman's paternal duties for him.

What was he thinking? He wouldn't *be* here when her father arrived. But . . . but he could go to London.

Tongues wagged quite freely in London's less salubrious gentlemen's clubs during the off-season, when there was little else to do but gossip. As soon as he returned to town, he would find this . . . this Marmeduke and have a conversation with him and make sure that the bastard understood the meaning of discretion. Because while Robin's reputation for seduction might be exaggerated, his reputation as someone not to be trifled with was not.

"What is my rival's full name, may I ask?" Somehow, he managed to sound no more than curious.

"Marmeduke, Lord Goodhue."

He frowned. He could have sworn he knew every roué in London. "I don't believe I've ever met the gentleman."

"I shouldn't be surprised. He rarely visits London, staying solely in Surrey," she replied.

"He lives near your family's country estate?" he asked. *Where* in Surrey? He'd always meant to visit Surrey.

"Not *near* our house. *In* our house. He became our permanent houseguest after having become insolvent a few years ago and having nowhere else to go. Indeed, my parents assigned him chambers right next to mine."

He stared at her, an odd sensation rising within him. Damnation, he believed he was *shocked*. He hadn't been shocked since he was fifteen and the Latin teacher's wife had offered him different sorts of lessons.

"Well, we couldn't very well put him in the servants' hall," she said defensively. "Though I have little doubt he'd much prefer it. The chambermaids are always threatening to give notice as it is."

It wasn't simply a marvel the girl's reputation was intact; it was a bloody *miracle*.

"Damn, you say," he muttered under his breath, and she burst out laughing. Her whole face bloomed with merriment, her eyes dancing, the laughter bubbling from her lips, her teeth flashing in an open grin. She took his breath away.

"Of course, as he's eighty-three years old and suffers from gout, he stands a better chance of winning the Derby than he does catching a housemaid," she managed to say between giggles. "Or me. Not that he'd ever make an attempt. He has some standards, as do all rakes." She gave him a sidelong glance. "Or so Marmeduke assures me."

She started laughing again and damned if he didn't join her. She'd been leading him along all the while, paying him back for making her praise his kisses.

"*Touché, ma petite,*" he said, when they finally stopped laughing. He offered her his arm and she took it, and once again they commenced their much-protracted journey down the frozen hallway.

For long companionable minutes they were silent and he drank in the sensation, the warmth of her fingers resting on his arm, the elusive scent of vanilla and jasmine that tickled his nostrils every so often, the simple pleasure of her company . . .

"It may be chilly, but Finovair does have considerable charm," she said after a while. "Yet I take it you think your bride will be happier in London than here."

He should have demurred, let her comment pass without replying but he needed to tell her—no, he needed to remind himself of how very far above him she stood.

"Bride?" he echoed. "My dear Cecily, I have even less to offer a wife in London than here."

Any other girl would have blushed or apologized or at the very least looked on him with distaste. After all, he'd just committed one of society's cardinal sins: he'd acknowledged his poverty. But he was growing used to the unexpected from her, and so it was now.

"But you must want to marry and have a family," she said earnestly.

"I must," he agreed. "But I have been told that when one takes a wife, one also has an obligation to take her wants into account, too. Wants I have scant hope of fulfilling. I may be a rake, Lady Cecily, but I am not a scoundrel."

She stared at him for a long moment and then her eyes flashed and she said, "I see. So, you see your future being similar to that of Marmeduke's?"

Hell and damnation, *no*. But before he could rebut this noxious notion, she hurried on in the manner of one trying very hard to be encouraging about a very dismal prospect. "Not that there's anything wrong with that," she said, adding under her breath, "I suppose."

Dear God, in her imagination was he predestined to go hobbling after chambermaids in his old age, gnarled fingers extended in hopes of pinching one last fleet-footed wench? Is that how she saw him? "You horrify me."

"I do?" she asked. "Why is that, I wonder?"

"I meant your vision of my future horrifies me."

"Oh? Why? Marmeduke's really rather a pet," she said. "He's a great favorite amongst my younger sisters."

The idea of dangling cherubic little girls on his knees while offering them well-censored bedtime stories about his youthful exploits sent nearly as great a shiver through Robin as the idea of him chasing chambermaids, and so he ignored her question, asking one of his own instead. "Do you have many siblings?"

"Four. I have two younger brothers, twins. They were sent to Eton last year and I miss them a great deal, as my younger sisters consider games that require physical dexterity beneath them. Though I think they would find such games delightful if they were any good at them," she confided with an arch twinkle in her eye that he found adorable.

"Have you any brothers or sisters?" she countered.

"No."

"But you had Oakley to keep tally of your sins?"

He smiled at that. "No. Not really." His smile faded. "Oakley and I were kept apart."

Robin hadn't met Byron until they were adults. After Robin's parents had died of influenza, pride, not compassion, had prompted Byron's father to pay for Robin's education. However, the old tartar had seen no reason that his heir should hobnob with some impecunious Frenchman's get. So while Byron went to Eton, Robin been sent to Rugby. He had never been invited to spend holidays at Oakley House. Instead, Rugby's headmaster had been paid to take Robin to his own home during those periods.

But there was no reason to bother her with such details.

"How many sisters?" he asked.

She regarded him thoughtfully for long seconds before answering. "Two. One is nineteen and the other, who is seventeen, was launched just this past season. Quite successfully, too," she said, with a touch of pride.

She loved them, he realized, her affection for her family wholly uncomplicated and honest, and she felt loved in return. It made him yearn to be included in her magical circle. He frowned at the thought: he'd finished with such nonsense years ago.

"Both have received offers of matrimony from gentlemen of whom they are quite fond," she continued. They were almost to the end of the corridor now. He could see the great stairway leading down to the inhabited part of the castle, a soft glow rising from the lower level. "They are all aflutter to marry and set up their own households," she said. "Alas, Papa will not hear of it."

"The young men are unacceptable?" Robin asked, feeling comradely toward these poor, unworthy swains.

"Not at all," she said. "It's just that my father is dreadfully old-fashioned. He refuses to let my younger sisters marry until I am off the market. In fact, that is why we are in Scotland."

At her words, something swelled in Robin's throat and his heart thudded dully in his chest. That explained why the Maycotts were here, hosting a house party: the earl was going to announce his daughter's engagement. Who was the bastard? Scottish perhaps, otherwise why drag society up here in the dead of winter. But *who*?

They'd reached the end of the gallery and were at the top of the staircase looking down into the foyer just outside the great hall. The sound of light laughter drifted up to them. Bretton and his ladylove. Cecily belonged down there with them, in light and warmth. Not here, in the chill and ruin.

"You are unflatteringly preoccupied, Robin," she said reproachfully. "I daresay you haven't heard a thing I've said."

Every syllable, every *breath*. He managed a smile. "Of course I have. You have come to Scotland to announce your engagement. "

"No," she said, her brow wrinkling. "I've come to decide *which* marriage proposal to accept."

"Which?" he repeated, dumbfounded. "There were so many?"

She tipped her head, watching him closely. "Five."

"Five?" Somehow he managed to sound only faintly amused, politely interested. Perhaps he should consider a career on the stage.

Five. And doubtless each one able to offer her the things any loving parent wanted for his child: security, wealth, consequence. Otherwise Maycott would have outright refused them. Still, *she wasn't promised to another.* Not yet.

"And," he said, careful to keep his gaze straight ahead of him, "does any one fellow stand above the rest?"

"No," she said with a small sigh. "That's the problem. There is not one amongst them for whom I care more than the others."

Absurd relief washed through him. He was craven. He was ridiculous. Still, it changed nothing.

The pain of that realization cut through him, sharp and deep. He mustn't let her see. He had pride, if nothing else. It had been the one thing he refused to compromise or cede in a short life filled with concessions and compromises.

"What do you think I ought to do?" she asked intently, her voice no longer light and careless.

This was one part he could not play. Yet play it he must.

"Well," he drawled, "if you postponed your decision for another season you could probably field another five offers. Then you'd have an entire cricket team and could just choose the best bowler."

Color washed delicately up her throat and stained her fine, pale cheeks. Wordlessly, she pulled off his jacket and handed it to him.

"Thank you, Comte," she said icily. "I shall take your suggestion under advisement." She turned to start down the stairs, taking with her every dream he never realized he harbored but which she had brought to painful light . . .

But not yet.

He grabbed her arm and with not a whit of expertise or urbanity, spun her back around and into his embrace. He tipped her over his arm, and his mouth descended on hers in a ruthless, hungry kiss. All the years he would not touch her, see her, be with her poured into that kiss; loss and urgency, anger and helplessness. Then, as quickly as he'd taken possession of her, he set her back on her feet and stepped away, his hands dropping to his sides.

For a long moment, they stood facing each other, each breathing heavily, their gazes locked in some undefined contest in which there would be no victor. He waited for her to castigate him, slap him, revile him, do any of the things she had every right to do not only now but in answer to his earlier kiss, too. But again, she didn't. She just stood there, shoulders back, head high, eyes blazing. He had no idea what she was thinking, feeling. Fury? Disgust? *Pity?*

Finally, he could stand it no longer. "Aren't you going to say something?" he demanded desperately.

"Aren't you?" she countered in the same tone.

God, yes, how much he wanted to speak, to swear fealty, explain what she'd done to him, plead for her hand. But he couldn't. It wouldn't be right.

"No."

Her head snapped back as if he'd struck her and his hand came up to reach for her . . .

But she was already running down the stairs.

Leaving him behind.

Chapter 23

What in the name of all that is holy was wrong with the man?! He kisses her not once but twice, then pushes her away both times—though she has made it as clear as day that she does not want to be pushed away—and then, in answer to her pathetically obvious attempt to rouse his jealousy, suggests she should try to field a cricket team. A *cricket* team! That was all he could say?

Cecily stomped down the stairs, her velvet skirts swishing angrily around her ankles. But her steps slowed as she touched her lips, feeling again his hunger, his fierce desire. Thank heaven the gallery wall behind her had held her up for that first kiss, for without its support she would have buckled under his sensual onslaught, and he'd supported her for the second, which was even more potent. Even now the memory made her knees weak and her breath come high and tight in her chest.

She realized now that he hadn't even bothered to embrace her during that first kiss. When he'd stopped, all she could assume was that he'd been somehow disappointed, that her kiss had been too *jeune fille* for his worldly palate, and so casting about frantically for something to say that would not sound horrifically unsophisticated, said the first thing that had popped into her head, some daft comment about how good he was at kissing. And for some reason, that had seemed to anger him. Almost to embarrass him.

What was she to make of that? And why had he kissed her again and why had that second kiss seemed so angry, yet so desperate? And what had he meant, "Aren't you going to say something?" *He* was the one who'd kissed *her*. And finally, most importantly, why the *hell* wasn't he following her now—

Oh!

She reached the bottom of the stairs and tripped over the hideous old dress's hem. Frustrated, she yanked at the skirts and in doing so dislodged the velvet bed hanging looped around her shoulders. It fell in a coil to her waist, sweeping the loose neckline off her shoulders before catching around her hips like a great velvet boa constrictor. She froze, afraid that any movement might render her completely topless.

Tears welled in her eyes. What had become of her? She looked like a musty Gypsy crone and she smelled like a wet dog. No wonder he'd let her go. She should probably be happy he hadn't given her a boot to the backside.

"Lady Cecily?" a tentative female voice hailed her.

Oh no. The last thing she wanted was an audience to her misery. Snuffling mightily, she dabbed at her nose trying to compose herself before turning around. Catriona Burns was coming toward her, her attitude cautious, her expression carefully bland. *Her* dress fit. A tear escaped Cecily's eye and dribbled down her cheek.

"Hello, Miss Burns," Cecily said, knowing she sounded brittle and false. "You are up early this morning." She looked away, trying to recover her poise, but her tears only fell more quickly. She ignored them as best she could. "It looks like it has the making of a lovely day." She sniffed. "Wouldn't you say?"

"Lovely," Catriona agreed, coming to her side. And, without so much as a by-your-leave, she snagged the loose end of the treacherous bed curtain and draped it back over Cecily's shoulders.

The unexpected kindness nearly undid Cecily.

"I believe we've seen the last of the snow for a while," Catriona said as easily as if returning teary gentlewomen to a state of modesty were an everyday occurrence. "What's already fallen won't last long. It never does. I expect within a few days most of it will have melted." She finished wrapping the curtain and stepped back, looking over her endeavors with a critical eye. "There now. How's that?"

Cecily looked down at her faded dress with its bilious embroidery and drooping roses, and at the ragged velvet curtain. "Awful," she said. "Simply awful," and then she clamped her hand over her mouth, staring at Catriona in contrition because she hadn't meant to be ungrateful, it was just that—

"It really is, isn't it?" Catriona agreed, her gaze on the dress. "Completely and unutterably hideous."

Catriona lifted her head, and something in her exaggeratedly woeful countenance made Cecily smile and then grin, and then the two of them were laughing like loonies.

"Now, we shall have a nice cup of tea and one of Mrs. McVittie's scones," Catriona said when their laughter had died down. She linked her arm through Cecily's, drawing her into the room where breakfast was being laid out. "And then you can tell me what all this is about."

And so Cecily did.

An hour or so later, Cecily sailed forth from Catriona Burns's bedchamber much restored in spirit and body. Catriona Burns, soon to become Duchess of Bretton— and a lovelier duchess one would have a hard time imagining—had found stacks of boys' clothing in the trunk brought to her room, including an antique tiger's uniform, and insisted Cecily try them on. Throwing propriety to the wind, she had, and was gratified to discover that she and the tiger were a similar size and shape except for a certain constriction in the jacket. And about the hips. And her backside. In anticipation of finally being able to get a breath of fresh air after being castle-bound for so long, she'd finished her toilette by donning a knit cap found in the trunk.

Bolstered by Catriona's encouragement and her own exhilaration at doing something as scandalous as wearing boy's clothing, Cecily struck out, determined to find her would-be lover and recommence her seduction of him. The only problem was she did not know where he might be and she could hardly ask someone where his chambers were. As daring as she'd grown these last few days, there were some lines she was not prepared to cross. That was one of them.

And she *had* become daring, she thought, walking along the corridor, cracking open doors and peeking inside. Who among her acquaintances would ever imagine she'd be so audacious, trading bon mots with a rake, planning to seduce that same rake, and donning boy's clothing preparatory to doing so? None.

In fact, for the first time outside the small circle of her immediate family, she felt wholly and comfortably herself. A chill traveled through her. What if she had never come to Scotland, what if she had said yes to one of those worthy men who'd courted her? What if she'd never been kidnapped and she had never met Robert Parles, Comte de Rocheforte?

She would have spent the rest of her days living a life removed from herself, experiencing emotions at a distance, cocooned and indistinct, like bumping a well-bandaged wound. Not *painful*, precisely, but not alive, either, a dull layer of conventionality and unmet expectation standing between her and her heart.

The chill grew deeper, colder. What if Robin refused her? What if he would not wed her? What then? Could she be satisfied with something less? Could she wed for convenience and hope that something more might eventually grow out of the union? Would she choose spinsterhood and the memories of a very intense, very few minutes over the promise of a family?

Her footsteps slowed and her earlier ebullience faded. She needed to clear her head.

She frowned and looked about. Lost in thought, she'd made her way toward the back of the castle, near the kitchens, and was standing next to a narrow window looking across a snowy yard toward the stables. Next to the window, a low door led outside.

She lifted the latch and pushed the door open, finding herself at the top of a short flight of stairs leading down into a thick blanket of snow. Above, the morning sun blazed in a robin's-egg blue sky, setting the pure white field sparkling. The tang of pine reached her nostrils and the sound of birdsong filled the air.

As she stood there, the stable door opened. A couple emerged, a tall blond man with his arm wrapped protectively around the shoulders of a red-haired woman. With a start, Cecily recognized Lord Oakley and Fiona Chisholm, whose hair tumbled down around her shoulders and whose laugh tinkled in the air as she looked up at him with a teasing expression. Even at this distance, Cecily could discern the tenderness with which he returned her regard.

There wasn't any possible way someone could misconstrue what Cecily was seeing. Blood rushed into her cheeks. The most disturbing thing was that she didn't really feel shock . . . she felt jealousy.

She started to turn away, embarrassed at having unwillingly encroached upon their privacy. But Oakley spotted her and raised his hand in greeting. Without saying a word to Fiona, he bent down and swung her up into his arms. She gave a little shriek, but by then Oakley was already cleaving a path through the thigh-high snow, making his way toward the door where Cecily stood.

A moment later he was standing just below her, showing no inclination to put Fiona on her own feet. "Lady Cecily!" he said, with a broad smile of a sort she had never imagined seeing on the earl's face.

"Lord Oakley." She inclined her head, waiting for him to chastise her about her apparel. But it instantly became clear that he did not care, perhaps did not even notice, what she was wearing.

"Good morning, Lady Cecily," Fiona said with a smile almost as large as Oakley's. Then she turned and gave the man holding her an entirely unconvincing scowl. "Lord Oakley, will you please set me down?"

"Lady Cecily," the earl said, setting Fiona on the step just below that on which Cecily was standing, "I would like you to be the first to know that Miss Fiona Chisholm had done me the great honor of agreeing to be my bride."

He lifted Fiona's hand and turned it over, bowing to press a swift kiss on the inside of her wrist. Fierce color flooded Fiona's face, and Cecily caught the burning look she bent on Oakley's white-gold head.

Due to some alchemy of the heart, Oakley must have sensed Fiona's regard, for he looked up at her. Their gazes locked for a second, and then she leaned just slightly toward him. He was still standing thigh-high in snow, but he snatched her off the step in a rough embrace and . . .

Oh my!

Uncertain what to do, Cecily cleared her throat. No one paid her any mind. She cleared it again. Louder. Oakley lifted his head at that, his expression irritated. "If you are cold, Lady Cecily, may I suggest that you retire to the sitting room?"

"Byron," Fiona murmured, "I confess that I am a bit chilled."

That was all he needed to hear to pull her tightly against him and sweep her up the steps. Fiona had time only to give Cecily an apologetic glance before they were gone.

Amazed by this unexpected turn of events, Cecily picked her way down a narrow path along the castle walls where the snow had drifted back up on itself, forming a little corridor. Apparently, the castle was a veritable Cupid's bower for lovers. Catriona and Bretton, Oakley and Fiona; why, she'd even seen Ferguson succumb to a romantic impulse and kiss Marilla Chisholm during their game of hide-and-seek.

The only one unaffected by all the carrying on was the famous rake himself, Robin, though she had to admit he'd not been entirely immune to the spell enveloping Finovair. He'd kissed Marilla or, she merely preferred to think, allowed Marilla to kiss him. And he *had* kissed her. Indeed, he had kissed her most thoroughly. It was just that he showed no signs of wishing to whisk her away to the stables, or sweep her up in his arms, or . . . or marry her.

She halted in her tracks, beset with frustration, and in doing so caught sight of a figure coming round the far end of the castle, heading for the stables. Her eyes widened. It was Robin. He glanced briefly in her direction, but did not pause. He'd apparently mistaken her for some poor stable lad his uncle had tricked out in antique finery in order to impress his guests.

Her gaze followed his progression, his greatcoat swinging from his broad shoulders, the high tops of his leather boots cutting through the snow, one gloved hand holding tight to the leather strap of the satchel slung over his shoulder . . . By God, he was leaving!

He couldn't leave. How was she to convince him they must marry if he was somewhere else? She had to stop him. But by the time she waded through all that deep snow—which was probably up to her waist—he would be long gone out the stable door at the far end. And if she hailed him, he might not hear, or worse, hear and ignore her.

Frantically, she looked about before being struck by inspiration. Jaw set with determination, she scooped up twin handfuls of heavy moist snow, packing them tightly into a ball, ignoring the biting cold against her fingers. Veteran of hundreds of snowball fights with sharpshooting younger brothers, Cecily worked quickly but painstakingly, because a loose, ill-shaped snowball was an imprecise missile.

Finally, she was satisfied, and none too soon. Robin was almost to the stable doors. She had one chance to stop him.

Offering up a quick prayer, she stepped forward, cocked her arm, and let fly.

The snowball sailed true. Barely an arc altered its swift trajectory as it hurtled unerringly toward her proposed target in the middle of Robin's back. Except . . . except it slammed into the back of Robin's head instead and, with an audible thud, burst apart.

For an eerie second, Robin seemed to freeze in mid-stride. Then, slowly, as though time was unfolding in molasses, the satchel slipped from his shoulder, his knees buckled, and he fell face-first into the snow, disappearing from Cecily's sight.

Her legs were moving before he hit the ground. She bowled into the deep drifts of snow, arms cartwheeling, certain that she had just killed the only man she would ever love.

Chapter 24

Cecily lurched across the snow-choked yard, finally managing to reach Robin. He lay motionless, facedown in the snow, one arm outstretched, the other crooked beneath his cheek. His sooty eyelashes lay thick against his cheeks. Not a breath stirred the snow near his lips.

She cried out as she struggled the last few feet to his side and was about to drop to her knees when a hand shot out, grabbed her leg, and jerked her off her feet. She landed on her stomach with a whoosh, something beneath the snow catching her full in the diaphragm, leaving her windless and dazed.

"Ha! You young limb of Satan! " Robin shouted triumphantly, dragging her toward him by the ankle. "A few smacks to your arse will remind you of the penalties for such jokes. For God's sake stop thrashing about and take your medicine like a man!"

She managed a high, strangled sound of protest. The soft hat she'd pulled down over her hair had shifted, covering her face so that she couldn't see him. Nor could he see her face.

"Fine then, you bloody bairn," Robin said, sounding disgusted. "I'll not lay a hand to you. *This* time."

He transferred his grip from her ankle to the belt around her waist. She felt him shift and realized in horror that he'd moved to sit astride her thighs. Still unable to choke out any coherent words, she thrashed with renewed vigor. With one swift movement, he grabbed her wrists, flipping her to her back and pinning her hands on either side of her head.

"Now, let's see your face, lad."

Locking her wrists together above her head with one hand, he flicked the hat from her head. Her hair caught in the knit of the cap and came unbound, falling free and pooling around her head.

He stared down at her, dumbfounded. "Mother of God. What are you doing here?"

"I had to stop you!" she snapped. "You were leaving. You were—you were *leaving*."

"Well, yes," he agreed, his gaze roving her face. He seemed to have forgotten that he held her prisoner, his hands still holding her wrists pressed into the snow, his thighs locked around her hips.

"Why?" she shouted.

"It seems the most advisable course of action. Your father will hardly like seeing me here. This way he won't."

For some reason, the sensibleness of his reply infuriated her. She bucked, trying to unseat him, and in doing so shoved her loins straight into his. At once she felt the evidence of his masculinity. Very stiff and obvious evidence.

He drew his breath in sharply through his teeth. She barely heard. The brief contact had incited a maelstrom of sensations at the juncture of her thighs, an ache between her legs that was a potent pleasure, a tickle that was a throb . . .

Swearing beneath his breath, Robin swung his leg from over her, rising in one fluid motion to his feet, as he snagged her upper arm and hauled her effortlessly upright.

For the first time, he seemed to realize what she was wearing. His eyes narrowed and his jaw set. "Where did you come by that clothing?" he demanded.

"Catriona Burns found them."

"And she gave them to you? To *wear*?" he asked incredulously.

"Yes," she said defiantly. "They are a sight more comfortable and two sights warmer than what I was wearing. And they cover me modestly!"

"That they do not," he ground out. "You are wearing boy's clothing. The jacket is too tight over your . . ." His gaze dropped to her breasts and he seemed to forget whatever he'd been about to say, ending with: "That clothing is too tight."

"Exactly," she retorted. "Being compressed into a masculine outline cannot be called provocative."

"I assure you, there is *nothing* masculine about your shape," he said grimly. "Those pantaloons fit your legs like a second skin from calf to knee to . . ." This time his dark gaze brushed where the material stretched across her groin, the look as effective as a touch in bringing the molten lick of desire rushing back. He turned his head, directing his gaze at the stable wall.

"What is wrong with that woman?" he muttered angrily.

"What woman?" Cecily asked, hands on her hips.

"Catriona Burns. I thought she had more sense. Is she trying to ruin you?"

"Ruin me?" Cecily echoed disbelievingly.

"Yes," he said, his gaze returning to her face. "You can't appear in public in that . . . those . . ." He waved his hand in the general direction of her clothing.

"This is hardly public, and yes, I can and shall," she assured him, her ire rising at his tone.

She had always done the acceptable thing, made the conventional reply, allowed herself to be guided by society's expectations and rules. But lurking in her heart all these years must have been a hoyden simply waiting for the right man to lure her out: a man who did not obey all of society's dictates, who recognized a person's value before being told her assets, who was quicker to laugh than to judge.

Robin was that man—even if he was currently doing a fair imitation of his cousin, Oakley. Or at least, Oakley as he'd been before he met Fiona.

"*No*," he said fiercely. "You shall not."

And with that he picked her up, slung her over his shoulder, and began making his way back toward the castle.

It was insupportable! Oakley cradled Fiona against his chest as if she were the most precious thing he'd ever seen, while Robin treated her like a sack of flour.

"This is hardly proper behavior, if that was what you were aiming for," she shouted, her long hair swishing like a pendulum across his broad back.

"I leave the *aiming* to you, Cecily," he replied. "You give me no choice."

"You still have no choice, unless you plan to strip me and redress me yourself!"

She probably shouldn't have said that. She felt the big shoulders beneath her grow taut, and the muscular arm around her thighs squeezed a little tighter.

"God help me," he muttered.

"What?"

"Nothing," he said.

"You mustn't go," she said, trying to wiggle free of his grasp.

His arm tightened again. "What?"

"You can't leave Finovair. You can't just run away!" she shouted, her exasperation clear in her voice.

"I am *not* running away. I have already explained—"

"If you leave, it will appear to everyone that you are fleeing, and if you are fleeing, everyone will assume it is for a reason and then they will make the very *worst* assumption." She braced her hands flat against his broad back and lifted herself up and craned her head around, trying to see his face. All she could see was a tightly bunched jaw in profile.

"Jesus," he muttered.

"It would be far better if you stayed and put a good face on the thing, don't you see?" she said, hoping the desperation she felt didn't find its way into her voice.

He stopped and made some harsh, strangled sound.

"Don't you agree?" she prodded.

"Yes!" The admission seemed torn from him. "Yes. I concede your point."

"So you won't leave?" she said, managing to break free and slide down his body. She felt every inch of that journey . . . her breasts pressed against his shoulders, then against his chest: all the hardness of him and the softness of her.

"Not at once," he choked, trying to pretend that he didn't notice the same thing.

"Not at all," Cecily stated, with a thrill of elation.

"I'll be leaving as soon as possible."

But the heat in his eyes belied his promise.

Chapter 25

That afternoon

Robin strode into the library and stopped short. Cecily stood in front of the hearth, silhouetted against the merrily burning fire. She still wore those damned boy's breeches, but had shed the jacket to reveal the fine, loose shirt beneath. Backlit by the glow from the fireplace, one could easily see every curve through the thin material.

And she had curves.

The effect was breathtaking. Her slight rib cage narrowed into her small waist before flaring gently out again in sweetly rounded hips. And when she bent to poke at the fire, he could see the way her breasts jostled ripely and the delicious manner in which the trousers' material stretched over her shapely derrière.

Future duchess or not, Catriona Burns ought to be put in the dock for encouraging Cecily's crime against a man's self-restraint.

"Hamish said you wanted to see me," he announced with ill grace. "Here I am."

She turned around, her eyes lighting up on seeing him. Why was she so happy? Because, he realized, she liked him. She not only liked his kisses . . . she liked *him*. Something hard and painful knotted in his chest.

"Thank you," she said, coming round the lumpy old sofa toward him. "I wanted to make sure you were all right. I do hope you understand that I didn't purposely aim for your head."

"Of course not. You needn't trouble your conscience. Byron has always claimed I have the hardest head in England. I'm fine."

She had a beautiful smile, gamine and spontaneous, and soon he would not be a witness to it. The claims that she was a cipher, a statue, and other, unkinder comments had all been proven false. She was nothing like her reputation, and there was little time left to revel in the company of the unexpected woman she'd proved to be.

One of Taran's men had returned at noon with the news that the snow was melting quickly and the passes would likely be cleared by the morrow. Maycott's men were undoubtedly already working on it. Her father would arrive and Robin would play the role she'd assigned him.

He would contrive to look exasperated and indifferent. He might try to keep Maycott from stringing up Taran—though at this moment he was not sure whether he wished to succeed—and then he would take his leave. Perhaps he might catch a glimpse of her someday in London, on the arm of whomever she married.

She stopped in front of him, her smile vanishing. "You are still angry. No, don't deny it. I can see it in your face."

Wrong, my girl. That's anguish, not anger.

"I expect I deserve no less," she said sadly.

"I'm not angry. I promise you. I am simply"—he cast about for some excuse for his dark expression— "distraught that you did not heed my advice and change into other clothing."

"You say this because you have a care for my reputation?" she asked. And then, with a heartbreakingly hopeful smile, "Or a care for *me*?"

A *care*. A tepid term for what he felt. But why make this harder for anyone, especially her?

"I don't want you to suffer any consequences for merely trying to keep warm," he answered.

"I will change as soon as we get word that a carriage approaches," she said. "But for now, well, what can it hurt?"

"A great deal," he answered. "You would not want it bandied about London that not only were you closeted for four days with men unrelated to you and without a proper chaperone, but that you also sashayed about in a pair of tightly fitted breeches."

She bit her lip, and he had the distinct impression it was to keep from laughing. He could hardly blame her. It was absurd but, damn and blast, he *had* become Byron!

"Who's here that would describe the scene?" she inquired. "Catriona Burns is distracted by her duke and upcoming nuptials, as is Fiona with hers to Oakley. And I do not think either Bretton or Oakley is the type of gentleman who'd waste his breath tattling about a lady's choice of clothing."

"What?"

"I do not think your cousin or Bretton—"

"No, of course not. I meant, what did you say about Miss Chisholm and upcoming nuptials?" he asked, frowning.

" 'Tis true," she said. "They told me themselves—or rather Oakley crowed about it—outside in the stable this morning just before you appeared."

His head was spinning. She must have read his confusion for she spoke again, in slow, distinct accents. "Lord Oakley has proposed to Miss Fiona Chisholm and she agreed to marry him." She gave a light trill of laughter as she crossed the short distance between them. "It looks like your uncle's mad plan has met with unexpected success."

She stopped and tipped her head back to look him squarely in the eye. "Except in your case, of course. And if I recall correctly you were the target of all his machinations. Ironic, isn't it?"

"Very."

"You must feel a bit left out," she teased.

"I am not the only one who failed to fall victim to his machinations. Marilla Chisholm has also escaped heart whole."

Cecily's lips flattened and her expression grew haughty. It seemed that she did not like Marilla. "Yes," she said, "though I doubt she's feeling precisely triumphant. But if you are congratulating people on not succumbing to Cupid's arrow, you must certainly add me to your list. I, too, remain unbetrothed."

"But that's only for the time being," he said, and before he could think better of it, added, "Have you given your choice any further thought?"

She regarded him with an unreadable expression. "Comte de Rocheforte, are you perchance offering me your advice? Your *real* advice?"

"Good God, no," he said, thunderstruck. "Of course not. I would never presume."

She laid her hand against his chest in an unconscious gesture of appeal. He felt the imprint of each finger. "I wish you would. I have only my sisters to act as my advisors—"

"And I am sure they are far better qualified than I to guide you. Besides which, they are privy to your innermost feelings."

"So might you be," she said, her voice low and husky. His heart thundered beneath her palm, and he was seized by the impulse to sweep her into his arms and kiss her far more thoroughly than he had in the frozen corridor above.

But he didn't move. He didn't say a word, and after a few seconds, she sighed, letting her hand drop from his chest.

"As far as being dependable counselors," she said, "they are silly girls, moved to raptures by the cut of a gentleman's coat or the way he sits a horse. The youngest fell in love with her young man because he styled his hair à la Brutus."

He could not help but laugh at that, and she grinned, edging closer once again. "You, though, with your reputation as a *bourreau des coeurs,* you can offer me invaluable insights: how to know if a gentleman will be faithful and guard my reputation, become a playmate, advisor, and tender lover."

He would. But how could he say such a thing? Everything about his past refuted that claim. And even if he were, how could he convince her father?

Lord Maycott, it's true I've bedded a fair number of women, but none of them were virgins and none of them were living with their husbands when I slipped under their sheets. All very up-and-up, don't you agree? And yes, my title was restored by a regime that could just as easily rescind it tomorrow. Still, it's a title, what? And no, I haven't any wealth to speak of, but happily, I will inherit this splendid castle, and there are a few rocky acres in Bordeaux that in, oh, a decade or so, may make enough profit to buy a small cabriolet. But in the meantime I daresay we'll make do with your daughter's dowry—not that I care about her inheritance. How could you possibly suspect otherwise?

He should have laughed at the thought of it. He should; he couldn't, had his life depended on it.

"Robin?"

She had no idea what she was asking him. He scraped the hair back from his forehead, looking anywhere but at her.

"Am I wrong, Robin," she said, "in thinking there is sympathy between us? That even in so short a time, we have recognized in one another a friend?"

He could not resist the appeal in her voice. He looked down at Cecily and instantly became caught in the somber depths of her eyes, her earnest expression.

"If I am wrong, pray, correct me now. I shall not take offense," she said. "Only be honest with me," she added, extending her hand.

How could he refuse her? He enveloped her hand in his own.

"You asked my advice. Here it is," he said. "Choose the gentleman whom your father most approves, a man who can command his respect, and to whom he will be overjoyed to entrust your future."

The firelight licked at her tresses, turning them into polished mahogany. "My father wants my happiness. He would approve whomever I loved."

He gave a short, humorless laugh. "I would not wager a single penny on that assumption."

He was pulling her gently but inexorably closer as he spoke, his body having a will separate from his mind. She showed no signs of resisting. But then, as she herself had said, he was good at this.

Of their own volition, his fingertips traced a path up the gentle valley of her spine to the back of her neck and beneath the heavy knot of hair, scattering the pins holding it in place. Her loosened tresses cascaded down over the backs of his hands, cool as silk and just as fine. A fragrance of lavender and soap, homely and yet incredibly erotic, rose from the unleashed tresses. Without thinking, he leaned closer to breathe in the scent.

She regarded him somberly, the delicate fabric of her blouse shivering with each breath she took. She wet her lips with the tip of her tongue, and his gaze fell on it like a thief on a jewel. In his mind he was tasting her again, plumbing the sweet depth of her mouth.

"He would accept my decision," she whispered.

His lips curved in a slight smile, distracted by her beauty. "Only if it were the right decision. Take someone like me, for example."

"What of you?" she asked, her body very still.

"What if someone of my stamp were to approach your father and ask for your hand?"

Her gaze searched his, but he barely noted it, drawing a feather-light stroke along the line of her jaw with the backs of his knuckles. Unable to stop himself, he went further, outlining the plump curve of her lip with his thumb. She trembled. He shifted closer.

"Let us say that some brain fever takes you and you are persuaded by whim or madness that you are in love with someone of my ilk."

"Let us say that," she repeated, in an odd voice.

"How would your father react?" He went very, very still, awaiting her answer as though his life depended on it, even though he already knew what it must be.

Her mouth curved in a partial smile, and she drew in her breath on a tiny sob and gave a small, shaky laugh.

"But the point is entirely moot," she said, eyes sparkling with . . . merriment? "I would never ask my father—"

"There you are!"

Robin's hands dropped and he fell back a step, feeling as though he'd taken a blow from a battering ram squarely in his chest. Fool. *Fool!*

"I have been looking everywhere for you!"

With neither interest nor urgency, he looked around. Marilla Chisholm sailed into the library. He greeted her interruption with a vague sort of relief. At least she'd spared him the remainder of that sentence: *I would never ask my father to accept a man like you.*

"I swear for so small a castle, people do a marvelous job of getting lost in it," Marilla prattled on. "But no matter, I found you. We are going to play a new game and we need you to— Good heavens!" She stopped dead, her eyes growing round. "Is that Lady Cecily behind you? Whatever— Oh!" Her hand flew to cover her mouth. "*Whatever* are you wearing, Lady Cecily?"

Cecily glared at Marilla.

"Now you know who would tattle about your apparel," he said softly before turning to Marilla. "Lady Cecily is preparing to enact a scene from *Romeo and Juliet* for tonight's entertainment. She is to play Mercutio."

"Oh," Marilla said, doubtfully.

"Wasn't it clever of her to dress as a young gentleman to bring veracity to the role?" he asked, the hollow in his chest growing with each passing second.

"I suppose," Marilla said grudgingly. "But we are not doing theatrics. I have another game and you *must* play," she said. "I refuse to leave unless you come with me." She glanced at Cecily. "You can come along, too."

"Thank you," Cecily replied, but her gaze never strayed from Robin's face and her brow furrowed as she regarded him.

Was his pain so evident? Poor dear girl. She had probably thought they would laugh together at the idea of him proposing to her and now he'd revealed himself, and being a tenderhearted young lady, she would be distressed that she had unwittingly caused him pain.

If he stayed here in the library with her, if he even refused to join the party, he had no doubt she would hunt him down and tender an apology, or worse, console him.

"We must hurry along. The others are waiting and you have no idea how long it took me to find them all and gather them into one place," Marilla said. "All these couples billing and cooing as if they are the only people in the world, and no one else matters or needs to be entertained." She sniffed.

"I suppose you haven't heard that Lord Oakley has offered for my half sister? Apparently, he must have some sort of fascination for women who wear spectacles. Rather peculiar, if you ask me, but I suppose there's no accounting for a gentleman's quirks." She shook her head, and without another word, hooked her arm through Robin's and began tugging him toward the door.

And he went.

Chapter 26

"The game is called forfeit," Marilla announced to the group. "And it is all the rage on the continent."

Cecily, seated in a big upholstered chair near the fire, was in no mood to play more of Marilla's games, but no one else seemed to share her reluctance. In fact, they all looked rather loathsomely happy and lighthearted.

Oakley was seated on a settee with his arm stretched along the back, Fiona tucked in close. Every now and again he would brush her cheek with the side of his thumb as though he could not get enough of touching her. At the other end of the settee, Catriona Burns occupied a similar position next to Bretton, and though Bretton managed to keep his hands off her, the look he bent on her was as telling and ardent as a touch.

Even Taran was in fine form. For once, he'd traded his ragged old kilt for a surprisingly clean one, below which his legs were properly hosed and gartered. On top, he wore a velvet jacket that, though a few decades out of mode, was at least well cut, and with an improbably snowy lace jabot at his throat, he looked nearly elegant.

Only one person in the room looked as dour as she felt. Robin stood beside the hearth, an arm resting on the high mantel as he stared into the fire. He hadn't even looked up when she'd entered the room, arriving late as she'd decided to heed his advice and change out of her boy's clothing. She'd done what she could for the blue ball gown but out of necessity had wrapped the velvet "shawl" around her shoulders again.

"And how do you play this game, lassie? Is there kissing involved?" Taran asked hopefully.

"It's not required," Marilla tittered, fluttering sidelong glances at Robin. "But I shouldn't be surprised if some merry souls didn't take advantage of a certain element of the game to steal a kiss."

At least, Cecily noted, Robin paid Marilla as little attention as he did to her.

"I like this game," Oakley declared. "How do you play?"

"One gentleman is chosen to leave the room. Everyone left selects something from their person and puts it on that table. When the gentleman reenters the room, he holds an auction for the various items that the rest of us bid on. The only rule is that you cannot use money as your currency. You must provide something you own, or offer an antic or a song or such. You can also bid to have your own item returned to you."

"Where does the kissing come in?" Taran demanded.

Marilla pretended a pretty fluster. "Well, I suppose if a person wished to claim something urgently enough, that person might be inspired to offer a kiss to procure it."

"It sounds disastrously dull," Robin declared flatly.

"Rob," Oakley said, sounding surprised.

"It does. Childish antics. We make eight. Let us play two tables of whist instead."

"I don't play whist," Marilla said, mincing to Robin's side and pouting prettily. "I so very, very much want to play. And I would be very, very disappointed if you did not join the fun . . . Robin."

"Good Lord, what's come over you, Rob?" Taran sputtered. "I have never known you to act so high on the instep. It's a simple game and the ladies are bored."

"I'm not bored," Fiona Chisholm said.

"I am," Marilla countered, glaring at her half sister.

"Fine," Robin said. "I'll play."

Marilla clapped her hands. "Oh good! We'll draw short straws to see who is the auctioneer."

She made quick work of shredding splinters from a piece of kindling and offering each gentleman in turn a chance to pull one from her fist. Robin drew the short splinter. Without a word, he stalked from the room, leaving the others to select what they wanted auctioned.

Oakley drew a small book from his waistcoat pocket and placed it on the table. Fiona made a sound of surprise, and though Oakley remained as sober as ever, he caught her hand in his and kissed it. When he released her hand, she removed her spectacles and set them atop the book.

"I don't have anything," Catriona Burns said, pinking up a little. With a rush of sympathy, Cecily realized she wore no embellishments other than a piece of satin she'd tied around her neck, the end of which disappeared beneath her modest neckline.

"Of course you do," Marilla said, sounding a bit irritated. "What's that around your neck?"

Reluctantly, Catriona pulled the ribbon from under her décolletage. At the end hung a man's heavy gold signet ring, its large sapphire incised with a beautiful portrait. But before Catriona had finished untying the ribbon, Bretton's hand covered hers, stilling her fingers. He bent and whispered something in her ear then reached into his vest pocket and withdrew a gold watch and fob. He set them on the table. "These will suffice for Miss Burns and myself."

"But they're a pair," Marilla protested. "You can't bid on them separately."

"Exactly so," Bretton said, escorting Catriona back to her chair.

"Some people must ruin everything," Marilla muttered, but was soon distracted by Taran, who strode to her side, stooped down, and with a flourish pulled a short-bladed *sgian-dubh* from the top of his silk hose. With a courtly flourish, he laid it on the tabletop.

"Now there, lassie," he told Marilla, "is the only thing worth a tinker's damn on this entire board."

Marilla picked up the small knife by its mother-of-pearl handle.

"Careful," Taran cautioned. "Play with a man's weapon and you might get pricked." His eyes danced with a lascivious light.

At this, Oakley, who'd been speaking to Fiona, swung around. "For God's sake, Uncle. Apologize at once."

But Marilla proved herself Taran's equal in mischief. Lifting the blade, she very deliberately and very conspicuously took her time sawing a tress of her hair off with it. Then she replaced the blade on the table with the casual observation, "That old thing is dull and in want of a good whetting."

Taran burst out laughing. Catriona bit her lip, Bretton looked bemused, Oakley coughed away a laugh, and Fiona looked away, but not in time to hide her smile. Cecily watched them, an unfamiliar wave of jealousy spreading through her.

They were all so happy, even Marilla, who'd not yet realized that the next gentleman on her list would no more accommodate her matrimonial ambitions than the former ones.

"What's your forfeit, Marilla?" Taran asked, when he could breathe again.

"Why, this lock of my hair," she said, holding up the guinea gold tress. "I should think anyone would recognize it as mine." She meant Robin, of course.

She looked up. "That's everyone. We can call Robin in and . . . Oh. Lady Cecily. I forgot about you," she said. "What are you going to forfeit?"

"I think this," she said, unwrapping the bed curtain shawl from her shoulders and letting it fall in a heap on the table.

"That? No one will bid for that."

"I might," Catriona said. "What good are jewels to a frozen corpse?"

"As you will." Marilla shrugged, then practically tripped over herself running to open the door and calling for Robin to reenter.

When he reappeared his former issues with the game seemed to have evaporated, for his expression was pleasant. *Determinedly* pleasant, Cecily thought.

"Remember," Marilla lectured him with mock severity, "You must make us pay very, very steep prices for those things we wish to secure."

"I understand," he said. "Let us begin."

He went over to the table and picked up Fiona's spectacles. "Here we have nothing less than a piece of magic. Nineteenth-century glass, I believe, rumored to allow its wearer to detect the very nearly imperceptible."

"How so?" Bretton called out, looking vastly amused.

"Why," Robin said, "legend has it that the current owner was even able to discern the heart beating beneath the wooden effigy of a certain earl."

At this Bretton burst out laughing and Oakley joined him.

"Well, as they are magic, how can I resist?" Oakley said. "I will offer my boots for them."

"Boots?" Robin scoffed. "Magic comes at a far greater price than a pair of Hoby boots, sir. Who else will bid?"

"As their current owner I must insist they are returned to me, for I am not done yet with my perusal of that earlish effigy you mentioned. I am convinced there is a great deal more yet to discover, and I am well and truly committed to the endeavor."

"I applaud your commitment, Miss Chisholm, but what forfeit will you give?"

"A kiss!" Taran shouted.

Robin grinned wolfishly at Fiona, who looked away, flustered. "Aye," he said. "A kiss might buy these spectacles. But whom should she kiss? I would, of course, suggest myself, but I would hate it to be said that I took unfair advantage of the situation."

"Since when?" Oakley demanded.

"The lass can kiss me!" Taran suggested magnanimously.

"Miss Marilla said the price must be high, not extortionate," Robin said, winning more laughter. "No, there's nothing for it, but that she must kiss Oakley to retrieve her glasses."

Oakley wasted no time in seeing that Fiona's glasses were returned. He surged to his feet, catching Fiona by the hand and hauling her into a tight embrace. Cecily glanced away; the passion in their kiss made her heart ache.

When Oakley finally released her, Robin shook his head. "Coz, you really must learn to attend. *She* was to kiss *you*. Not vice versa."

At once, Fiona stretched on her tiptoes, clasped Oakley's face between her hands, pulled his head down, and planted a hearty buss upon his mouth. "Satisfied?" she asked, with an unexpected note of coquetry in her voice.

"My dear, alas, I am in no position to answer," Robin replied rakishly. "That is a question for Oakley."

Cecily's heart thudded dully in her chest. She wanted a lifetime of Robin's roguish smiles and unaffected humor, his teasing laughter and warmth.

Next, he picked up the watch and fob. "What am I to make of this? Is it one or two pieces?"

"It is two pieces that must perforce be bought together," Marilla explained.

Robin snorted derisively. "One need not guess whose idea this was. You always seemed to me a possessive sort, Bret."

"Always," the duke agreed amiably.

"And I suspect any attempt to outbid you would be futile."

"Entirely," Bretton agreed. "You might ask Miss Burns to offer a kiss."

"No. I don't think my sensibilities could tolerate another such exhibition," Robin said.

"I'll bid a dance. A dance with the comte," Marilla said, standing up as though Robin's acceptance were a foregone conclusion.

The little group broke into a smattering of approving applause.

Cecily did not think she could bear to watch Marilla in Robin's arms. "I will bid a dance, also," she said. "With the laird of Finovair."

This met with even greater approval. Soon, everyone was bidding against one another, the antics growing ever greater. At one point, Taran even bid to waltz with Hamish, sending the entire company into gales of hilarity. Bretton finally announced he would throw himself on the altar of ignominy in order to spare the ladies so haunting a spectacle, and recite Lord Byron's latest poem in order to win the bid.

Robin awarded him the auction, and Bretton rose to his feet and proceeded to recite . . . something. Just what it was would forever after be the subject of much debate, but whatever it was, it most decidedly was *not* written by Byron. There were naiads in it and a few fauns, a character named Despot, and a whole gaggle of talking swans. And it was set in some country that rhymed with "puce."

The rest of the auction went much the same, everyone seeming to have a grand good time. Not unexpectedly, Marilla continued to bid her lips, her limbs, and her company to Robin for the various items. And Cecily continued to outbid Marilla's offers with her own, and from there the others inevitably joined in to bid all sorts of japery and antics. Fiona balanced a spoon on her nose; Taran sang "The Bonnie Lass of Fyvie" in a very credible baritone, and Cecily juggled three pinecones.

When, near the end, Marilla bid a kiss to retrieve her hank of hair and Taran was the only man who took her up on it, she was a good enough sport not to pout but to give as good as she got—and Cecily was surprised at how good what she got looked to be.

Finally, only Cecily's shawl remained on the table.

"Do tell us what wondrous thing you have there, Comte," Miss Burns encouraged.

"This?" Robin said softly. For a moment he simply ran a finger along the velvet nape, his expression softening. He lifted it up, swishing it lightly in the air. "This is most rare, indeed. A relic, in fact."

"But what *is* it?" Fiona asked, dimpling.

"I believe this once cloaked the form of a creature as rare in these parts as hen's teeth."

Cecily's heart began beating faster. His voice was warm and sad, wry and bittersweet.

"What creature is that?" Marilla asked.

"Why the *Angliae optimatium heres.*"

"What's that?" Taran demanded.

"The English heiress," Fiona translated with a laugh.

Cecily felt warmth rise in her cheeks and looked away.

"Rob!" Oakley said in a low voice. "You've embarrassed Lady Cecily with your reference to her wealth."

The smile stiffened on Robin's dark, handsome countenance. "That was never my aim," he said. His gaze caught Cecily's and he inclined his head. "My pardon, Lady Cecily. But you must certainly know that your value far exceeds anything that can be counted in coin."

"Fine," Marilla broke in abruptly, "Robin's made a pretty apology. Now who is going to bid on that?"

"I'll kiss Miss Marilla Chisholm for it," Taran offered.

Marilla giggled.

Catriona raised her voice and said, "What of you, Rocheforte? I heard no rule against the auctioneer bidding, and you have yet to do so. Surely you must want to possess so rare a relic?"

She caught Cecily's eye, her own shining with a teasing light.

Cecily's heart trip-hammered in her chest and she found herself holding her breath, waiting for Robin's reply.

He had gone very still at Catriona's words, staring at the tawdry piece of cloth he held as though it were gossamer that might dissolve before his eyes. Carefully, almost reverently, he replaced it on the table, smoothing a fold away. He looked up.

"I am afraid I have nothing of value with which to barter, Miss Burns. Neither goods nor talents."

Cecily's heartbeat slowed to a dull, heavy thud as her throat constricted with tears she refused to shed.

Catriona frowned, her expression uncertain. "Surely there is something . . ."

He shook his head. "Nothing. Besides, the point is moot. I would never aspire to something so far above my touch."

So that was it, then. He could not be more clear: she'd receive no offer of marriage from Robin.

She didn't even realize she had stood until the book she'd won dropped from her lap. And then she was running out the door, Catriona Burns calling after her.

Catriona.

But not Robin.

Chapter 27

Cecily avoided the stairs; she couldn't go to her room. Kindhearted Catriona Burns was bound to look for her there, and Cecily did not think she could face the other girl's pity. Better to be unavailable until she could mask her heartbreak.

Instead, she headed for the small family chapel next to the great hall, one of the few other public rooms still in use in this part of the castle, though gauging from the dust on the pew cushions, "use" was a relative word. Like many castle chapels, it rose two stories tall, its height divided horizontally by a small second-floor balcony that overlooked the altar so that the lord and lady could attend daily services directly from their chambers. A wooden staircase led to the balcony so Cecily climbed it, not wanting to be seen by anyone passing the door opening onto the corridor.

The dust lay even thicker above than below, coating a pair of wingback chairs set well back from the wooden rail and a bench that might have served the lord's children, which now lay toppled on its side. Cecily sought refuge in one of the oversized chairs, curling her feet beneath her and huddling deep into the corner.

What was she to do now? How was she to return to her former life and go about the business of choosing a husband, when the only husband she wanted would not court her? She had done everything she could to charm, beguile, and befriend Robin. Nothing remained in her arsenal of feminine weapons.

Since birth, she'd been taught that whatever a lady wanted, she must wait until it was given, be it a pony, a dress, a party, or a husband . . .

Not that a lady need be entirely passive. But Cecily *hadn't* been. She had followed Robin, kissed him, worn boy's clothing, tried to rouse his jealousy in her pursuit of him. What more could she do?

And why would he not propose? Because she was too rich, too English? Because he was too poor, his title too French? Because she was a virgin, or because he was so patently not a virgin . . . None of that mattered.

The only reason she would accept was that he did not love her. But he did! She knew it. Her heart could not be so blind, her soul so deaf. When he had looked at her this evening across the room, the pitiful shawl in his hands, she had been as certain of his feelings as she was of her own . . .

"No! I'll not be quiet!"

Cecily lifted her head from her arms. The voice from directly below her had been Taran's.

"Then at least do me the courtesy of coming in here and not shouting so that all the world might hear you!"

Cecily froze. *Robin.*

"Why should you care?" Taran demanded, his voice growing louder as he entered the chapel. "The world already knows you're a heartless bastard. Nothing I can say will surprise a one of them."

Robin's reply was terse and unintelligible.

"I know you and Byron think I'm nothing but a half savage," Taran went on, "but at least I don't reduce lassies to tears."

"Do you think I enjoyed that?" Robin ground out.

"How could a man tell with you? Always ready with a quip and a laugh, and all the while the lassie looking as pale as the survivor of a massacre."

"You overstate the case." His tone was thick with emotion.

"The hell I do!" Taran shouted. "That she has feelings for you is as clear as fresh blood on new snow . . ." He trailed off and when he spoke again, his tone had changed from bombast to true shock. "Dear God, laddie, ye dinna *actually* seduce the poor wee creature? I know I encouraged you to do so, but only if you had honorable intentions. If you dinna plan to marry the girl, then you are a bloodier blackguard than I—"

"Stop! I did not seduce her!" Robin thundered. "For the love of all that's holy, what do you take me for?'

"Who you are," Taran snapped in reply. "*What* you are."

For a moment Robin was absolutely silent. Carefully, Cecily shifted in the chair, craning toward the rail to hear better.

"My past has nothing to do with Cecily and myself," Robin said. "I would never do anything to harm her. *Never.*"

Cecily's heart began to beat faster. She slipped from the chair to her hands and knees and crept to the rail to look down. Below, she could see Taran standing halfway down the short aisle leading to the altar. Before him, black curls gleaming in the afternoon light streaming through the chapel's rose window, Robin paced like a caged beast.

"Cecily, is it?' Taran asked musingly. "Well, it looks like for all your proposed good intentions, you've mucked up a grand bit, laddie, for the lady is heartsore and that's a surety."

"No," Robin said emphatically. "She's not."

What did he mean? How could he make such an assumption?

"You're wrong," Taran said flatly. "I saw her watching you this afternoon. She could fain take her eyes from you."

"No." Robin stopped pacing, raking his hair back with his hand. The very set of his shoulders suggested resignation and weariness. "This afternoon I asked her to pretend that she loved a man like me and tell me how her father would react if that man asked for her hand."

"And?" Taran prompted.

"She said the point was moot, because she would never ask her father to approve someone like me."

What? No. *No.* She hadn't! Cecily's brows furrowed, thinking back fiercely, trying to recall her exact words before Marilla, with her impeccable sense of timing, had interrupted them. Robin had just said, "Let us say you are in love with someone of my ilk," and she had agreed, and then he had asked how her father would react and . . .

Her eyes flew wide. She had said the point was moot, and been about to say she would not ask her father's permission because the only thing that mattered was if he loved her. But those words were not what Robin's imagination had supplied. He had heard what he thought he deserved to hear.

"I don't know why she would say such a thing when it's so clearly a lie. Maybe she's afraid of her parents. But if you were man enough, you'd find the way to persuade her to ignore her parents' wishes and elope with you."

"Dear God, Taran, have you not heard a thing I've said? Do you not understand? *I love the girl,* damn you and your plans and your machinations! I love her. I would never come between her and her family. I would never ask her to elope. Indeed, I would never . . . I should never have . . ."

Cecily's heart began beating madly, a heady warmth rushing through her, filling her. The very blood in her veins seemed to carry joy with it, suffusing her every fiber with happiness.

Below her, Robin's hand clenched into a fist at his side. "If she were my daughter and a man like me pursued her, I would horsewhip him within an inch of his life. I would sell him to a press gang and hope he died on foreign soil in some futile war." He laughed bitterly. "But, as has been said, the point is moot."

"It's only moot if ye don't do something aboot it, lad."

"Enough," Robin said, his voice weary. "Your man returned a few hours ago. The pass will be open by daybreak. I'll stay to see that no one suggests there be any reason I should have left, and after that, I'm gone."

Without another word, Robin brushed past Taran and disappeared, his uncle following.

On the balcony above, Cecily dropped back on her bum with a thump. Her hands slipped from the rail to her lap, her unseeing gaze fixed on the small marble altar below.

Robin loved her. Her heart swelled anew at the thought, became complete and whole and filled with unlimited potential, the future suddenly an invitation to a glorious adventure, the rest of her life a love story waiting to be told. Whatever her father's objections, however reasonable and heartfelt, they would somehow find a way past them.

The only question now was how she would find her way past Robin's own objections.

Her gaze drifted to a chapel window, the bare vines outside covering it like latticework, and suddenly, she knew: she was going to climb the ivy.

Chapter 28

Late that evening

C ecily bullied Hamish into bringing her hot water, then washed off all the chapel dust, then offered Mrs. McVittie her pearl ear bobs to tell her where Robin had his chambers. The scrawny, stooped old Scotswoman cackled like a witch and asked what she would do with pearl ear bobs and then, with a toothless grin, told her the location anyway.

But now, creeping up the cold stone staircase, shielding the flicking candle with her hand, it occurred to Cecily that the old lady might have been teasing her, because why would Robin stay in the abandoned part of the castle?

The corner room above the bailey tower, the old lady had said. Well, here she was and there was the door leading into that room, a thin line of light delineating the bottom. She pulled the blanket she'd draped over her shoulders closer and, taking a deep breath, pushed the door open.

Beyond was a small chamber, lit by the glow from embers in a tiny hearth in the opposite wall. It was a monkish room with only a few pieces of furniture. A large wingback chair stood facing the hearth, turned away from her and a narrow bed had been pushed hard against the wall.

She did not see Robin at once, and for one terrible moment thought he'd left after all. But then she saw a man's hand appear over the arm of the chair, the long fingers curling over the carved end.

"If that draught is you, Taran, come to lecture me some more, go away," Robin said tiredly. "If it is Hamish, leave the bottle on the table, and my thanks. And if it is Marilla, I am sorry, my dear, but I am not receiving tonight. Or any night. Or day, for that matter."

She took a breath. "What if it is Cecily? How is she to act?"

The fingers tightened reflexively over the chair's arm. For a moment he did not reply, and then in a very careful voice he said, "Sensibly. By leaving. At once."

She smiled at that. "But it turns out I am not sensible. Or dutiful. Or circumspect. Or any of those things for which I have been admired. So I believe I will stay." She let the blanket slip from her shoulders to the floor.

He stood up, slowly and without turning at once, as though carrying with him a great burden, and once erect pulled back his shoulders. He was wearing only a white lawn shirt, the sleeves rolled up over muscular forearms, and a pair of skintight buckskin trousers that showed his athletic figure to great, distressingly great, advantage. A little thrill raced through her at the sight of his tall, broad-shouldered form silhouetted against the fire.

Then he turned and saw her. The mask he'd composed failed him at the sight of her, for she wore only an antique chemise of the softest, sheerest linen, the deep, rounded neckline edged in lace, the sleeves falling free to her wrists. His eyes burned in his pale face and a muscle jumped at the corner of his hard jaw.

"Cecily. You must leave," he said. "Please." But in his expression she read everything she needed to give her the courage to stay.

"No," she said. She moved to his side, tipping her head to look up at him. He stared silently back.

"I am cold, Robin," she said.

Still mute, he pulled his discarded jacket from the back of the chair and draped it over her shoulders. She shook her head, her eyes never leaving his. "Still cold," she said.

She stepped right up next to him and wrapped her arms around his chest and pressed herself tightly against him. The muscles in his chest jumped into tense rigidity. She laid her head against his shoulder. The rightness of it was startling. Every bit of tension, every last bit of doubt dissolved into his body's warmth and heat and strength. She sighed, a soul finding its moorings, a homecoming and an awakening all at once.

"For God's sake, Cecily," he finally rasped, "please. What is this?"

His heart thundered beneath her ear.

"I love you," she said. "I love you, and I want you to marry me. Marry me." She would never have imagined herself saying something so bold, so extraordinarily forward. A woman should make her plans and then wait for a gentleman to fall in with them. She did not . . . climb the ivy. Yet it felt right, perfect. In fact, the only possible thing she could say.

A shudder ran through his big body. She rubbed her cheek against him, her eyes closing as she luxuriated in the sensation of being this close, this connected.

"How can you ask this? What has happened to make you forget your situation, your family, your name?"

"You," she replied simply.

He put his hands very lightly on her shoulders. "You are the most extraordinarily forthright young lady I have ever known."

"Not to everyone. But always to you. Loving you has made me so."

"So many sins on my head," he murmured, his breath stirring the hair at the top of her head.

"I would never recognize myself in the woman wrapping her arms around you, unconcerned with anything other than the fact that your arms are not around me. Why aren't you holding me, Robin?"

"Because if I embrace you, I am afraid I will not be able to find the will to let you go."

"Then embrace me. "

His hands slipped from her shoulder, crushing her to him.

She laughed shakily. "See? I warned you. I am without shame, capable of anything where you are concerned. And you, what are you capable of?"

"Too much, I fear."

"I don't know that is true," she said, tipping her head back to study his face, her unbound hair cascading down over his arms. "Are you capable of living on my wealth? Of enduring my father's suspicion and my mother's mistrust and society's worst speculations? Are you strong enough to endure the whispers that may follow us for years before they fade, if ever they do? Because that is what marrying me will mean."

He released her but did not step away, reaching up instead to cradle the back of her head with one hand and tip her chin up with his other. "It was never myself I wished to spare."

"I know," she said softly. "I will not lie to you, Robin. I would just as soon none of those things happen, and everyone we loved would bless our union and be confident of our future happiness. But the alternative is to live without you, and that I cannot do."

In reply, he dipped at the knees and scooped her into his arms, his mouth descending hungrily on hers. She wrapped her arms around his neck, trying to get closer. His mouth still closed on hers, he moved to the chair and sank down in it, holding her on his lap.

"I have spent a lifetime training myself not to want what I could never have," he said, and dipped his head to feather kisses along her lower lip. She arched in his arms and he splayed his hand between her shoulder blades to support her.

"But then you arrived," he said, "and played havoc with my will. Every barrier, every defense, every bit of common sense, and every hard-learned lesson has been shattered by your smile, razed by your glance."

She smiled, joy slowly blooming in her heart. "Then you'll marry me?"

In answer, he covered her mouth with his own, kissing her with a thoroughness that left her shivering in his arms. "Oh yes. There's nothing for it now, my lass. I'll ask your father and then we can only hope he's fool enough to agree, because it won't matter if he does not.

"He could spirit you away, wed you to another man, secret you in a French nunnery. No matter how long it might take, no matter what I must do, I would find you.

"Because, you see, the only thing stopping me before was the idea that you would be happier without me. But now I know you love me and so nothing will stop me until you are mine, by fair means or foul."

"I do not think we need to elope just yet," she teased in a shaky voice, because if she did not tease him she might cry, and there were far better things to do this night then cry.

"Unless there is no other way, we are not going to elope at all," he said severely. "I intend to stand before your family looking for all intents and purposes like the most brazen and bald-faced fortune hunter London has ever seen and pledge before God and gawkers my undying love and devotion and care of you, and it will not matter to me a whit who believes me. Except for you, Cecily. That, I own, I must have."

"I do," she said.

"Good," he said, looking amazed and bemused, a man who has just heard a death sentence commuted into an extravagant reward. Then shaking his head slightly, he gently clasped her shoulders and lifted her upright on his lap. "And now, my beloved, you must leave."

Her mouth dropped open. "*What?*"

"You must leave," he said. "Because I do not want anyone in this castle saying you were forced to marry me because I'd seduced you."

"*You* seduced *me?*" she echoed. She scrambled around in his embrace until she sat straddling his lap, her hands flat against his chest. "No one who'd seen the concerted effort you have put into avoiding me these past four days would even consider the possibility."

He stared at her, apparently having a hard time coming up with a response. She felt the hard evidence of his arousal, and heat rose and flowed up her chest and neck into her cheeks. It was beyond arousing. She wet her lips with the tip of her tongue and his eyes narrowed, his gaze falling raptly on her mouth.

"No, indeed," she said, breathless and exultant. " 'Tis I who've seduced you, and everyone here knows it. Besides," she said, "I have discovered I do not care what others think."

He groaned, his eyes slipping shut and ground out, "And I have discovered that I do. At least where you are concerned."

She frowned, leaning forward, and pressed a soft, clinging kiss against his lips. He shuddered.

"What matter?" she murmured. "We are to be wed anyway, are we not?"

His arms slipped around her, crushing her to him. "Yes. Yes. And yes," he said, giving in to the irresistible temptation of her mouth before tearing his mouth free. "But," he said, "and I cannot believe I am about to say this—truly, if Byron were dead I would swear I'd been possessed by his stiff-rumped spirit—*but* I want you speaking your vows at the altar knowing that you do so only because you love me, not because you were compelled by a rash decision made in a moment of passionate excess and are afraid you might be pregnant."

"I would very much like to experience your passionate excess." She sighed, leaning forward for another kiss.

He pulled her close and bent her over his arm, his mouth plundering hers for long, erotic moments before, with a groan, he lifted his head. "You have no concept of what you are doing to me, or the effort I am exercising. But I swear soon enough you shall.

"There will be a better time and better place for these things, my love," he said, his dark eyes narrowed but unable to hide the hunger burning within them. "Long, passionate nights followed by languid days when we will be undisturbed while we teach each other about desire and pleasure." He dipped his head, once more sipping a kiss from her lips before jerking his head back, breathing hard.

"I want to explore every nuance of lovemaking with you. Enjoy every taste of you." He nibbled the tender flesh at the base of her neck, traced the tip of his tongue beneath her chin to the corner of her mouth. She arched into it, her eyes closing in a swoon of pleasure.

With a low, strained chuckle, he pulled her upright, catching her face between his hands and gazing deeply into her eyes. "I will not hurry one second of that maiden exploration, my beloved. Because I have never been in love, you see, and when we do make love, my darling, my wondrous Cecily, I do not want anything interfering."

She burrowed her hands beneath his shirt, astonished and aroused by the satiny smooth texture of his skin stretched taut across the hard pectoral muscles. "What would interfere?" she asked, breathing hard, riveted by the idea of knowing him, this man she loved, in every sense.

"Well . . ." He hissed with pleasure as she raked her teeth lightly along his jawline.

"Well?" she echoed. He tasted subtly of soap and smoke.

"Taran," he gulped. "He might pop in for a nightcap. Then I'd have to kill him."

She froze.

"Dear God, what a hideous notion," she said, her ardor momentarily doused. "I counted you a great seducer, but I see now you can kill passion as easily as you engender it."

But then his arms came round her once more, pulling her back into his embrace, and ardor burst into flame anew. She wrapped her arms around his neck, whispering, "But for now we can still practice a bit, yes?"

"Oh yes," he said, laughing as his mouth settled over hers. "Oh yes . . ."

Epilogue

Amid hollered threats, imprecations, and vows to unman any men they found near their daughters, the rescuers leaped from their horses and barreled into Finovair, heedless of the fact that no one barred their way and that, in fact, Hamish held the castle's ancient portal open for them.

Finnian Burns led the charge, him having only the one bairn, and thus feeling both the insult and the fear the greatest. Jamie Chisholm was close at his heels, bellowing for his Marilla, while at his side strode the Earl of Maycott, looking justly grim, as everyone knew how much he doted on his eldest daughter, Cecily. Behind them crowded half the men of Kilkarnity, ostensibly to see that justice was finally done to that old brigand Taran Ferguson, but in actuality because nothing near so exciting had happened in the parish in thirty years and they wanted a front-row seat.

The small horde swept down Finovair's high, empty hall, wrenching open the doors to every hidey-hole, cupboard, and room, one after the other as they hunted down their quarry until finally, they stood before the last door in the corridor, the one leading into the dilapidated family chapel.

"They'll be no sanctuary in there for you, Taran Ferguson!" Chisholm cried out, and kicked the heavy oak door with all his might.

Unfortunately for Chisholm, the door had not been latched and the violence of his kick sent him flying in and sprawling face-first on the chapel floor. Burns and Maycott, who'd endured four days of Chisholm's bombast and bluster, and had both come to conclusion that those four interminable days might well lead the list of their grievances against Taran, stepped over him and into the chapel, followed close by the men of Kilkarnity.

Whereupon they all stopped in their tracks.

Standing with their backs to them, facing the altar, stood eight people, four tall men and four ladies in evening attire, while at the foot of the altar stood Father Munro, still wearing the greatcoat Hamish had tossed over the old priest long before daybreak this morning when he'd kidnapped the man from his cozy bed, dragged him up onto a saddle in front of him, and galloped all the way from Kilkarnity to Finovair.

Now, all eight turned around to look at them, variously reflecting amusement, cool appraisal, and steely resolve, yet, oddly enough, also in each face a full measure of indisputable happiness, the happiest of all looking to be the old reprobate Taran, who might as well have been rubbing his hands together, his gloating was that evident.

"What the devil is going on here?" Chisholm, who'd picked himself up from the stone floor, bellowed.

With terrifying hauteur, the Duke of Bretton lifted one dark brow and intoned, "We are having a wedding. Sir."

At which the handsome, black-haired devil standing beside Lady Cecily added, "Rather to say, we have *had* a wedding. Sir."

"Whose wedding?" Finnian Burns demanded.

"Mine," said Duke of Bretton. "To Catriona." He smiled broadly. "Father-in-law."

Burns reeled back under this pronouncement as if he'd been kicked in the chest by a mule, falling into the waiting arms of the Kilkarnity men behind him, more than one of whom had the sense to whisper to their fallen comrade, "A duke, Fin. A bloody rich duke!"

"And mine, also," the darkly handsome man said before Burns had recovered, "to the Lady Cecily"— words that set Earl of Maycott starting forward in alarm, for now he recognized the man holding his daughter's hand and remembered his reputation. But Maycott's steps faltered to a halt when he saw the beatific expression on his daughter's face.

He opened his mouth to speak, but whatever objection or comment he might have made was forever lost when the icily handsome Earl of Oakley spoke.

"And mine," he announced, his gaze never straying from the face of Kilkarnity's most famous romp, Fiona Chisholm. "To the Countess of Oakley, my own Fiona."

"Fiona?" squawked her own father, dumbfounded. "Not Marilla? Are ye mad?"

"Quiet, Jamie," one of the Kilkarnity men hissed, "ye have a son-in-law what's an earl," while behind them, the much recovered Finnian Burns beamed with paternal pride at his new son-in-law, the duke, until Maycott turned to him and in voice heavy with irony said, "Don't think this means you're shut the cost of a proper English ceremony, Burns. That'll come later."

To which Burns, who was known far and wide to have deep pockets and short arms, shot back smugly,

"Unless a bairn comes first." Meanwhile Chisholm, heedless of proffered advice, burst out, "But what of Marilla?"

At which point Taran, the instigator and author of all this fascinating drama, stepped forward—though later reports claimed he wisely kept his muscular nephews Lords Oakley and Rocheforte between him and Chisholm—and said, "Well, Jamie, since ye're of a mind to know, I'm glad to be telling you—"

But Marilla, who had no patience with, well, anything, burst out with obvious glee, "I am wed, too, Father! I won't have to leave Scotland and I shall have my very own castle!" She grabbed Taran's arm. "So come and kiss your new son," she crowed.

Chisholm's eyes grew as wide as saucers, and all about the room, everyone fell dead silent. Then, with a roar such as hadn't been heard since Braveheart's time, Chisholm launched himself at Taran, going straight through the laird's nephews—well, not truly through, as both men stepped neatly aside—aiming for Taran's neck and . . .

. . . And all merry hell broke loose.

Witnesses at the pub that night all agreed that Taran made a fair show and acquitted himself well for a man of his years. The laird wasn't there to dispute it, since he was dancing the bedtime waltz with the prettiest girl in the county, even as her da sat gazing into a glass of whiskey and shaking his head.

Those who believed in fairies and suchlike—and since the Scots aren't fools, they know right well that magic has its place—well, those folks said later that a strange moon shone over Finovair Castle that December, a lovers' moon, a blue moon, a spoonin' moon. Other said the Seelie Court had come riding in on that winter storm, their steeds as white as snow itself, and their laughter falling like blessings down Finovair's old chimneys and turrets.

Whatever magic took hold of Finovair castle that December of 1819, the four couples who fell in love there never thought of that storm without a leap of the heart.

More to the point—and sure evidence of the magic if ever there was—some nine months later five new bairns squalled their way into the light of day. That would be one each for the noble parents, and a set of red-faced, lusty twins for the laird.

Beautiful, those babes were. And strong. And—or so their parents said—canny. And—so the Ferguson oft proudly said—loud.

But mostly, they were blessed . . . as is every child born to a couple who love each other with the kind of passion that only grows deeper with time. Neither the laird nor his male guests were the sort to babble much poetry, but there wasn't a one of them that didn't, now and then, drop a kiss on his wife's sweet mouth and make her a promise: "And I will luve thee still, my dear, Till a' the seas gang dry."

> Till a' the seas gang dry, my dear,
> And the rocks melt wi' the sun;
> And I will luve thee still, my dear,
> While the sands o' life shall run.

HARPER LUXE

THE NEW LUXURY IN READING

We hope you enjoyed reading
our new, comfortable print size and found it
an experience you would like to repeat.

Well – you're in luck!

HarperLuxe offers the finest in fiction and
nonfiction books in this same larger print size and
paperback format. Light and easy to read, HarperLuxe
paperbacks are for book lovers who want to see
what they are reading without the strain.

For a full listing of titles and
new releases to come, please visit our website:

www.HarperLuxe.com